Amber Shades of Grey

Amber Shades of Grey

Lindsay Dias

To Jordan—
Happy Birthday!!:)
Enjoy the book!
Love—
Lindsay

iUniverse, Inc.
New York Lincoln Shanghai

Amber Shades of Grey

iUniverse books may be ordered through booksellers or by contacting:

iUniverse
2021 Pine Lake Road, Suite 100
Lincoln, NE 68512
www.iuniverse.com
1-800-Authors (1-800-288-4677)

This is a work of fiction. All of the characters, names, incidents, organizations and dialogue in this novel are either the products of the author's imagination or are used fictitiously.

ISBN-13: 978-0-595-39557-6 (pbk)
ISBN-13: 978-0-595-83956-8 (ebk)
ISBN-10: 0-595-39557-0 (pbk)
ISBN-10: 0-595-83956-8 (ebk)

Printed in the United States of America

For

Haley, Rocco, and Milania

PROLOGUE

Dear Readers:

I look out my window at the world before me and wonder what my life would have been like if I was born into another family. Many people have thought the same things; I am one of the unlucky ones who really mean it. But then I think to myself, what is unlucky? According to Merriam-Webster dictionary, unlucky is defined as: "Marked by adversity or failure, likely to bring misfortune, having or meeting with bad luck or producing dissatisfaction". The first definition explains my life perfectly, I was born into adversity and failure, therefore the mark was set upon me while still in my mother's womb.

I never understood how objects, animals and even days could be considered unlucky. If a ladder is in your path and you walk under it, will you be hit by a car while walking across the street? How can a black cat crossing your path bring you bad luck? How can opening an umbrella inside a closed structure cause your good luck to change suddenly into bad? If you accidentally break a mirror, are you really doomed for seven years? And why, is Friday the 13th so unlucky?

My life has never been a lucky one, but in many ways I have been lucky. Throughout my childhood I have been let down by those who I have trusted the most and I have been left with a broken heart. Other times I have been blessed with love and happiness. I express my thoughts and opinions in writing and by writing I have healed my broken heart and have moved on with life. I am thankful for being able to share myself through this novel and hope that it will change people's perceptions of others, and allow them to see other people for who they are and not what they look like or who their parents may be.

Everyone who ever looked at my sister or I with pity or dislike read this and realize that your thoughts of us were wrong. The next time, look more closely at those around you, you'll be surprised at what you find.

I sit in my study, which is painted in a pale shade of yellow with mahogany furniture and a playpen in the corner. In it smiles the most beautiful little girl ever to be born. I look into her eyes and know the life I have lived was for a purpose and she is it.

This is my sanctuary, my soul, my heart; this is the life of Amber Katherine Jacobs.

Entry 1: <u>August 2002</u>

When a child is born into the world they should have a full, happy life to look forward to. A life with a mother, father, siblings, friends, love interests, and people in their lives who give them inspiration; a life with all of this is a happy one indeed.

Some people come into this world with all those people in their lives and more. Others don't have the luck of that and are born into already broken homes. A single mother, a mother who has all the odds against her and for some reason or another gives the child up for adoption, and still some are expunged from the world before they are even allowed to kick inside their first home. I am not saying anything is wrong with any of the situations I have mentioned, I am just stating facts. I wish I was born to any one of those women.

As I have been told, my life at the beginning was perfect, a mother and father who loved me, a grandmother who spoiled me with everything she could give and at two years old I was given a baby sister, Alicia. My memory does not expand to that time in my life for it has grown through the years and those memories are hidden in a deep cavern of my mind. I wish I could get those years into my head and keep them there for eternity. To look back and remember I was once loved.

Entry 2: <u>September 2002</u>

When Alicia was born things started going downhill. The meaning of life had changed for me. That was the beginning of hell, the beginning of something I would end up hating, resenting, and most of all wishing I was never a part of. The stress of having a toddler and an infant was too much for my mother, and my father was never home. Before Alicia's birth he had always been there for us after work and on weekends, and then when she was 3 months old he started working late. I went from having a daddy to being by myself with my depressed mother and crying sister.

There have been many times when my mother told me stories about those days when my father was "fucking every woman who walked by" and his neglect of his wife and children. When I was four and Alicia two my father left. He walked out the door with two suitcases and without a word. He didn't even say goodbye. He drove away from our house leaving his two young children without a father and his wife standing on the doorstep in complete disbelief. That was the moment the not so perfect world had flipped over and there was no way it was turning back.

My mother stood there for a long time. At four years old it felt like one week but in reality it was two hours. When she finally came back inside she had tears in her eyes and a vacant expression on her face. She locked herself in her room and left my sister and I in the living room without dinner. Alicia and I slept on the couch that night, starving and afraid. The next morning we had breakfast and our mother gave us baths. We started our new lives as a family of three.

Entry 3: <u>September 2002</u>

Weeks turned into months and my father never called, never sent cards. Alicia, my mother and I hadn't heard from him in four months. I always wondered where my daddy went, but never asked. I believe that even at four years old I knew that my mother would be hurt and upset if I asked about him. Alicia would once in a while say "daddy, daddy" in her tiny voice.

My fifth birthday came and went, Alicia's third birthday passed by, and my parent's wedding anniversary flew past and still no call. And so another year passed. My mother was deeply depressed every day, and with each day without him she got worse.

Entry 4: <u>May 1986</u>

Today was my sixth birthday and my dad came to the house. He had been gone for two years, five months, three days, four hours, and twenty-three minutes, and he had come home on my birthday.

I remembered him only vaguely and was still angry with him for leaving so I stayed in my seat and didn't utter a word. Alicia didn't remember him at all. The entire house went silent, my mother dropped a plate. I remember this day like it was yesterday. The memory of my sixth birthday is engraved into my being, like a permanent tattoo.

"David," my mother had said at his arrival. She was speechless at the sight of her husband who had left so long ago without a word.

"Shelley," he responded. They stared at each other for what seemed like eternity. I had never been in my house when there was complete silence, you could cut it with a knife. What had happened to them two years ago? Alicia, who craved attention anyway, started singing away with a spoon to her mouth. She also began screaming, "I want cake!" over and over again. I tried to quiet her but she wouldn't listen.

"Hey Alicia, do you remember me?"

"No, who are you?"

"Well I'm your daddy. I had to take a long trip but I came to say hi to you and your sister."

"My daddy doesn't love me anymore, he's not coming back to stay here," she said with the spoon still in her tiny hand. Her brown hair was pulled back into a ponytail and she was wearing a pink dress with a flower design.

"Of course your daddy still loves you, I always will sweet pea. And no I'm not coming back to stay here, but I want you and Amber to come live with me."

"What?" screamed my mother who didn't like the idea of anybody taking her children away from her. "What gives you the right to leave here for two years without one phone call and then come back here and all of a sudden you want to take my children away from me!"

"They are my children too Shelley."

"Bullshit! They stopped being your kids the moment you stepped out that door." Her face was red, her anger showing through her emotions. She was ruining my birthday.

"Shelley, calm down. Can we talk in the kitchen? I don't think it's appropriate for me to tell you this in front of everyone, especially the children."

"I'll tell them anyway," she said but still walked into the kitchen. She was furious and my father was extremely embarrassed. They were in there for a while. My grandmother cut my cake for me and gave Alicia a piece. I didn't want cake, I was mad at my father for coming here and making my mother ruin my party. The kitchen door swung open after I finished opening my presents, my father walked out; he was crying. He waved goodbye to Alicia and me and then walked out the door.

I stood up and walked after him. Leaning my face against the glass door, I watched as my father left for the second time in my life. Tears rolled down my cheek. His car drove away, the same route as the first time. This time he said goodbye, but he didn't say "Happy Birthday."

When would I see him again?

I was six years old. My birthday was ruined. My father was gone again. My mother was still in the kitchen.

"See, I told you he didn't love me anymore," my sister said as my grandmother wept.

Me? I leaned on the glass door, angry and sad.

"I hate you, Daddy." I whispered.

Entry 5: <u>May 1986</u>

In the days following my father's abrupt departure, my mother sunk into a deeper depression. She wouldn't eat unless someone fed her, and she wouldn't take care of us. My grandmother had to come and stay with us. I loved my grandmother; she was so beautiful, so intoxicating. We were her little angels and we knew just which way to push her to get our own way. We wanted cookies; they were in the oven within five minutes. We wanted a new toy; where's the car? She took care of us while my mother sulked in her room. I didn't know exactly what happened in that kitchen, all I knew, it was horrible.

On a Friday night, two weeks after my birthday my mother came out of the room, dressed from head to toe in black. She had a black tank top on with black leather pants and black army boots. Her blonde hair was pulled up into a bun and she had her diamond earrings on, the ones my father had bought her when I was born. She had make-up on which looked horrible. Her lips were covered in a hot pink shade and her eyes were painted with blue powder.

My grandmother walked into the room and looked at her with disgust. "What are you doing?" she asked. "Where do you think you're going dressed like that?"

My mother, dressed like a vampire, gave her a look of contempt.

"I'm 37 years old. I think I can go out looking however I want without my mother criticizing me. You can't tell me what to do anymore, Mom. I'm all grown up now." She opened her purse and took out her car keys. "But if you must know, I'm going out. I need to get out of this house. It's making me sick. It reminds me of that bastard, and right now I need something else in my life. Something better. Don't wait up."

Mom looked at me.

"Amber, you take care of your sister, okay? I'll be back late so I want you in bed by 8:00. Bye."

"Shelley," my grandmother hollered. "You need to snap out of this and get on with your life; you have two children who need you to be here for them. You aren't the only one who lost someone you know!"

My mother didn't answer, she just went out. I had never seen her like that before.

"Grammy, is mama leaving like daddy?"

"Oh Amber sweetheart, no, she'll be back later on tonight. But, let's watch a movie! Would you like that?"

Alicia and I both decided on watching "The Sound of Music" and we all sang the songs until the movie's finale. Alicia went to bed at 8:00 and I was allowed to stay up until 9:00 to watch some television with my grandma.

We talked about my father and how I felt about that and about my mother. I told her that I was very sad about my father leaving; I didn't understand why he left. She told me that it wasn't my fault and that he loved me very much. I didn't believe her though, if he loved me why did he leave? She explained my mother was going through a difficult time and I should give her time to recover from the trauma of the whole situation.

"You know Amber, being a single parent is very hard work. Just give her time, she'll be okay and she'll go back to being your mom."

"I don't want her to be my mom; I want you to be my mom. Can I move in with you?" I asked with all the hopes a six year old can have about wanting a better life.

She told me that I couldn't come live with her, she was old and she wasn't able to take care of a young girl all the time. Why couldn't she make an exception? I wouldn't be any trouble; I just wanted to be happy. My grandfather had died before I was born and she had been living alone for all that time.

"I'm sorry sweetie, but you wouldn't like living with me, I'm no fun. There are no kids in my neighborhood for you to play with."

She didn't know I didn't have any friends in the neighborhood; they all thought that my family was weird. We were the outcasts of the group, the "deformed" Jacobs family who lived at 784 Woodland Avenue. Stay away folks; they'll bite!

Entry 6: <u>May 1986</u>

I awoke in the middle of the night to a screaming fight between my mother and grandmother. It was late; I had been asleep for a very long time. My eyes were blurry and crusty, my mouth was dry and I was still half asleep. Why were they yelling? What time was it? I rubbed my eyes and opened my door a little. My mother was standing in the hallway, she was wobbly, and she couldn't seem to keep her balance. My grandmother was standing next to her holding her up, trying to keep her steady. My mother was pushing her away, angry at her for trying to help. My mother was yelling, and she sounded different, her words weren't all there, she was talking like Alicia used to talk when she was two years old.

"What the fuck are you doing? You're ruining my life. I'm grown up and you can't tell me what to do. Why don't you leave me alone?!"

"Look at yourself Shelley. You're drunk. You're unable to stand by yourself and you're totally incapable of taking care of yourself, never mind two young children. Maybe I'll take them home with me tomorrow and let you work out whatever you need to work out."

I was so happy, for one fleeting moment I smiled. My grandma was going to let me and Alicia live with her! I couldn't believe it, I was out of here. I was leaving and going to live with the one person who I loved more than anything. I couldn't wait to tell Alicia. She was still sleeping, and since grandma said she was going to take us with her tomorrow I thought I'd let her sleep until morning.

"You fucking think I'm letting you take my kids. That's a joke," I was back at the door watching them. She almost fell over again. "I wouldn't let him take them and I'm not letting you."

"Think about the kids for a second, stop thinking about yourself. When you become a mother you have to put your needs aside and theirs ahead of you. I knew this was going to happen."

"What? You knew he was going to leave me for another woman? You bitch!"

"No, I didn't know he was going to leave you but I knew that you shouldn't have ever been a mother. You have always been unstable Shelley. Do you remember when you became pregnant with Amber? Do you remember what I said to you?"

"No, and I don't give a shit."

"Well you are going to listen to me. I told you that having kids isn't going to make up for the love you needed from everybody else. Having kids is a full time job, a position not to hold lightly. I told you that kids deserve all your attention and you can't just have them for yourself. There are other ways to find love in your life, babies aren't the answer."

"I've learned that. They don't even like me, so don't tell me about my life and how to live it."

"They love you! They don't think you love them. You need to show them."

My mother was slowly losing it. She was holding herself up against the wall for support, her hand on her head. She was very volatile.

"Get out of my house, I want you out now. And, I don't want you to come back."

"You don't mean that Shelley, I'm your mother and Amber and Alicia's grandmother, they need someone in their lives who cares about them."

"Like hell I don't mean that, if I ever see you near my kids again I will call the police. And if you come within fifty feet of my house you will regret it. Now get out of my house."

My grandmother started crying. She had been humiliated and banned from seeing her grandchildren. "Ok," she said very quietly, she was defeated. "I'll go. Tell Amber and Alicia I love them dearly." She said looking at me. "Tell them I will always love them, and always be there for them. Even if they can't talk to me or see me I am there in their hearts and souls. Pray to God and I will hear them, tell them they are my life, my reason for being. Goodbye Amber, I love you." My mother turned around and looked at me, a fury in her eyes. I have never seen that. Ever. I was afraid. I shut the door and crawled into bed. I brought the covers up to my forehead and I wept. I could still hear them through the door.

"Goodbye Shelley, I love you dearly, and if you change your mind don't be afraid to call me. I am always here for you."

"I won't change my mind, now get out."

My grandmother left my house, we were alone again, the three of us. Only now I didn't want to be here with my mother. I wanted to be somewhere else, somewhere far away. Maybe I'd join the circus.

Entry 7: <u>May 1986</u>

That night was the first of the many nights my mother came home like that.
We were always stuck in the house with "Beverly the babysitter," who didn't
care for us very much. Our mother was never the same. I wanted her back to
the way she was before, even if she didn't pay attention to us. I would much
rather her not pay attention than not acknowledge our existence.

Each night was the same, Beverly would come over around 6:00 p.m. and
my mother would go out with her new friends. They would drink until 3:00 in
the morning when she'd come home and pass out on her bed. She and my
grandmother formed an agreement, my grandmother could see us whenever
she'd like but couldn't come over after 4:00 p.m. They weren't on the best of
terms but Alicia and I could still spend time with our grandmother. She taught
me what to do if my mother ever was in trouble. I learned how to dial 911, but
only in case of an emergency. And, after calling 911 I should call her. I now
knew her phone number, which I used almost every night when Beverly was
kissing her boyfriend Jordan. He came over many nights after my mother left
and he'd leave before she returned. My mother didn't mind him visiting she
just made sure she never saw him.

Entry 8: <u>August 1986</u>

Tonight, three months after the fight my mother came home at her usual time. Jordan had left and Beverly was lying on the couch watching television. She seemed worse than she had been in the last months. Her eyes were bloodshot, her nose was bleeding, and she was throwing up all over the house. She fell over more than once on the way in. It took her ten minutes to get the money out of her wallet to pay Beverly. When I got older I always wondered where all the money came from.

That night she went into her room and shut the door. I followed her in and she looked at me. Without saying anything she fell to the ground, but this time she didn't get up. My body shook, my mind went blank, and I started to cry. Alicia came in, she knew what to do. She grabbed the phone from the nightstand in my mother's room and handed it to me. She was still too young to know numbers. I dialed 911 and told the operator my problem.

"My mom, she came home, she's drunk, she's on the floor and she's not getting up."

I gave the lady our address and she said she'd have someone there right away. I hung up on her before she could tell me what to do. Nerves were boiling through my body.

I called my grandmother like she said. She was groggy from sleep but she promised to come right away. The ambulance arrived within minutes from my call and my grandmother was right behind them. The EMT's put my mother on a respirator and wheeled her out to the ambulance. My sister and I were crying in our grandmother's arms. After we were in my grandmother's car she drove to the hospital. I remember all I was thinking was how my mommy was going to die. She was going to leave us forever. Even though she was never really there for us, never home when we needed her Alicia and I always loved her, she was of course our mother, the reason for our being.

We sat in the waiting room while the doctors and nurses worked on saving her. The room I remember was large, with chairs lining the walls. Magazine racks sat in the corners and in the middle of the room was a table with books to read while waiting. In the corner farthest from the entrance was a tiny table and bookshelf, next to it a box of blocks. Alicia and I played with the blocks until the boredom overcame us and we moved on to the books. We each took turns making up the stories to the pictures featured on the paper pages. We read every single book on the shelf.

"That was hundreds of books, huh, Amber?" asked Alicia.

I responded, "No, only one hundred," as if I was smarter and knew how many books were actually there.

With all the books read and the blocks played with we had nothing to do. The two of us had exhausted our limited amount of options and now had to sit around watching the many other people around us.

In the corner seat where we were just playing a large man with white hair was sleeping, his mouth wide open as drool dripped from the corners of his large red lips. He was snoring and his belly was rising with each breath he took. The people around him were staring with annoyance. Across the room an old woman sat with her husband, they both sobbed and held each other. Her nightgown was faded; the flowers on it were barely visible. At one point during our wait a doctor came in and the old couple stood up. The doctor explained to them that he was sorry but their efforts didn't work, their son had passed away. The woman curled into her husband and he held her tight.

Alicia fell asleep on the floor, and my grandmother was reading a magazine. A teenage boy sat in the seat next to me. His arm was bleeding and he looked to be in intense pain. He had blue eyes and blonde hair, and he was tall. He noticed me staring at him, he talked to me.

"Hey kid, what, you've never seen blood before?"

"What happened?" I asked.

"I was shot with a gun. Someone didn't like my friend so he shot him."

"But if he shot your friend how come you're bleeding?"

"You're a smart kid. I went to stop the bullet from hitting my friend, his name is Jim. I didn't stop it though, it just hit me in the arm and then the man shot Jim."

"He's not very nice."

"What's your name kid?"

"Amber."

"That's a pretty name, my name is Tristan," he told me with a twinge of pain. "What are you waiting here for?"

"My mother is sick, the doctors and nurses are going to make her better."

The nurse stuck her head in the room and called him in. It was his turn to get fixed. "Hey kid, I hope your mom's okay. Give me five."

I slapped him five with his good hand and he returned the favor. "Tell Jim to get better," I said to him. "Bye Tristan."

Tristan waved to me and he was gone. I was happy; I had made my first friend. The doctor came in a little while after Tristan left and told us my mother was going to be okay.

"Hey, you did a very good thing calling 911, who taught you that?" he asked kneeling down to my level.

"My grandmother. Is my mommy okay?"

"She'll be okay sweetie; she just had a little too much to drink. She must have been thirsty."

If he was trying to make me feel better it wasn't working. I already knew she was drinking alcohol. I knew it was bad for you, I knew the dangers of it; they shouldn't have told me about it they should have told it to my mother. She needs to know it, so maybe she would stop.

We couldn't go see her that night, she was resting, so my grandmother carried Alicia to the car and I walked beside her. When we arrived home I helped put Alicia into bed and I got into my bed. My grandmother tucked me in and kissed me on the forehead. Dreamland was my next destination.

Entry 9: <u>August 1986</u>

It is the following morning and we went back to the hospital to visit my mother. Her hospital room smelled of urine and disinfectant, I cringed at the horrid smell. The curtain was drawn for my mother's roommate, a woman who had been in a car accident and was recovering from the trauma.

We walked past the curtain and came face to face with my mother. Flowers were sitting on the windowsill with hopes of recovery and good health. Balloons were floating high above the bed where my mother was lying. She was wearing a hospital gown and covered with the blanket. She had an IV in her hand and heart monitors covering her chest, the "beep…beep…beep" of the machine echoed through the small room. She had tubes in her nose helping her breathe, and a table of food was resting next to her; she hadn't touched it.

My grandmother walked over to the bedside and caressed my mother's forehead. My mother turned away, my grandmother looked hurt and disappointed. My mother didn't say anything for the hour we were there. She seemed sullen, depressed, annoyed at the very thought that she was alive. She was not at all happy that her children and her mother were there by her side loving her and wishing she was better; wishing she would come home and take care of them. I hoped with all my heart that the old mother had died and a new mother was coming home, so far it wasn't working to my favor. Not only did she not change, from the looks of it she got worse.

We were about to leave when my mother spoke for the first time since we arrived. Immediately my grandmother was at her side, convincing her everything was going to be okay, she was loved and cared for. My mother started to cry, she grabbed my grandmother's hand, but she didn't look at us.

"Why did this happen?" she asked, her voice trembling.

"Shelley, you need to stop drinking or else the next time this happens you might not make it. You're lucky Amber was there, that she knew what to do. If she didn't call 911 you would have died."

"Am I? Lucky? I would have been lucky if she didn't follow me around all the time."

"Don't say that Shell, they need you here, they need you to be there for them."

"They have you don't they? They'd be fine without me. Everything would be better if they weren't mine, if I weren't around."

I stood there holding Alicia's hand and realizing that our mother didn't want us. We were termites, eating up the structure of her body, chewing away until there was nothing left. She didn't want to be our mother, she couldn't stand the sight of us, and I was sad. My mother would rather be dead than love her own children. My four-year-old sister and I stood there as my grandmother cried and my mother talked about death.

Entry10: <u>August 1986</u>

My mother was allowed to return home today; she was still weak and disoriented. She permitted my grandmother to stay for a few days, just until she was capable of walking around and doing things herself. My grandmother was thrilled to be around us, she loved taking care of us, and we loved having her there.

This first week of my mother's homecoming was great, I felt like a normal six-year old. Alicia and I played outside in the backyard; we received great presents from my grandmother and my mom's friends. The dinners were delicious, baked ham, spaghetti, turkey and mashed potatoes, and my favorite, macaroni and cheese. I was happy; my mother had even joined us outside and played catch with us. If only life could stay like that, happy and perfect. But, pretty quickly the week ended, my mother was better, and my grandmother went home. I thought that maybe it would be okay; maybe my mother would take care of us and love us.

I was wrong. Just like so many times in my life, I had jumped the gun and wished for the best, and it turned out to be the worst. She went back to her lifestyle before the hospital stay. She was gone every night, drinking and partying. Beverly was over again with Jordan. I had to do my homework by myself, no help from anyone.

Entry 11: <u>October 1986</u>

I had been back in school for a couple of weeks and first grade wasn't any better than kindergarten. The kids didn't talk to me; they played with each other leaving me in the playground by myself. The teacher didn't make any effort in helping my social situation; she hardly talked to me herself.

My mother, for her own selfish reasons had developed a reputation for herself, and in doing that she brought her children down with her. She was the alcoholic, the person in the town to be talked about, looked down on, and stayed away from. Everybody in town knew about her drinking, her late nights, and her hospital visit. Parents of the children in my class told their kids to stay away from me, I was trouble, and I was the alcoholic's daughter. Nobody knew me for my personality, who I was inside. They knew me for what my mother was.

I wasn't acknowledged as a child, a person, a living, breathing human being. I was categorized in the dirty, unwanted, invisible, person who shouldn't be in the world category. I was the underdog of everything I did, school, sports, and piano lessons.

Entry 12: <u>December 1986</u>

One this specific day in the month of December a new boy came into class. He was cute, brown hair and brown eyes. His name was Chris. Being new in the school he came to me first, I was stunned. Nobody had ever come over to me to say hello, but Chris walked straight to me, only me. It was raining outside; a dreary day so recess was inside. I was by myself as usual playing with a doll, pretending it was my baby.

"Hi, want to play?" he asked me. I of course nodded, being deprived of socialization for too long I didn't quite know what to say. "My name is Chris," he said to me.

"I'm Amber, what do you want to play?"

"Let's build a castle with the blocks, and then we can knock it down." Typical boy, always into construction and destruction. He grabbed the blocks and threw them around on the floor. We got the yellow hard hats out of the blue box and put them on right away, we were well on our way to building the biggest and best castle ever made. Chris and I formed a barrier from the rest of the class and brought trucks and fire engines inside. The two of us played for the rest of the day, building castles, knocking them down, building them again, and knocking them down. That was the first time I had ever enjoyed school.

For the rest of the school year Chris and I hung out and played together. He was my best friend. I had wondered why he was my friend when he knew nobody else played with me. It was just in his nature to form an alliance with those in need of love and attention. Whenever I was home with Beverly while my mom was drinking I thought about what Chris and I would do the next day in class.

Entry 13: <u>January 1987</u>

Today was Alicia's fifth birthday. She had a party and I wanted to invite Chris. I was also afraid to invite him, what would he think when he was thrown into the fire to see first hand what it was like inside the burning volcano? Would he run or would he stay, to be beside his friend?

The day came for the party. Chris arrived a little late, his mom lost her way. This was the first time I had ever had a friend over my house and I was anxious. I cleaned my room, and I made my mom promise she wouldn't ruin the day. She kept teasing me about having a boyfriend. "He's not my boyfriend," I yelled, furious at her for even thinking that. Alicia was excited; she had a lot of friends over from pre-school. She was popular. Kids that age didn't exactly listen to their parents when they were told not to go near certain children.

Chris's sister Janie was there for the party, she looked a lot like her brother. My grandmother was there, passing out cake, singing happy birthday, entertaining the children and helping with presents and clean up. Alicia was thrilled with all the toys she received, the stuffed animals, Barbie dolls, board games and coloring books with crayons. Our grandmother bought her a beautiful baby doll, I loved it and so did Alicia. I had written a poem for Alicia and was bubbling to read it out loud to her.

It was my first piece of work, my first inclination to what I wanted to do with my future. A sign of true talent, pure joy in my life. It was finally time. Alicia had quieted down her guests and I stood up in front of everyone, my mother, my grandmother, my best friend, a group of four and five year olds, and my sister, sitting on a stool with a paper crown upon her head. I became very nervous; I started to shake with fear. What if nobody liked it? And, I was only six so the poem wasn't up to par with Edgar Allen Poe, or William Shakespeare. My grandmother told me not to worry and to just read without fear, read like I was the only one in the room. I tried:

"My sister, her birthday is today; she is small and pretty and doesn't smell like hay. What should I say? Happy Birthday Alicia-ay!" My grandmother helped me write it, the poem wasn't too spectacular but it awarded a round of applause and a hug from my sister. She loved it, and hung it up on her wall in our bedroom.

After my poem was read and finished Chris and I played outside for a little while until he had to leave for home. The house emptied as each child took their party favor and left, their parent in tow. Finally all the children were gone and my mother, grandmother, Alicia and I were left in the small ranch style house cleaning up the mess. I enjoyed myself immensely that day. My mother was sober, she was cheerful and most importantly, she was involved in my sister's party. That was the great thing about my mother; she was always attentive on our birthdays. She loved decorating and baking the cake, it made her feel like a whole person.

The four of us had a nice dinner out at my sister's favorite restaurant and then my grandmother took Alicia and me to a movie. Another surprise and wonderful thing that happened to us that night, my mother came to the movie too. She didn't pass us off on another person so she could fulfill her needs and wants.

Entry 14: <u>February 1987</u>

As a young child who didn't comprehend the seriousness of alcoholism, I was naive to the facts. I thought that if she didn't drink one night then she wouldn't drink anymore. The end of her sadness was cured by Alicia's birthday, a time when she could begin doing things by herself. My mother no longer had babies as children, she had two children who could act and be independent. This would help wouldn't it? And maybe, just maybe my father would know this and come back to us.

Everywhere we went we attracted the looks of the other people surrounding us, but the night of Alicia's birthday party I didn't care. They could have stared forever and hated us for all it was worth and I didn't care less, my mother was with us and she was coherent in her thoughts and emotions. She wasn't looking for an escape, her full attention was exactly where it was supposed to be, on her two children. My heart was soaring, my sadness lifted for that day. It had been the best day of my life. The world seemed to have stopped that day, in my little mind that was what my life was like for normal people.

Entry 15: <u>August 1987</u>

I remember that the day after the party our twisted life started again, the life where our mother was missing. My father was gone in reality but my mother was gone figuratively, her body was there, her mind wasn't. Months passed, my birthday came and went, the summer passed with no change. Chris and I played at my grandmother's house and over to his house but never at mine. My house was considered the devil's playground; no child would want to spend a minute there. One hot summer day in August Chris's mom took him and I to the zoo for the day, we had a very good time. The animals were all out, the elephants squirting themselves with their trunk, the hippos were bathing in the water and the polar bears were swimming in their tank where Chris and I had our faces up against the glass windows.

Entry 16: <u>September 1987</u>

The summer was what I called semi-fun. I had a lot of fun while away from my mother, away from the home I had lived since birth. I was seven now, a big girl, someone with her own mind and I was testing my limit with my mother. That summer I got into a lot of trouble, I was getting into places I was forbidden from going near and I was rebellious against all those who were in a place of power. Alicia and I, although close, were always arguing about this or that, we both thought we were right and wouldn't back down to the other. The bickering between us caused my mother to have a horrible headache and to surrender to her room, where she spent most of her days. Nights she was still heading out to her comfort, the bars, to booze away with her friends.

The Friday night before school began she brought home her friends for a poker game and drinking. She had never brought home the alcohol before, it was always consumed outside the house, but now she didn't care. She had considered us old enough to deal with her drinking in front of us. My grandmother tried to argue, she disagreed about my mother's whole lifestyle but this was the last straw. My mother threatened to ban her from seeing us again so in turn my grandmother shut her mouth and walked away, aggravated. That night they played poker and drank a great deal of alcohol. Alicia walked in, I tried to stop her but she was a stubborn child. She didn't listen to our mother, or grandmother—why would she listen to me?

"Hey look, it's a little person! Hey little person, how are you?" some man by the name of Frank said while patting her head. I felt like screaming, "She's not a dog!" but I kept my mouth shut. Alicia acted as if she were a little princess who deserved all the attention from everybody. She was a very precocious child, acted like she was twenty-five. She reminded me a lot of my mother.

"What's that you're drinking?" she asked curiously.

"Well aren't you the curious little monkey!" said another man, Bruno, the guys all called him. "This is beer, can you say that? B-E-E-R."

"I can say beer, I'm not a baby." Alicia rolled her eyes and flipped her hand. Nobody treated her like an infant.

"Do you want a sip," asked Bruno.

"Don't give her that, she's too young," my mother said without real authority.

"Come on mama, I want just a little sip." Bruno gave my five-year-old sister the bottle and she took a large sip. "I like it."

"Oh do you? You know what kid? I like you. Hey Shelley, you got a great kid here."

"Yeah, she's the good one. She's not like my oldest. Amber is very quiet, and I don't think she has a very good vocabulary. Alicia here is gifted, aren't you Lishy?" my mother squeezed her cheeks together and formed a fishy face with her mouth. "Ok, let mommy go back to her friends now. Why don't you go play with Amber, she needs you to be her friend. Amber only has one friend," she mentioned to the others. "Poor thing, she's not very social. Okay Lish, go play."

I wasn't social, I was never taught to be social, and what was she talking about I didn't have a good vocabulary, I was seven years old. I was extremely angry at my mother that night. She had made fun of me in front of all her friends.

"Amber, wanna play dolls?"

"No," I said taking out my anger on Alicia. "Leave me alone, bitch." And I pushed her away. I had heard my mother call my grandmother 'bitch' on many occasions, I had picked up on the fact it wasn't very nice to call someone. It was a very opportune time to use it. See mom, my vocabulary is just fine.

Alicia looked like she had been punched in the face. Her tear ducts went on full force and her lip quivered. She stood there in shock and disbelief. She hadn't seen that coming.

I stormed into my room and slammed the door, gaining a scream from the person who calls herself my mother. I buried my face into the pillow sobbing. I called my grandmother; I was distressed and knew she would know exactly what to say. She answered on the third ring.

Entry 17: <u>October 1987</u>

My grandmother was the strongest person I knew, the greatest person in my life and I loved her with all my being. If I could call one person in the world the greatest good, the one human with all the qualities of a saint, that would be my grandmother. Like Mother Theresa, she helped others with no expectations of receiving anything in return. Like Martin Luther King Jr., she wanted equality between all races. According to her we were all the same, no matter what differences we held within us. Each and every individual had feelings, felt love, hatred, sadness, and happiness. It didn't matter what color the skin was, everybody's blood was the same color: red.

My grandmother was the one person I looked to in times of need, she was the true caregiver of my sister and I. She went to the parent/teacher conferences at our schools, and acted as our guardian when we were in trouble. She gave us advice on life, school, boys, friends and family. Her views and beliefs were her life. If she didn't stick up for what she believed in she would have been heart broken.

Every Wednesday she would go to the library and read books to young children, and every Thursday she taught a class to teenagers who were interested in babysitting. She was a member of the organization for families who had lost someone, and she was the president of a local group advocating gun control in the United States. She had told me once that she was sick of hearing about all of the deaths in the world caused by guns, and if she could do one thing in the world it would be to make it more difficult for people to obtain a weapon.

When she was young, she led a life anyone would have wished for. She was born in Italy where she lived until she was 18 years old. She left Italy to travel the world, and to learn about other cultures and lifestyles. She came to America on her twentieth birthday and took English classes. She learned the language rather quickly and fell in love with her teacher, Steven Martin. He was five years older than her, but to my grandmother age didn't matter. He was handsome, "a sight for sore eyes," she told me. His blonde hair was long and wavy and he had the most beautiful blue eyes she had ever seen.

"We fell in love the moment we met, but he had a girlfriend and I didn't speak English very well." A few months went by and his girlfriend broke up with him. She learned the language and became an American citizen. They began dating when she was twenty-one and he proposed to her on her twenty fourth birthday.

"He was so romantic, your grandfather. He took me to this expensive restaurant and treated me like a princess. During the dessert he had this man come over to our table and play a song completely in Italian. My heart was bursting. I knew the song; it was of love and devotion. And he said to me 'Maria, I've loved you since that first day you walked into the door. Love shows us the way and makes sure all obstacles in its path are rapidly pushed away, and I am eternally grateful for you showing me the light of life. I couldn't possibly bear living my life without you in it. Waking up in the morning in an empty bed is the worst feeling, when I know you could be there next to me. It would do me the greatest honor if you would be my wife.' Of course I said yes, who wouldn't? He was a charming and handsome man. And he was all mine."

After their wedding my grandmother became pregnant and had her first child ten months after the special night. Anthony David Martin was born followed by their second child Christopher Mark Martin. When my grandmother was thirty-five she found out she was pregnant again. My mother was born nine months later.

Death, pain and suffering seemed to follow my grandmother wherever she went. When my Uncle Antonio was eighteen and Uncle Chris was sixteen a drunk driver driving 95 miles an hour hit the car from behind. My uncles died instantly. My grandparents were devastated.

Ten years later my grandfather had an aneurism in his sleep. My grandmother, so strong, so brave was left alone with a sixteen-year-old daughter to raise. Being a single mother wasn't easy for her, and the fact that my mother was always acting out didn't help. On more than one occasion my grandmother had to drive twenty miles to the jail facility and bail out her daughter who had been arrested for one thing or another. The only trouble my mother didn't get into was drinking. She had been only six when her brothers were killed and she still felt their spirits around her. She didn't want to make the same mistake the boy had done.

When my mother met my father she calmed down a bit, he was her love. She had finally found something worth settling down for, something happy in her dark world. My grandmother felt a large boulder lift from her shoulders and her heart, for now she didn't have to worry about her only child left.

She was thrilled when I was born, and when Alicia was born she was even happier. My grandmother now had two grandchildren to look after, and then she could let them go home. We were her pride and joy.

All the worry came back when my father left. She knew my mother wasn't stable; she wasn't sturdy enough to take care of herself, never mind her two kids. When my mother started drinking my grandmother could only think of her two sons. She never in a million years thought her daughter would resort to alcohol when she knew the damage it could do to people, whether they are directly or indirectly related to you.

My grandmother was strong; she was a powerful woman, with emotions made of steel. She could weather any storm, she could live through anything. Death came to her door and took away three of the most important people in her life and she stood there and looked on. Death passed her by, she was meant to be there for me. God somehow had a reason for her to stay on this earth. She didn't allow death to hurt her, to bring her down. She was valiant. She knew everything. She was my savior.

Entry 18: <u>October 1987</u>

I remember how her voice sounded through the small microphone inside the receiver of the telephone in my room. She sounded different, her voice was shaky. I was nervous, scared to no end. What was wrong? "Hello Grandma, what's the matter," I asked. I was still crying from the episode between my mother and sister. "Amber, I love you. Please know that I love you so much." Her voice was weak, breaking up in certain areas. "I know grandma. I love you too."

The other end was silent for a moment; I called her name over and over again. Maybe she dropped the phone. "Amber, I want you to be brave okay? You take care of your sister and your mother. I love you."

What was she talking about? Why did I have to be brave? Why did I have to take care of my sister? And my mother?

"I love you too Grandma."

The line went dead. I knew something horrible just happened. I just didn't know how horrible it had been. I told Alicia about the phone call and we told our mother. She brushed it off as something my grandmother was doing to get us to be more sympathetic to her. We went to bed, confused and scared.

Entry 19: <u>November 1987</u>

The next morning when we awoke our mother told us that our beloved grand-mother had a heart attack last night and had gone to heaven. My eyes welled with tears and my body ceased to move. I felt as if someone had thrown a base-ball at my chest and knocked my heart out of its place. The one and only per-son who cared about me with all the love in the world—no strings attached, was gone forever. God wasn't doing his job, he had forgotten the pain I was in all day every day and took away the only person who meant anything to me.

I remember the funeral as surreal. I felt as if I was somewhere else, in a dif-ferent time, a different place. The mass held many people who my grand-mother had touched during her life. I had never seen so many people in my life, and here they all were honoring my grandmother. Alicia was quiet for the first time in her life. She was sitting with me in the pew, her eyes distant and saddened. The casket was in front, feet to the altar and head to the door, as if she had walked in alone to attend her own funeral services.

She was buried next to my grandfather and her two sons. We all stood by her grave and prayed for her, prayed that her soul would make it to heaven and her family be able to move on with their lives, if that was at all possible.

We went to a dance hall for the reception. Alicia and I sat in the corner by ourselves. There were several old men and women who were friends with my grandmother who came to offer their condolences. We said thank you and they left. For the first time in my life I had no one to talk to, no one who understood what my life was like. I was angry at her for leaving me and I was angry at God for taking her away from me, and I was angry at the people who didn't save her.

Entry 20: <u>November 1987</u>

The weeks following my grandmother's death were horrible. I felt alone. There was no one to talk to and no one talked to me. My mother continued her alcohol abuse and her parties at our house. The fact her mother died didn't seem to affect her and it bothered me to know that. According to my mother, now that I was seven and a half, I was old enough to become a slave. Every time she needed something: a glass, her booze, food, I would be the one to retrieve it for her. The roles were reversed, I was the mother and she was the child. Alicia would always be on my mother's side, she would boss me around as she got older and she would hang around the gang who was over every night. Everyone loved her; she was the mascot for their poker games. "Go team go!" she'd yell with a large smile on her round chubby face. "Who do we love," the others would ask. And Alicia would respond in a cheer, "A-L-I-C-I-A, ALICIA!" Make me sick.

Entry 21: <u>July 1989</u>

The years passed by without a change, I was still the grown up and Alicia was still the baby and my mother was the teenager who didn't care what others thought. School never got easier and the kids never talked to me. Chris and I were still best friends and did everything we possibly could do together.

When I was nine-years-old and in the fourth grade, my mother came home drunk as usual, but there was also something else in her eyes. Something she hadn't done before.

For the longest time I couldn't figure out what type of alcohol she was drinking that made her eyes watery and red. I had to find out from the girls at school who were gossiping.

"I heard Amber's mother takes drugs," said one girl.

"Eww, my mom says drugs are bad. No wonder Amber is weird; her mother is stupid," said another. My eyes had burned with hatred, embarrassment and disdain.

"Here she comes," the third girl of the group said. They had seen me walking toward my classroom. "Let's get out of here, NO WE DON'T WANT ANY DRUGS," the girl screamed my way. I hid my face in my books and walked faster into the room where I took my seat in the back. Stares and giggles followed me wherever I went that day; I couldn't escape.

At lunch I sat at the table closest to the door and ate by myself until Chris came by with his tray. I told him about the incident in the hallway and he told me they were being dumb. That helped a little, besides I had the best friend anyone can ever have so it didn't matter what the other people said. As long as Chris was my friend nothing else mattered.

Every day of fourth grade gained me another few people talking about my mother and her way of life. The same as before, they didn't try to get to know me as a person, they just knew my home life and that frightened them. They didn't want to be friends with me for reasons I had no control over. I couldn't force my mother to stop drinking, stop taking drugs. I was only a child and my mother never listened to me about anything. Each day I hated waking up and going to school, I hated being the only one in the world. I was lonely, I wanted friends, I wanted to go out to the movies, to birthday parties and other events the local children were involved in.

My mother's problems prevented me from being the child I was meant to be, the child God had made. My mother never knew what I went through at school, nor did she care. She made it a point to make sure Alicia and I didn't talk to her about school. As she put it, "I've already lived through my share of schooling; I do not need to be bothered with more."

Being so young I didn't know how money came into the household, I only knew we had clothes and we had food, most of the time. Now that I look back I don't know how my mother paid for any of the necessities; food, clothing, school books, etc. or the late nights she spent on the drugs, alcohol and the stuff she splurged on that encumbered our survival. She didn't work, and she didn't get any money from the deaths of my grandfather and grandmother. My father was paying child support but that didn't cover the costs of her needs and wants, just ours.

I believe my mother duped him into giving her more money. She is a very persuasive person. As I got older I believed she told my father that Alicia and I were spoiled kids who needed every material object known to man and she couldn't give it to us because he didn't pay her enough. My father, probably filled with guilt would give in to her and pay her more and more money, and each day that passed he would believe we were terrible children and that was why he stayed away. He didn't know she had a drinking problem, or that she was a drug addict.

Entry 22: <u>February 1990</u>

My mother was very greedy, she would always think of what she wanted before she had even one ounce of a thought about her children. During the month of February, about one month after Alicia's eighth birthday I was told that I would be able to read one of my stories out loud to the entire school, and could possibly be rewarded a trophy if I won for most creative. I told my mother and she said she would be there. I was excited, I loved writing and I couldn't believe my mother was going to be there cheering me on.

The day was approaching rapidly and I still hadn't chosen which story I was going to read. This had been a tough decision for me; I knew that everyone would be laughing at me even if they liked what I had written. Chris helped me along with the process and we chose the perfect story, a story about a girl who wanted her mother to stop killing herself. It was a sad story, a story that paralleled my life in some way. The mother in my tale would smoke and drink and she didn't care. She had tried to kill herself on four occasions but never succeeded. My hope in reading this would show my mother what she was doing to me, maybe she would realize the pain and suffering she was putting me through and she would stop. I also prayed that my fellow classmates would understand that I was just another kid like them who had a troubled mother; hopefully the other kids would realize that I was not my mother and they would accept me for who I was.

The day finally came and I was backstage rereading the words on the paper when Chris came to me. He was also reading one of his accomplishments. "Hey, I just want to wish you good luck," he said to me. "And, don't worry about your mom, just read it."

"Thanks Chris," I responded.

"Amber Jacobs," the teacher responsible for the contest called out in her squeaky voice. "Amber Jacobs, it's your turn."

I scrambled to my feet and took the stage overlooking my peers and their families. What was I thinking? I looked into the curtains; Chris was giving me thumbs up. I half smiled at him. I looked out over the crowd, glancing around for my mother. I didn't see her but believed she was there behind the shadows watching me read the story I wanted her to believe in as much as I did.

After I read, the crowd was silent. Did they like it? I looked around once more, still unable to find her. I didn't know what I was supposed to do so I walked off the stage. There was no applause but there were also no boos. I won first prize that night. I won a trophy and a check for fifty dollars. I had never had that much money in my lifetime, what was I going to do with it? I knew I wasn't giving it to anyone.

Chris won second prize and a girl named Emily won third. I walked out to the lobby with Chris and his mom but it seemed I was wrong, my mother wasn't hiding in the shadows, she wasn't there. My heart was broken, she had promised me. Chris's mom drove me home. Beverly was there with Alicia, she told me that my mother went out and she wouldn't be home until later. I should have known. Her greed had taken over, had consumed her whole and nothing could stop it. She needed that drink, she craved that joint, but her daughter could wait.

I went to my room and shut the door. I looked at my trophy and put it away in my closet. I didn't want to remember this night at all. I won and lost at the same time, it was a very bad feeling.

Entry 23: <u>February 1990</u>

The Monday following the contest at school changed everything for me. Kids came up to me and said I did a good job, they congratulated me. They still didn't talk to me but they liked my writing. That made me feel better, it made me feel like I belonged in the world for a reason. I was put on the earth to write, to change people's lives through my talent. Finally, an outlet for me, something to put all my anger, disappointment and sadness into. I smiled.

Entry 24: <u>May 1990</u>

The school year had ended, and it was May before I knew it. It was time for me to turn ten-years-old. My mother decided on taking me out to dinner with Alicia and Chris. I was so excited, a special dinner just for me, and I could invite my best friend. I wasn't keeping my hopes up that my mother would keep her promise; I had been hurt too many times in my short life to be that stupid. But the day came and the dinner was still on.

It was a Friday night, and it was the most beautiful night I had seen in a long time. The sky was clear, lit up by the tiny bulbs of gas-stars. The breeze was just right for the hot weather we had been experiencing. I was dressed in a knee length skirt, my favorite color, blue, and a blue sweater to match. My feet sported brand new flip flops that my mother had bought me just a week before. I had been bugging her for new shoes, my old ones were ragged and gave the impression that I just came out of a cardboard box. The soles were falling off and the toes had holes in them. I sometimes would stick my big toe through them. Alicia was wearing a pink dress and Chris was dressed in khaki pants and a white button down shirt. My mother actually looked beautiful for once. Her hair was down, resting on her shoulders and she was wearing a navy blue dress with pearls around her slender neck.

The night was starting off on the right foot. I couldn't believe it, not only was my mother taking me to dinner for my birthday, we looked like a happy family. I prayed the night would stay like this.

Dinner was fabulous. The restaurant was an upscale and classy place which featured a jazz band with Cassandra Blanc as the lead singer. Her soulful voice resonated through the room, grasping the attention of all attendees. The room we were in, nicknamed the "dark room" was burrowed in the rear of the building hiding us from the rest of society. It was entitled the "dark room" for many reasons. The walls were covered in a dark mahogany wood paneling and the floor was hidden underneath a maroon colored rug. Along the walls were photos that had been taken of the surroundings of our small town and of the occupants of it. Babies that were born, Weddings held at the restaurant, the owners, and a gorgeous painting by Jon Luc DeAregalla. Jon Luc was a well-known artist who lived an hour from our house. He was also a regular partier at the "Jacobs Club for drinkers."

We took our seats at the table to the rear of the room. All in all there were about eight other tables, all full, in the tiny room. Chris and I sat next to each other and Alicia on the other side. My mother sat in the middle of her two daughters. She was perched with a cigarette in her hand and an ashtray close by.

The waitress came by a minute later and asked if we would like to start on any drinks. I winced at the word. I ordered a coke, Alicia a root beer and Chris a sprite. As I knew my mother, she ordered a vodka tonic, on the rocks, her drink of choice. I hoped that she would only drink that one drink that night, which wasn't the case. I wanted to open my presents right away so my mother consented and gave me the present she had purchased first.

The box wasn't wrapped and there seemed to be no card attached, didn't matter, it was the thought that counted. The box was small, and I opened it slowly, afraid of the contents. It was beautiful. Inside was an antique ring, with my birthstone embedded into the casing; emerald. "It was your grandmother's; I thought you should have it since you loved her so much. The two of you had the same birthstone, isn't that something?" she said after she took a long sip of her third drink. "Don't lose it now Amber, she would be very upset."

I cried. I missed my grandmother and wished she was here to share this with me. The ring immediately went onto my finger. "Don't worry mommy, I won't lose it. Thank you." I said to her, as if she really cared. She smiled and said Happy Birthday.

Alicia gave me her present next. Hers was wrapped, haphazardly though, wrapped all the same. The box held a doll, her name was Olivia, and it was Alicia's old one from when she was a baby. She hadn't exactly loved the doll but she hated to part with any of her toys so it was very special for me. "Thank you Alicia,"

She got up out of her chair and walked over to me to give me a hug and a kiss on the cheek. Although bossy and sometimes cruel I loved my sister. Chris's present was last. His was wrapped and it had a card. The card read:

"To a Birthday Girl who is the Best…" and the inside, "Have a Happy Birthday and all the rest!" He wrote inside, "Dear Amber, I hope you have a happy birthday, Love Chris." I would save this card for eternity.

The present was incredible. I had never received such a wonderful gift before and I was thrilled. The red leather cover with the word 'journal' engraved on the front came into view first and I immediately ripped the rest of the paper off. On the bottom of the journal, engraved in gold lettering was my name, Amber Katherine Jacobs. I was so excited. Five hundred pages of nothing that would soon become greatness. I could write down my thoughts in a nice book now instead of on scrap papers of loose leaf from my notebooks. I gave him a huge hug and thanked him profusely.

Dinner came to our table on a large brown tray on one hand of our wait-ress. Her name was Priscilla, I knew because my mother was calling her over every five minutes for a drink. By the end of our dinner she was causing a scene. Her words were slurred, as they were every night, and her actions were all over the place. Everyone in the room was staring at us, and there was no hiding. She couldn't seem to control the volume of her voice, screaming her thoughts as if she was the only person in the room. It was time for dessert and she was up, yes my mother was standing up with a glass of vodka in her hand hollering above the conversations of the other patrons.

"Today's my girl's birthday! Can you believe it? She's ten years old! You're not a little girl no more," she said as she squeezed my cheeks until blood trick-led from the cut she inflicted from her long fingernails. "Give my girl a fucking cake Priscilla! What are you fucking stupid?"

I tried to hide; I slumped down in my chair hoping I would disappear. Chris was looking around the room at all the people. Who knew what he was think-ing. Alicia had tears in her eyes. Although she loved the party scene and she was an extremely outgoing girl, when in public she always became embar-rassed. Priscilla came in with a chocolate cake with one candle on top, illumi-nating the frosting.

"Well it took you long enough, what were you doing, giving your boyfriend a blow job?" my mother asked laughing, sounding like a hyena. Priscilla put the cake on the table while everyone sang happy birthday to me, she looked as if she was going to cry. Out of everyone my mother was the loudest, most obnoxious person in there. Her drink was spilling everywhere. Her arms were flailing about, up, down, right, left, round and round. She turned around and noticed everyone staring at her, took her long enough.

"What are y'all staring at? This aint no freak show," she said in her loudest voice. She walked up to the nearest table where an old couple sat, sharing what should have been a romantic evening uninterrupted by crazy people. "Hey old man, aren't you going to wish my daughter a happy birthday?" The man looked over to me and raised his glass, saluting me and wishing me happy days. He looked rather frightened of my mother; she had that way about her. "That's better. Y'all have a wonderful evening now ya hear?" she said. Since when was she southern?

After we all finished our dessert my mother drove us home. Yes, in her drunken state she drove with three young children in the car. It was a miracle nobody was hurt. Chris was dropped off at home and his mother waved good-bye. I never thought about what she was thinking letting my mother take care of her son for so many hours. She was probably a very naive person who thought that my mother could be responsible once in a while. If she spent one second in our house she would see the light. We arrived safely at our house.

In bed that night I had cried. The night had started off with a bang and ended with an explosion. Why couldn't we have been a normal family? Some birthday, I thought.

"Hey Amber, I'm sorry your birthday was ruined," my sister said.

"It's okay. It's not like I've had everything I've ever wanted before."

"I love you," she said to me in all honesty. She really was the sweetest person I had known, when she actually acted like herself. I admired Alicia more than anyone; she was strong, valiant, and most of all brave. She was the total opposite of me, not afraid of anything, could conquer every obstacle set in front of her if she wanted, and she was beautiful. She looked like our long lost father, her reddish hair flowing down her mid-back and her brown eyes shining with life. Her personality was extraordinary. She could make friends wherever she went and everyone seemed to flock to her. Me on the other hand had brown hair and brown eyes, people stayed away from me, and I only had two friends; Chris, and Alicia. "I love you too Alicia," I responded.

She crawled into bed with me and hugged me, reassuring me about life, about family. We both had gone through too much for young children, too much hurt, too much pain, and too much neglect. We held each other and cried, comforting each other, taking away the numbness of the unfairness of life, if only for a fleeting moment. That night brought us together again. We had been too far apart for too long. I missed my sister, my friend and now I had her back, and I was never going to let her go again.

Entry 25: <u>August 1990</u>

The summer months hurtled us into chaos and multiple parties. Alicia and I, not wanting to spend too much time at our house spent most of the summer at Chris's house playing with him and Janie. Chris was our savior, without him we would have been trapped in that house with our captor and her prison guards.

It was the beginning of August and school was going to begin in a few weeks. Chris and I were starting the fifth grade and Alicia and Janie were going into third. Janie had blonde hair like her brother and blue eyes. She and Alicia were excited to be in the same class that year, they talked about it non-stop.

One day we were playing tag outside, having a good time. During lunch Chris told me that his mother had gotten a job and they would have to move.

"Where?" I asked. "We're moving to California," he told me, his eyes focused on his feet. My heart sank deep into the depths of my soul. We wouldn't be able to hang out. There wouldn't even be times when either of us could make it to visit. He wasn't close, it was a two day drive to California and there wasn't even a remote chance my mother would opt to drive me there.

"You know, Alicia's going to be upset that she won't have Janie in her class," I said trying to sound as if I didn't care I wasn't going to see him anymore. "Has she heard yet?"

"I don't know. I think my sister is going to tell her today." "When are you leaving?"

"Next week." He started biting his lip, a habit that informed me he was nervous and upset. He had done that since the day I met him five years ago. "But we can still write letters to each other, ya know, pen pals or something."

"Yeah," I agreed.

A pen pal wasn't the same as real friendship to me. I was angry at him for doing this to me, for leaving me to fend for myself. He knew my situation and he should have forced his mother to turn down the job to stay here. If our friendship had meant anything to him he would have done that for me. His mother had a perfectly good job and it wasn't a necessity to get a new one.

I also didn't want to lose him as a friend; he was the only one I had, so I kept my anger inside. I didn't let him know anything. I was also worried about my next year at school. Who would keep me company while I endured the endless remarks kids made about my family.

"Hey Amber," Alicia said. The girls had come out from the kitchen and had joined us. She sat behind me and rested up against me, and Janie did the same with Chris. From the sounds of things it seemed as if Alicia hadn't yet found out about the sudden loss of a good friend.

The rest of the day went by in a blur. I tried to have a good time but the thoughts of Chris leaving encumbered my being. The four of us played more tag and then a game of hide and seek. Dinnertime was approaching so Alicia and I left. What route we took I didn't know. One minute we were playing the next minute we were walking through the door into our hell.

Our mother wasn't home so we were left to fend for ourselves. I made us both peanut butter and jelly sandwiches and a glass of milk. We finished our summer reading, watched a little television and went to bed.

The next morning I told Alicia about the move and she was upset. As I suspected she hadn't known and she had gone to her room and sulked in her pillow. She had made a vow never to talk to Janie again, maybe if she ignored her she would stay. I convinced her not to do that and by mid-afternoon we were back at their house.

Every day that week we spent with Chris and Janie. Their mom was very lenient with all of us and knew how important our friendship was. We practically slept over every night. Moving day was coming closer and closer and nothing we could do would stop it. It was the end of August and school was to begin the following week, without our best friends we didn't know how we were going to survive.

Their house was filled with large brown boxes and the remaining furniture they hadn't packed yet. Chris's room looked empty without his posters on the wall and quiet without his stereo blasting. It was the last night I would see Chris for a long time and both Alicia and I were spending the night. Our mother didn't even ask where we were going.

Chris's mom called up to us to tell us dinner was ready so we stumbled down the stairs to the dinner table. Chris's dad, Charlie was sitting at the head of the table, he was cutting the turkey. Chris's mom Maureen was in the kitchen preparing the last minute dishes. Janie and Alicia hurried in from playing in the backyard and sat in the two seats to the left of Charlie. Chris and I helped Maureen with the rest of the food and took our places at the table.

"Well tonight is a very special and sad night," Maureen said as she sat down. "We are no longer going to live in this lovely town and will leave behind two very special people. None of us will ever forget Amber and Alicia and we hope to remain friends for life. Amber," she said to me, "you have been a dear friend to Chris and I pray that the two of you will keep in touch. You can call any time and we will be pleased to get many letters from you. Chris is lucky to have you in his life and I know he wants to hear from you. Alicia, we welcome your letters and phone calls as well. Janie found a great friend in you and she would be heartbroken if she lost you. Now, let's enjoy this wonderful turkey dinner. We will celebrate our own thanksgiving tonight.

"We will go around the table and each one of us can say what we are grateful for. I'll start; I'm grateful for this meal, for my husband and my children. I am also thankful for having Amber and Alicia here to share this with us."

"I'm thankful for Amber and for dinner and for Janie and Chris and for you Maureen and Charlie," Alicia said. "I'm thankful for turkey, and horses, and for my mom and dad and Chris. I am thankful for Amber and for my best friend Alicia." "That was nice Janie," Charlie said as he patted her on the back. "I am thankful for everything we have and for my lovely wife and her new job. I am thankful for my two beautiful children and our health. I would like to thank God for Amber and Alicia for being with us tonight and for the last five years."

"I'm thankful for Amber being my friend and for the food and my family," replied Chris.

I wasn't feeling too thankful that night; I was too wrapped up in my own feelings of despair and abandonment. So far all the men in my life had left me, both of my grandfathers who died before I was born, my father, and now my best friend. But I didn't want to feel like the only one who wasn't grateful so I found my voice inside of me and I repeated what they had all said, except I didn't elaborate on anything. I kept it simple. "I am thankful for Alicia and all of you and Chris." "Well that was nice now wasn't it?" Maureen said as she placed some mashed potatoes into everyone's dishes. 'Not really,' I thought to myself.

The dinner was excellent; turkey was my favorite food. Maureen had cooked some broccoli casserole which I had never tasted before, it was incredibly good. The flavor of the casserole, potatoes, turkey, beets and stuffing filled my mouth with happiness and I forgot for an hour that Chris was leaving. We cleaned up our plates and awaited our dessert, triple fudge brownie cake. I couldn't believe how big the fluffy cake was and it melted in my mouth it was so delicious. I had two pieces.

With the kitchen clean and our bellies full Chris and I went up to his room to play a board game. The only game he didn't pack was Monopoly so we set up the pieces and chose our figurines. I was the horse and Chris was the shoe. Alicia and Janie came in and begged to play with us. Janie chose to play the wheelbarrow while Alicia was the hat. Chris was the banker as he was the best in math between the four of us and we began play.

An hour later Janie and Alicia became bored with the game and left to go play house in Janie's room. Chris and I were left alone to finish our game. He took over Janie's place as the lead and I was losing, as usual. It was finally quitting time, although monopoly was a great game there's only so long one can play without it becoming monotonous.

"You know Amber; I wish I wasn't going anywhere." "Me either. I'm going to miss you." "I'm going to miss you too. But, we'll still write and talk on the phone all the time right?" "Well I guess. I don't know how I'm going to call you; my mother probably won't let me. And, I don't have any money for stamps or envelopes."

"I'll call you then, and we'll figure out something about letters. Here I got you a present," he said reaching under his bed bringing out a neatly wrapped gift.

I opened it, inside was a box of envelopes, a roll of stamps and stationery set with angels riding winged horses. It was beautiful, I loved it. "Thank you Chris," I said as I pulled him into an embrace. "You're my best friend."

"You're welcome. I wanted to tell you before I left that I like you Amber. I like you as a girlfriend."

This caught me by surprise and my body tensed. Out of all the times we've spent together he picked that night to tell me, the night before he left for good. Many emotions swelled my soul and I didn't know what to say. I was angry at him for waiting until now, happy that he told me and that he felt that way, and sad to lose him. "I like you too," I managed to say. He kissed me on the cheek and then on the mouth, it was the first kiss for both of us and it was an awkward 10-year-old kiss, but one I would remember for a long time.

We went to sleep around 11:30 and woke up early the next morning. I walked downstairs and forgot where I was. The downstairs was empty except for a few small items. There was a large moving truck in the driveway; two men were loading the furniture into it. We sat on the kitchen floor and ate blueberry muffins for breakfast and then played a final game of tag outside.

"Hey kids, we have to get going," Maureen yelled from the patio window.

"Bye Amber," Chris said. The time was here and I stood looking broken. "Don't forget to write." He hugged me tight and we both cried. He kissed me again and then he said bye to Alicia. The four of us walked to the front yard and stood on the steps next to the rose bushes we had helped Maureen plant. Chris and Janie got in the back of their car and waved goodbye. Maureen and

Charlie gave Alicia and I hugs and a kiss on the forehead and wished us good luck. They drove away with the moving truck in tow; Alicia and I staring after them.

Entry 26: <u>September 1990</u>

Both Alicia and I were devastated when they left and couldn't stop thinking about them for the months to come. School had started and it felt strange to be there without Chris. The desk where he would have sat held another student, Andrew James. He was new to the school and already had become the most popular boy in class. That one year at school without Chris seemed like a lifetime and my soul ached for him. I missed my best friend and wished he was there to keep my company during the classes I hated.

Alicia had made new friends and though she still missed Janie she had gotten through the third grade with flying colors. She was very bright and received all A's on her report card. The only class I enjoyed was English and received my one and only A in that subject. On each assignment handed back to us my teacher, Mrs. Jessimy wrote "Amber, you should pursue a career in writing, you have a way about you," followed by a smiley face and a 'way to go' sticker. That class always made me smile and wish for it to never end.

The remarks about my family never ceased and caused me to hide in the corner of the cafeteria away from the other kids in order to eat my lunch in peace. I never understood why they never harassed Alicia, I was a tad jealous of that and wished they would stop bantering me. Why couldn't I be normal like everyone else? Why was I chosen to live a life of solitude, neglect, and abuse? I often thought to myself that God had a bigger plan for me and I should accept my life and all the obstacles that were in my way. My life was like a track built around a football field, it kept on going around and around; it never ended at a single destination. Around the track yellow and white hurtles were strategically placed so I would have to figure out a way to jump over them without knocking them over.

I continued to circle trying to find my destination but yet it wasn't showing up anywhere. The same environment shined into my eyes and I wondered if I was lost. My mother was always at the same point, right next to the largest hurtle, which stood six feet high, impossible to jump and always in sight.

The fifth grade ended and it was graduation day. I was moving up to the middle school and I was scared to death. In just three short months I would be in a brand new school with many of the same people and new bullies to torture me. It would also be the first time in a long time that Alicia and I wouldn't be in the same building. She needed me, I was her older sister, her protector; or was it the other way around? I admitted to myself it was I who needed her.

Entry 27: <u>July 1991</u>

My eleventh birthday came and went as if it never arrived and it was finally the middle of the summer. Only one and a half months left until the dreaded day. On July 29th my mother had her friends over as usual. They were drinking and smoking and disregarding anything that we said to them. Nobody cared if we had any food or water and we were left to feed ourselves; it was a good thing we were used to it.

"Could I interest you in a history lesson about France?" asked Jon Luc, who was one of the frequent partiers at our house. Neither Alicia nor I liked him all that much.

Our mother was looking at us, hoping we'd be polite to her friend. We nodded.

He went on for close to two hours about the past, present and future of France. We learned about King Louis XIV's fear of bathing and his insistence on importing mirrors from Italy to place in his castle and how his home was now famous for "the hall of mirrors." We were told of the Louvre and the famous paintings found within the walls. The cathedral of Notre Dame, and its beauty and elegance as well as the Eiffel Tower were now implanted in our minds and we were actually fascinated by the stories of his travels.

Jon Luc would adjust his glasses accordingly as he told of his youth growing up in the popular city of Paris and of the encounters he came across. Although we still couldn't stand him we sat there and listened intently to his stories of love, adventure, and heartache. He told of his first love to a woman named Catherine whom he loved tremendously. One night he had come home to find her dead, suicide. Her father had forbidden her to see him and it had ended like the story of Romeo and Juliet except he didn't end his life. Instead he rose above it and moved far away to a foreign land to find the most beautiful woman in the world; our mother.

That was when we lost interest. Alicia and I said thank you to Jon Luc just for the sake of being polite and went to our room. While lying on our beds I wrote in my journal and then wrote a letter to Chris. Alicia wrote a letter to Janie. I allowed her to use some of the stationery paper I had received on the last day with my best friend. I was coming close to finishing off the packet of flowered paper and was saving up to buy some more. Under the bed I had a shoebox in which I saved every letter Chris ever wrote to me.

In his letters since his departure he had told me that he loved his new house, his room was big and his driveway had a basketball net. His new school was "all right, considering it's a school," he had mentioned. He had made new friends but I would always be his best friend forever. I couldn't help but get angry when he mentioned Sara, Nick, or Josh. I had to admit, I was jealous.

My letters were always the same. I wrote to him, expelling the hurt inside of me onto the paper. I wondered how he still wrote back to me. The letters were always depressing and filled with hatred toward my mother. I informed him I was on my third journal since he gave me the beautiful engraved one. My second journal and the one I had written in only a few minutes ago weren't half as nice as the one I received from him.

The letter I wrote to him on the night of the history lesson wasn't any different. I wrote and told him about Jon Luc and how he had enlightened us with his vast knowledge of his home country. The story on paper helped Chris understand what France was like and how I wanted to visit sometime in my future. I also made it clear that I still despised Jon Luc and no matter how interesting his stories were he would never gain a place in my heart or in my life.

Alicia told Janie about her new friends and how they had gone roller skating the other day. The ice cream wasn't as good without her there to have fun with. I could tell Alicia missed her best friend more than she said. She didn't want anyone to know that she was hurting, she had been like that since our father had left. She had made a new best friend Ally who was always spending time over our house. She wasn't replacing Janie but she formed a new place in Alicia's life that was blocking a leak from draining out of her heart.

I finished writing the letter to Chris with a tear in my eye, and signed it in my usual signature. With the envelope sealed, a stamp in its rightful place and both Chris's address and mine on the thin slice of paper I was ready to go to sleep and mail it in the morning.

Entry 28: <u>September 1991</u>

Alicia and I had begun our new school year in separate schools. It was horrifying to us that we wouldn't be able to see each other during the day and we dreaded the day that we took different busses. I remember the middle school loomed ahead of me as the yellow bus bumped along the windy road. I knew that this school wouldn't be any different than the elementary school I attended for five years. The kids wouldn't like me any better. Just because I was in a different building didn't mean I would have a better experience.

The first day proved my point. I stepped into my homeroom and the teacher was taking attendance. I sat down next to a girl who had fiery red hair and a boy who had his head stuck in a comic book. I put my head down when the teacher spoke up.

"Hello, I would like to welcome you to the sixth grade, my name is Mrs. Palmer and I will be your homeroom teacher for the school year. I hope you all enjoy your time here and know you can always come to me if you need help with homework. Now, let's go around the room and introduce ourselves. I'll start. As I have mentioned my name is Mrs. Palmer, I am married and have two girls who are both currently attending college. My favorite thing to do is work on my garden at my house."

Everyone in class introduced themselves and I was trembling in my seat wishing I wasn't there.

"My name is Reese McCarthy, I have two dogs and three cats and a snake named Boa. I play baseball and soccer and when I get to high school I am going to play football."

"My name is Olivia Miller, my mom just had a baby girl and her name is Rebecca. We call her Becky for short and she is so pretty."

The introductions went on for five minutes, but not long enough for me to get out of it.

"My name is Chad Oliver, and I am currently working on my own comic book series about a boy who saved the world when he was only five years old," said the boy next to me. "When I get older I will become famous and be well-known for comedy."

"Ok, thank you Chad. Now, how about you?" Mrs. Palmer said as she pointed to me.

I raised my head a little higher and softly said, "My name is Amber Jacobs and I have a sister named Alicia who is in the fourth grade. I enjoy writing and reading." My face burned as my cheeks lit up crimson rose.

"Amber, you forgot something," a girl by the name of Aubrey said to me. "Mrs. Palmer, Amber's mom is a drug addict and an alcoholic." She stared at me again with a grin. I slumped low in my chair hoping I would disappear.

"Now Aubrey, that isn't very nice to say. Apologize to Amber."

"Why? It's true."

"You know sometimes people have problems that are nobody's business but their own. You shouldn't judge people by their problems but by their personality. Do you think it's fair that you said that about Amber's mother?"

"No, I'm sorry Amber."

I knew she hadn't meant it; she had just done what the teacher had said for her to do. What a way to start the day.

The bell rang and I started to leave homeroom to go to my first class when Mrs. Palmer took me aside.

"Oooh, Amber's getting in trouble on her first day," laughed Aubrey.

Mrs. Palmer looked at her and Aubrey left the room leaving just the teacher and myself.

"Amber, is everything okay at your house?"

"Yes," I lied. I didn't want to be separated from my sister. I knew that in most cases children who were taken away from an abusive family were placed in foster homes and that most of the time siblings had to be separated. "Everything is fine. Aubrey doesn't know what she's talking about."

"Okay, but if you ever need to talk you can always come to me."

"Thank you," I said. By this time kids were coming into the room for first period. I left and walked down the room towards my math class.

The rest of the day didn't get any better. I had to bring my lunch into the bathroom because there weren't any empty seats where people would let me sit. So I sat in a smelly stall eating my self-made peanut butter and jelly sandwich and strawberry juice box feeling sorry for myself.

The last class of the day was my English class and I was looking forward to it. English was the only class I looked forward to. Since I learned how to read and write I found my escape from the harsh reality I was living.

My teacher, Mr. Darcy was very nice and also very intelligent. He was tall, young, and handsome. His dark hair was always brushed and perfect and his smile told everyone that he wasn't a mundane teacher but a fun one. Although English was my favorite subject I still positioned myself as far away from the teacher as I possibly could and kept my mouth shut.

That first day Mr. Darcy handed out note cards where we wrote down our information, our address, phone number and homeroom number as well as

homeroom teacher's name. Again we all went around the room and said something about ourselves. Great way to end the day. After introductions we went
over the basics of the English language and had a spelling bee; I won as usual.
He placed a book in my hands and I was on my way out the door as the bell
chimed.

Entry 29: <u>October 1991</u>

The weeks following that first day passed by as if everything were normal, but I knew all too well it wasn't even half way there. Mr. Darcy had noticed my writing ability and was in the process of trying to convince me to take this after school writing program for the gifted. I continuously turned him down. I didn't need any after school program to have more people make fun of my mother and my lack of confidence and social skills.

He never understood why I always said no and I wasn't about to tell him, if he really wanted to know he'd find out himself. And sure enough he did. In October he pulled me aside after class and told me he talked to my homeroom teacher and she had informed him about my family life. I couldn't believe he would do something like that. How could he snoop around in business that wasn't his? I was ashamed. I liked Mr. Darcy I thought he was a nice guy and a great teacher and I respected him.

I clammed up when he talked to me about it. I shut down my emotions and a glaze formed over my eyes. He must have sensed that I wasn't truly listening to him so he stopped talking and just looked at me with his arms crossed. He stood up to his full height and I could not help but feel intimidated and frightened that he was going to do something awful to me.

"Amber, I know how bad you must feel about this but you don't have to. If you talk about it I or someone else could help you. Does she abuse you?"

"No," I said emphatically.

"Good. Does she leave you alone for long periods of time?"

"No, she's always home. She's at work during the day when Alicia and I are in school and at night she stays home. And whatever everybody says she's not an alcoholic and she's not into drugs at all."

"She's not? I've heard from a credible source."

"Look!" I yelled. "Kids don't like me very much; they all think I'm weird so they make up stuff about me so that nobody likes me. My mother is normal and she loves us very much. I hate it when people talk about her like she's a bad mom, it hurts my feelings. She's the best mom, and she's my best friend besides my sister." I knew I had to say something that would make him believe me. I knew what I said was a lie and that I shouldn't have said it but again, I didn't want to be separated from my sister.

"All right, but if something happens you can come to me, I will help you."

I didn't understand why all of a sudden people cared about what happened to me. I didn't know if I liked it or not. I wanted people to care but I also wanted people to just leave me alone and not interfere with my life.

I nodded and left the room. No need to waste words on something I was never really going to do. The hallway was buzzing with activity, lockers clanging shut, friends whispering to each other about a secret they possessed, footsteps running to their designated classroom, and teacher's scratching the chalkboard with a stubble of a piece of chalk. I didn't want to face another class, more looks my way, another teacher looking beyond my abilities as a student and only seeing a girl who has a terrible life. I just wanted to be done with all of the day to day crap I had to deal with.

Only one more class and I would be finished for the day only to start another one tomorrow. It was volleyball day in gym and I was placed on the team with Jenny and Chad who were dating, as well as Catherine, Alec, and Noah. The opposite team was a much better one than us; Kim, Will, David, Shannon, Becky, and Lucas.

We played two games both of which my team lost. I didn't care much; I just wanted to leave school. I didn't necessarily want to go home but school was worse for me than home, at least Alicia would be there.

The bell rang and everyone rushed out of the gymnasium. I gathered my jacket and books from my locker and headed home. On the way I watched as the leaves on the ground danced with the wind as the sun seemed to put a spotlight on the dancers. I passed through the same park I did every day and noticed a young man on one knee on the ground asking his girlfriend who was sitting on a beautiful park bench to marry him. The tears of joy formed an outline around her eyes and she placed her right hand over her mouth stifling the tiny noises she was making as he placed the diamond ring on her left ring finger. She said yes and they embraced. It was a nice thing to see and I smiled. I hoped that their lives would lead them to happiness.

I stopped looking at the newly engaged couple and proceeded on my path to eternal hell. Dogs barked, children screamed, teenagers talked on the phone, and I walked steadily along the windy streets until I finally reached the house where I lived. The lights were dark in the family room and I found that odd. I didn't know what was going on, my mother never shut off the lights unless she wasn't home.

I opened the door and flicked the switch, immediately the light above my head came to life and the front hall was immersed with the shiny yellow glow of the 60 watt light bulb. "Hello," I yelled hoping for a return answer. Nothing.

Alicia wasn't home yet from soccer practice and my mother wasn't home either. I shrugged it off thinking she was probably at the liquor store stocking up for the next month. I did my homework and watched some television.

Around 6:30 Alicia was dropped off by her friend's mom and still our mother wasn't home. We couldn't figure out where she was nor did we bother to try to find her. Alicia did her homework and we both played a board game and watched a movie. By the time we finished it was 10:00 and we were both exhausted beyond belief.

The next morning we awoke to a vacant house, we couldn't understand where our mother was. We went to school and went through the mundane tasks we had to in order to pass our classes. When we went home she still wasn't there. We were both worried by now; she hadn't disappeared for more than a few hours before.

"Where is she?" asked my sister.

"I don't know, but we can't tell anyone she's not here, they'll separate us and we'll never see each other again," I responded.

"But what if something happened to her?"

"Who cares," I shrugged and went into the kitchen to do homework. That night I had to finish the book I was reading and write a book report on it. I loved to read so this assignment was fun for me but I still had history and math to do on top of it. I was more worried about finishing my work than whether or not my neglectful mother was alive or dead.

Alicia went into her room and blasted her music. She was mad at me for being so nonchalant about our missing mother but I didn't care. Lately I hadn't cared about anything except about my sister. She was the only person in the world that I loved, the only person I would die for. Sometimes when she cared too much about what was going on with our mother I would get angry. I couldn't see the reasoning behind why she cared so much. My thoughts were if she didn't care about us why should we care about her. My sister obviously thought differently.

Entry 30: <u>October 1991</u>

A week passed and still our mother hadn't shown up. At that point I had become really worried. I was scared; not that something happened to her but that without her home something horrible would happen to Alicia and I. I knew in my heart that I had to tell someone about the missing person but I was scared. Alicia was also scared. She had been having nightmares since the third night of freedom and had slept with me in my bed ever since.

That day at school I told my English teacher about what happened. He had an extreme look of concern on his face as I went through my story of how my mother hadn't been home since nine days before. "Well Amber, I'm glad you came to me and told me. Why didn't you tell someone sooner?"

"I'm afraid; I don't want to be separated from my sister. What is going to happen to us?" I asked with a tone of trepidation in my voice.

"You don't have to be scared; I will do everything I can to make sure that you and your sister are together during this time. I will have to call some people and have the police search for your mom in case something happened to her." He must have sensed my nervousness and assured me that my mother was going to be okay. "I'm sure she's all right, it's just a formality. Anyway, is there anyone who you can stay with?"

"Well my grandma died a few years ago."

"How about your dad? Is he around?"

"I don't know. He left when I was four and I haven't seen him since. I don't know his number."

"Well you understand that I have to call social services to place you in a foster home. I can't allow you to stay at your house alone for any longer than you already have. It's against the law for children to be home by themselves. A good friend of mine is a social worker and I'll give him a call and tell him about you. I'll make sure everything turns out okay for you."

"I understand Mr. Darcy, thank you," I said as I bowed my head in embarrassment. Now what would the kids say? "Can I go home and pack first?"

"Yes, I'll tell my friend to come pick you and Alicia up at your house at 7:00 is that okay?"

"Yes, thank you very much. I really appreciate what you are doing." Tears streamed down my face and I clenched my hands into fists as I walked out of the room towards my next class.

After school I told Alicia about my conversation with Mr. Darcy and she started to cry. She was upset that we would have to leave our house and only take a few of our belongings but she also knew that we were better off with adults taking care of us. We sat in the family room for the next hour waiting for someone to come pick us up. We looked around memorizing the house and its components. That hour seemed like an eternity and finally the front door bell rang. I walked to the door and unlocked the dead bolt and pulled back the chain. I closed my eyes as tears escaped my eyelids and I prayed that our mother was on the other side of the door.

I opened the door slowly and a tall chubby man stood with a clipboard in his right hand. He was balding and had round black glasses covering his blue gray eyes. His suit seemed too small for him and his black and white checkered tie reached the middle of his beer belly. He smiled showing off crooked teeth and cherry bubble gum. I shuddered and let him in.

"Hello, you must be Amber? John told me all about you. My name is Chuck Diggins. I worked it out where a husband and wife will take both you and Alicia. They are very nice people."

"Thank you Mr. Diggins. This is Alicia. Our stuff is all ready."

"Okay, let's get it into the car and head off."

We walked outside and I locked the front door. "What's going to happen to our house?"

"Well, it will stay there and it will belong to your mom and the two of you so when y'all return home you'll have a place to live."

"Oh."

The car sat at the end of the driveway like a lonely child waiting for his parents to take him home. The trunk opened with a pop and Chuck placed our suitcases in the empty space. I sat in the front seat and Alicia in the back. We were both solemn, and we watched as our house became smaller and smaller with distance.

"Well, let me tell you a little about your foster parents. The woman, Kira is a real nice lady. She was a teacher at the local elementary school until she had her first baby Bailey. She never went back because she loved being a mom. Bailey is two years old, you'll love him, and he's a great kid. Mark is a real estate agent. He's not around as much as Kira wants him to be but they're in love. He's a nice guy too, I'm sure you'll like him. He's a great dad. You two are their first foster kids and I know that you will all get along."

Alicia and I were quiet; we both didn't really know what to say. Never once did I wish that we were with our mother but I didn't want to go live in someone else's house with strangers either.

Chuck pulled up to a beautiful white house with black shutters framing the windows. The front door was painted bright red with a welcome sign hanging in the center. The walkway was filled in with tiny stones, larger rocks served as step stools. There were balloons on the mailbox that was an exact replica of the house. The yard was big and beautiful. Both garage doors were shut and the porch lights were lit for the new family members. Chuck grabbed our bags and we walked to the front door together.

My insides were all tangled and my heart was melting. I was nervous about meeting Kira, Mark and Bailey Warner but was happy that Alicia was able to come with me. Thoughts encumbered my brain; would they like us? If they didn't what would happen? Would we like them? What would our new schools be like? Would the kids be the same as our old classmates? I was shaking inside and out when Kira opened the door and smiled.

She was beautiful. Her smile showed the love and kindness she possessed. She had short brown hair that was accentuated with blonde highlights. Her large brown eyes displayed knowledge, strength, courage and confidence. She was tall and very fit. Bailey was right behind her hiding behind her legs. He had brown hair like Kira and the same large eyes. Only his eyes were blue like Mark. Bailey was dressed in his feet pajamas that sported baseballs, bats, and baseball gloves. His diaper made a squishy noise as he walked and his pacifier held firm in his tiny mouth. Mark was standing to the left of Kira and he smiled down on us. He had blonde hair and blue eyes and he was taller than his wife. I felt awkward around him as I had never lived in a house with a man before.

"Hi there," Kira said to us. "Why don't you come in?"

"Thank you," Chuck said in his loud booming voice.

We all stepped inside where I looked around. The hallway we stood in was elegant. The walls were painted yellow and there was a gorgeous portrait of Kira, Mark and Bailey when Bailey was a newborn hanging on the wall opposite another portrait of Kira and Mark on their wedding day. The living room, which was on our right, was covered in a deep maroon paint. The couches were displayed in perfection and the white satin curtains bordered the windows beautifully. Down the hall the family room lingered in view. Toys were strewn about and the television was playing "Spongebob Squarepants."

We walked deeper into the house and ended up in the large kitchen. On the table were two dishes of meatloaf and potatoes and a glass of milk next to each dish.

"Are you hungry? I made this special for both of you. I hope you like it."

"Meatloaf's my favorite," Alicia practically yelled. She was always so outgoing. I just smiled and sat down. We ate our delicious food in silence as Chuck talked to Kira and Mark put Bailey down for bed. With our dishes and glasses empty, our bellies full, Bailey in bed and Chuck gone Kira and Mark took us on a tour of the rest of the house and showed us where we would sleep.

"I hope you two feel welcome here. I want you to know that our house is your house now and whatever you want you can have. If you need to talk to someone you can always talk to me or to Mark. I am very happy to have you girls here with us."

"Thank you Mrs. Warner," I said quietly.

"Oh Amber, please call me Kira. Now, do you two need anything else? Do you need to take a shower? Do you want a snack, a glass of juice?"

"No thank you, I'm fine. Umm, what school are we going to?"

"Well, Monday you will start at the middle school down the street and Alicia you will begin at the elementary school."

"Is that where you taught?" Alicia asked.

"Yes, in fact your teacher is my good friend Mrs. Dennis. She is a great teacher; you will have a lot of fun with her. And the kids around here are really nice. I still get Christmas cards from my students."

"Do you miss teaching?"

"Yes I do, but I love being home and being a mother to Bailey. Okay, why don't you get ready for bed and I'll come and tuck you in."

Alicia went to the bathroom to brush her teeth and put her pajamas on while I opened my suitcase and took out my journal. I opened it up to an empty page and started writing. Kira was in the doorway watching me. I could see her expression through the tiny mirror on the nightstand in my room. She looked sad and concerned for me. I hated when people watched me, especially when I was writing, it made me self-conscious.

"Amber, can I talk to you for a minute?"

"Sure," I said putting the pen in the middle of the leather bound journal and closing it. "I know that this is hard for you, to not know where your mother is and to be put in a strange house in a strange place with strange people. I want you to know that I am here for you. I will listen to you whenever you want, no judgments." She put her hands in my hair and brushed it away from my face. She continued to play with my hair as she talked. "You don't have to worry about your sister or you because I will take care of both of you and love you as if you were my own daughters. I already do love you and Alicia; as soon as I saw you I knew that you were both very special. I can never replace your mom and I'm not going to try but I want you to know you can trust me. Whatever you tell me I won't tell anyone, not even Mark."

"You can replace my mom if you want; she's a bitch and I don't care if I ever see her again. I am sad that I had to leave home, I love my house." I started to cry again.

Kira kissed my forehead and hugged me tight. She wiped the tears from my eyes and I saw that she had tears forming in her own. This made me even more upset. To know that I caused her to cry stirred something deep inside me, which made me cry harder. Alicia came into my room and saw us both in tears. She came over and wrapped her short arms around both of us. We stayed like that for a few minutes until I was calmed down. Alicia went into her room and I stayed in bed. Kira went and tucked Alicia into her double bed and came back into my room to say goodnight.

"Amber, I'm going to let you get to writing in your journal so I'll just tell you that in the drawer I wrote you a letter, I also wrote Alicia one. I want you to read the letter tomorrow or whenever you get the chance. Goodnight. Have sweet dreams." She kissed me on the forehead again and started to walk out.

"Goodnight Kira, thank you for letting us both stay here."

"I wouldn't have it any other way." She turned off the big light and shut the door behind her leaving me writing in the tiny glow of the bedside lamp. I smiled as she left and knew I liked it there.

Ten minutes after Kira left Alicia opened the door a crack and peeked in my room. When she noticed I wasn't asleep she crept inside and shut the door quietly. "Can I sleep with you tonight?" she asked.

"Yeah sure," I said patting the bed signaling for her to sleep next to me. "What's the matter?"

"Nothing, I can't sleep. Kira's real nice."

"I know. I really like her too. We should be good for her and Mark. Isn't Bailey adorable? I can't wait to play with him."

"He's all right I guess. Do you think that our new schools will be good?"

"I hope so," I said honestly. "I hope that the kids won't make fun of me. Maybe I'll actually make friends at the new school."

"I know you will." Alicia nestled up to my shoulder and her eyes fluttered open and closed. "I miss Mom Amber, where is she?"

"I don't know where she is, but we are better off with Kira and Mark where we don't have to worry about food or drinks," I said. She hadn't heard me. I shut off the light and fell asleep. That night I dreamt of a future of happiness.

Entry 31: <u>October 1991</u>

The first morning I awoke to the smell of bagels toasting and eggs frying on the stove. Alicia wasn't in the bed and the door was slightly ajar. I heard Bailey crying from the kitchen and I heard the front door shut as Mark left for work.

I stayed there in bed for a minute longer looking around the warm room and I couldn't help but be happy. For once in my life I didn't have to worry about Alicia or myself. After using the bathroom I walked downstairs and found the best sight I had ever seen. Alicia was sitting at the table making faces at Bailey who was laughing at her as if he'd never seen anything so funny before. Kira was at the stove frying eggs. She was wearing a flowered apron over a pair of blue jeans and a red turtle neck sweater. Her hair was perfect and her makeup looked as if it was painted on.

The toaster popped and she quickly grabbed the two halves of the bagel and placed them on a dish. It was amazing; I had never seen someone move so fast. With a snap of her wrist she turned over each egg and placed a piece of cheese on top where it melted with ease. Next to the eggs were three pieces of ham sizzling from the heat. The meal smelled delicious.

I stood at the end of the stairs memorizing that morning for fear of never seeing it again. I must have stood there for two minutes before anyone realized I was there.

"Oh, good morning Amber, did you have a good sleep?" Kira asked me with a large smile on her face.

"Yes, thank you."

"I am making bagel sandwiches for breakfast, I hope you like them."

"They smell really good," I said as my stomach rumbled. I sat next to Alicia and anxiously awaited the bagel sandwich.

The tastes of egg, melted cheese, ham and the crusty outer layer and the soft inner layer of the bagel abducted my taste buds and held them hostage. "This is really good," I mumbled with food filling my mouth.

"I'm glad you like them." Kira smiled. She had the most infectious smile that lit up the room. I smiled back my cheeks bulging with bagel sandwich and finished my breakfast within seconds. I gulped my glass of orange juice, washing every last bit of food down my throat. I stood up and brought my dish and glass to the sink and started to wash them.

"You don't need to do that, I can do it. Why don't you and Alicia take Bailey in the family room and play with him."

"Okay," I said. I took Bailey out of his high chair and the three of us played hide and seek. Alicia was with Bailey while I looked and then while I hid they tracked me down. We played the game for an hour and a half. Finally Bailey didn't want to play anymore so we watched some television.

When Bailey went down for his nap I wrote in my journal and Alicia rode Kira's bike around the neighborhood. The bike was a little too big for her but she didn't care.

I remembered the letter Kira had mentioned the previous night so I opened the drawer of my nightstand and took out the flowered envelope. On it Kira had written: For Amber Katherine Jacobs' eyes only. I was intrigued so I slipped my finger in the corner and ripped the top layer open revealing a beautifully hand written letter on matching paper. I read it carefully and slowly;

Dear Amber,

On this day I knew you and Alicia would be joining our family for either a short or a long time. I have always wanted many children and was excited when my son Bailey was born. Now that he's older I wanted to help others. I wanted to share everything I could with someone who needed it badly.

You see, when I was a baby my mother gave me up for adoption. She wasn't ready to be a mother. She was sixteen when she got pregnant and couldn't afford to take care of an infant.

My mom, the one who raised me, she is a wonderful person. She was a foster mother like I am now, and when I came into her house she had already begun raising two boys, Ben and Taylor. When I arrived at 4 months old Ben was eight and Taylor was eleven. My mother wanted to help children who needed a home so she applied to be a foster parent. Immediately she was given to me and she fell in love. When I was five years old she knew she wanted to adopt me so she filed the appropriate papers and I became Kira Lynn Brandon.

I was so happy. My mother is my inspiration and I admire her so much. I wanted to help others like she helped me in my time of need. I applied to be a foster mother just last week; I wasn't expecting anyone to be placed with me for a while but when they called me and told me that two sisters needed a place I knew this was my chance to help you and Alicia.

I heard about your situation Amber, and I am so sorry that your mother left. I know that she loved you so much from what I have read. You had the privilege of being raised by her as I did not. Your mom didn't leave because she didn't love you anymore and her leaving is not your fault. Please understand that, you had nothing to do with her troubles. I ache thinking that you have this guilt burying you deep in the sand and I want to take all of your pain and suffering away.

Your mom will be back some day, they will find her and I hope you can forgive her. Forgiveness is the key to happiness and that is what I want for you two girls; happiness.

I was told you have a gift, writing. I am so glad that you have an outlet for your pain and I know you will use that and help yourself. I would some day love to read one of your stories, which would be wonderful but until then keep writing. If you ever need to write I want you to do it, no matter when. Don't stifle your creativity.

I am going to reiterate this to you; I want you to come to me if you are ever feeling sad or lonely. If you ever need to talk to someone and nobody's around I will be there no matter what. I am here for you Amber always remember that. Even when your mother comes back and you and Alicia go back to living with her I will still be there for you. I am just a phone call or a letter away.

I love you already,

Kira

I folded the letter and placed it gently back into the envelope. I finally had someone who I could trust, who I could talk to. My eyes were watering as I placed the envelope into my journal and continued to write. In the journal for that day I wrote about my present home and how I wanted to stay there forever. I wrote about how Bailey laughed as we hid under the table and how Kira made her bagel sandwiches and how much I loved her even though I had only known her for one day. For the first time in a long time I was happy and I could picture a life worth living. I couldn't believe it was finally happening to me. I smiled as I put the pen down and went downstairs.

Entry 31: <u>October 1991</u>

On the following Monday Alicia and I started our new schools. I was petrified; thoughts bombarded my mind of not being accepted and not doing well in my classes. Kira told me that the kids were all very nice. I was still anxious but I knew that Kira wouldn't lie to me or hurt me in any way so my nerves eased slightly.

I put on some beige corduroy overalls and a light blue long sleeve shirt. I put my long brown hair in a ponytail wrapped with a light blue ribbon that Kira had bought me. As I tied my brown boots Alicia came in my room.

"Amber, I have to go on the bus now; I wanted to say have a good day at your school."

"Thanks Alicia, you have a good day too. But I'm not worried about you; you'll make friends in the first five minutes you're there," I said.

"You'll make friends too. Remember that they don't know us so show them that you are a great person and then you'll make friends."

"Thanks." I hugged my sister and she left showing off her brand new backpack.

"Hasta La Vista Baby," she shouted to me as she scurried down the stairs.

I laughed inwardly. I grabbed my bag and went to get my lunch that Kira had made me. "I'm ready," I said nervously.

"Well don't you look beautiful," she said with her famous smile. "Before you go, I want you to have this," she handed me a gold chain with a cross dangling from the end. "My mother gave this to me the day I was adopted and I want you to have it."

"I can't take this, this necklace is special to you and I'm not your real daughter. You should save this for when you have a girl."

"No, I want you to have it. Every time you look at it you can think of me. Also, when you look at it you remember that you are a wonderful little girl, and whoever makes remarks to you that you don't like, it's them that have a problem not you."

"Thank you," I said not knowing what else to tell her. She gave me a big hug and then scooted me out the door. I was on my way to the day that would tell me what my life was going to be like while living with the Warners.

The middle school looked like a normal school. It was built with reddish brown bricks and had a baseball field in the rear. Everyone was talking and making plans for parties. The corridors were loud and filled with sixth, seventh, and eighth graders running from their lockers to their homerooms. I found the office and announced myself. The lady who was standing there was short with white hair and large round glasses.

"Hello, can I help you?" she asked me with her squeaky voice.

"Yes," I stuttered. "This is my first day at this school; my name is Amber Jacobs."

"Ahh yes, I have been waiting for you. Your homeroom is room 48 and the teacher's name is Mr. Matthew Colliky. Here's your schedule."

"How do I get to room 48?"

She looked at me with annoyance. "Go out the door and take a left it is your third door on the right hand side." With that she turned around and continued to file.

I found the room and sat down near the back. Mr. Colliky sat at his desk with his nose in a pack of papers. He adjusted his wire-rimmed glasses and made faces as he corrected papers. His eyebrows shifted and he nodded his head in agreement as he wrote some notes on a piece of paper.

I looked around at the other kids in the classroom. The boy sitting to my left was dozing off drool dropping from the corner of his lip. I laughed at the sight. There was a girl on my right reading a book intensely. The girl in front of me had long blonde hair that she wore in a French braid tied by a pink ribbon at the end. She turned around and smiled at me. I smiled back politely and wondered if she was going to be my first friend in this new school.

"Hi, I'm Lilly, what's your name?" the girl asked.

"Amber."

"Are you one of the girls who Mrs. Warner is taking care of?"

"Yes, did she used to be your teacher?"

"Yes. She was really nice, my favorite teacher. I wish I was still in the fourth grade so I could have her as my teacher forever. Sixth grade is hard."

"My sister is in fourth grade. She has Mrs. Dennis."

"My brother Carson had her, he said he liked her. He isn't here today, he has a cold."

I smiled. I was very happy to finally be talking to someone my age that didn't know and didn't care about where I came from. I knew Lilly and I were going to be really great friends.

"What's your first class?" I asked.

"I have Math first, and then history. What about you?"

"Well I have English first but I have history right after. Maybe we're in the same class."

"Is your teacher Mr. Rose?"

"Yes."

"Then we're in the same history class," she smiled excitedly.

"Can I sit next to you?"

"Sure."

She turned back around to finish what she was doing and then the bell rang for our classes. I gathered my book bag and stood up to leave.

"I'll see you in history," she said to me as she waved.

I waved back smiling. "See you there."

I was so thrilled to have a friend that for the first time in my life I had trouble paying attention in my English class. My teacher was going over a story that they had read in the previous class and I was trying to take notes on the subject but I just couldn't wait for history class. Then the bell rang and it was time.

I found Lilly in the front of the room. I immediately felt my body slump a little. I never sat in the front, always the back. I didn't want to sit in the front but I also wanted to sit next to my new friend. I stood in the back deciding on what course of action I was going to take when Lilly spotted me and called me over. I walked slowly to the desk next to hers and sat down looking around at all the strangers that from my point of view were staring at me.

"I saved you a seat," she said. "How was English?"

"It was good. It's my favorite subject. I love to write and to read."

"History's my favorite subject, our teacher is so cute! Do you have a boyfriend?"

I looked at her in confusion. "Umm, no. My best friend Chris moved away a couple of years ago. We're sort of boyfriend and girlfriend. Well, at least we were before he moved."

"Well Amber, there are a lot of boys you can meet while you are here. I'll introduce you to a bunch of my friends at lunch."

Suddenly the teacher came into the room and took his position at the front, right in front of Lilly and me. I was mortified. This was the first time in my life I had been this close to a teacher during the actual lessons. I was shaking and felt as if my face was burning.

He started teaching us about the History of the United States and we took notes. Lilly was right, our teacher was really cute and I couldn't keep my eyes off of him. I now realized that being in the front wasn't as bad as I thought it was going to be. I actually liked the front row and decided that I would sit there in every class.

The rest of the morning went by without incident and I was heading for lunch at 12:30. I again sat with Lilly. She introduced me to her friends, Jason,

Patrick, Riley, Olivia, Greg, Jeff, Jack, and Rachel. For the half hour I sat in silence eating my lunch and listening to the nine of them talk. I was having fun listening to them and knew that in a few days I would be involved in their conversation.

"Hey, look who's coming in Lilly, your boyfriend and his sister," said Rachel.

I turned to see a boy and a girl walk into the cafeteria. They both had dark hair and were rather tall. They didn't look to be in our grade, maybe a grade or two older.

"Who are they?" I asked.

Entry 32: <u>October 1991</u>

I learned that they were Beckah and Dylan York. "They are the most popular kids in school," Lilly informed me. "Beckah is a year older than us and Dylan is in our grade."

"Yeah and Lilly has a major crush on Dylan."

"Shut up Rachel, he's walking by us."

"Hey guys," said the handsome Dylan.

"Hi Dylan," Lilly said shyly. He smiled at her and continued walking past. Beckah didn't say anything. "Well, he is hot." They all giggled except for me. I was watching the famous York siblings walk to their table.

"If Beckah's older than Dylan why are they sitting together?"

"They're best friends; they are always together except in classes of course," responded Jason.

"So, are you friends with them?"

"Well we talk to Dylan but Beckah doesn't talk to us. She doesn't even know we exist. She's totally into herself."

I looked over at the table to the far left and watched Beckah as she laughed with Dylan and a few other kids. For the first time in my life I felt this pang of wanting. I wanted to be friends with Beckah. I wanted to be friends with Dylan, and I wanted to belong.

When I turned back around to finish my lunch Lilly was looking at me with a tint of anger in her eyes. I just finished peeling my orange and I ate the tiny slices. Everyone else started chatting again. The bell rang and we had to go to our last three classes.

Lilly was also in my health/gym class and my home economics class. My last class of the day was art. I sat down in the back corner closest to the window and waited until the rest of the students arrived. Just as the bell rang Dylan walked in and out of all the seats left, he sat next to me. I was shocked, and also a little nervous. I prayed that Lilly wouldn't walk past the room and suspect me of going after the boy she wanted to date. Because of this I tried to avoid him at all costs. Whenever he would talk to me I would answer him with blunt yeses and nos. For the first half of the class we conversed in that way and then I started to warm up to him. I didn't want him to think I was being rude.

"So, I saw you sitting with Lilly at lunch today. Are you two friends?"

"Yes," I said. "Today's my first day and she talked to me in homeroom. We are in a lot of the same classes."

"Where did you move to?"

"Well, I'm living with Kira and Mark Warner for right now. My mom left my sister and me so Kira and Mark are our foster parents."

"That sucks, I'm sorry."

"I don't care; my mother isn't a very nice person. Kira is the nicest lady."

"I know. I had her for a teacher when I was young. She was my favorite. Beckah had her too, and sometimes she baby-sits for Bailey. Her and Mrs. Warner are friends. How old is your sister?"

"She is going to be ten soon."

Just then the teacher interrupted us and told us to stop talking for fear of detention. We stopped for a few minutes and continued to paint the group of still objects located in the center of the room. They were placed in the center so that everyone would have a different perspective on the objects and therefore, have different paintings of the same objects. I wasn't a very good painter and it was evident by my misshapen drawing. Just when we thought that the teacher had resigned herself from watching us we began our conversation again.

"So, what kind of music do you listen to?" Dylan asked me.

"I don't know all kinds I guess. What about you?"

"I like Aerosmith and Kiss. They are my two favorite bands, the way Steven Tyler gets up there and just rocks, it's totally awesome! And Gene Simmons is just great. I love it when he sticks out his tongue, it's so long!" He stuck his tongue out as if to show me how the lead singer of Kiss does it. His tongue however wasn't that long. "My dream is to see either band in a concert, which would be so rad. I actually sing in my own band, we're called 'The Lids,' you should come and see us play."

"Sure. Can Lilly come?"

"Sure, if she wants to." He looked disappointed and I felt a pain in my heart for my new friend. If Lilly ever knew that Dylan wasn't interested in her she would be devastated.

This time the teacher walked over to us and told us that it was our last warning. We were to stop talking or we would be peeling onions in the cafeteria on Saturday afternoon. We stopped for the remainder of the class.

Entry 33: <u>November 1991</u>

That weekend Kira dropped Lilly and I off at Dylan's house to watch his band play. Lilly was so excited I had asked her to come. The anger at me from lunchtime that day was completely gone and her eyes just glistened with happiness. His mother answered the door and led us into the basement where a loud thumping was heard. The floor under our feet was vibrating and we were anxious to see if they were any good.

Beckah appeared from a hidden room and grabbed a soda from the refrigerator. She smiled at us and disappeared as quickly as she came.

"Don't mind her, she's upstairs with a couple of girlfriends," said Mrs. York.

The stairs leading into the basement were hidden underneath a pumpkin orange carpet which made both Lilly and I cringe with disgust. We grabbed the banister and walked down into 'The Lids Arena' which was written on the wall at the bottom of the stairs. The basement was obviously a hangout just for Dylan and his groupies.

"Hey ladies," Dylan said as he walked up to us. He had a black electric guitar slung over his shoulder which was attached to a black amplifier next to the large speakers. How could anyone stand being in this house with all the noise? "Take a seat in the audience and enjoy the show."

"Thanks Dylan," Lilly said flirting. We sat down and prepared ourselves for whatever was to come.

Sitting behind a white and silver drum set was a boy with blonde hair that reached his shoulders. His name was David but everyone called him Dusty. Playing lead guitar and vocals was Dylan, who was the heartthrob of the group. Playing bass guitar was a short stubby boy named Greg who seemed a little geeky to be part of a rock band. With curly fire red hair and deep blue eyes with freckles covering his face playing the rhythm guitar was a boy I had recognized from my first day. His name I found out later was Crispin. I thought it was amusing, sounded like a cereal brand. The final member of the band, Frankie, was a girl; she had jet black hair that was cut in blunt layers. She wore black pants and a black t-shirt and covered her face with dark eye shadow and black lipstick.

Lilly and I looked like teeny boppers who were following the band because of a gorgeous lead singer. Dylan started up by announcing himself and the group, his voice booming from the microphone.

"Hey there rockers, we're here to rock you," he screamed and hissed and then continued. "We are 'The Lids!!'"

The drummer slammed his sticks onto the round base of the drum followed by a loud clang from the cymbals. Both Crispin and David started plucking the strings on their guitars and the music was just loud noise. I tried my hardest not to look horrified; Lilly just sat there with a smile on her face stretching from ear to ear, her eyes locked on Dylan. Her dream guy was standing there bobbing his head to the 'music.' He made two movements with his right hand causing more noise to echo through the speakers. His head was looking down at the guitar and his feet were glued to the floor.

Finally he lifted his head and looked at his audience. His face contorted into what he would later call his 'rock band look.' Just before he began to sing he arched his back and caused more loud noise to come from the black boxes. Then he opened his mouth. I was afraid of what was going to come out of it, but I was surprised. Dylan had a really good voice. Lilly was in her glory watching him sing and play his instrument. I didn't know if she actually heard any of the actual music or if she just tuned it all out and concentrated on how good looking Dylan was.

"They are SO good," Lilly screamed to me. "Don't you think?"

"What?" I yelled back to her.

"DO YOU LIKE THEM?"

"Yes, they are very good," I lied.

The band played two songs for us and then shut off their equipment. The room was quiet but my ears were still ringing from the volume of the guitars.

"So, what do you think?" asked Dylan.

"You were great Dylan, I loved it," screamed Lilly; she wasn't used to quiet yet.

"Thanks, how about you Amber, did you like us?"

"Yeah, you were pretty good. You have a really good voice."

"Thanks," he said with a smug look on his face. He brushed back his hair with his left hand and turned to the band, "great job guys! Let's go get a soda."

The seven of us went upstairs where Mrs. York handed us each a soda. On the table she had prepared a plate of crackers and cheese and a bowl of chips. Lilly sat next to Dylan who was sitting next to Dusty. Greg sat on the other side of Lilly so I took a seat next to Frankie who was indulging herself with a handful of greasy chips.

"Where's your bathroom," I asked quietly.

"It's up the stairs yo," said the curly red head, Crispin. "Walk up the castle steps and pass Queen Beckah's room. The dungeon is on your right, and the outhouse is across on your left. Beware of the grumpy old lion though, he doesn't like trespassers."

"Thank you." I did as he told but stopped right after Beckah's room. She was in there with two of her friends. I usually didn't spy on people, I thought it was rude but this time I couldn't help myself.

"So, then Regina liked Bobby and Bobby liked Cassie. Regina got all like mad and jealous so she spread that awful rumor about Cassie. Can you believe that?" some girl said.

"Regina should get over it, he'll never go out with her, she's ugly."

"No, she's not ugly, she's FUGLY!" They all laughed.

"Come on Bridgid, who do you like?" asked Beckah.

"Nobody," she responded slyly.

"Whatever, tell us."

"I don't like anyone, so stop."

"BRIDGID! You can tell us, we won't tell anyone, we promise."

"Pinky swear?"

"Yes," both Beckah and the other girl said and then proceeded to interlope their pinky fingers with Bridgid.

"Well, he's younger than us, but he's so cute."

"Yeah…what's his name?"

"Dylan," she whispered.

"WHAT? You like my brother?"

"Shhhh…you promised you wouldn't tell anyone Beckah, please don't."

Beckah laughed. "I crossed my fingers, how about you Beth?"

"I did too," Beth laughed.

"You are so mean," Bridgid whined. I could hear the sadness in her voice. I felt bad for her. What Beth and Beckah were doing to her wasn't very nice and I knew that if I were in Bridgid's shoes I would be crying by now. "I called my mom to pick me up. I don't want to stay here anymore."

"Don't Bridg, come on we're just joking."

"Don't do that again, it's not funny. Plus, you know I wouldn't tell anyone who you like Beckah."

"Who do you like?" responded Beth.

"I'm not telling. Bridgid, why did you say anything?"

"Sorry."

"Beckah, why did you tell Bridgid and not me? We're best friends."

"Sorry, I just don't want anyone to know. I only told Bridgid because she knows him personally. You don't know him he goes to another school. We met at the mixer last year."

"Ohhh, I know who it is." Beth started laughing. She was rolling on the floor her blonde hair falling in her face. Beckah's face looked like she was going to break out in a rage any minute now. I didn't want to witness that so I went to the bathroom.

On my way out Beth and Bridgid were no longer in Beckah's room and Beckah was sitting on the edge of her bed with tears in her eyes. I felt bad for her, in almost the same way I felt bad for Bridgid.

"Excuse me, you're Beckah right?"

"Mmm hmm," she sniffled.

"My name is Amber, I'm Lilly's friend. We came over to watch your brother play in his band."

She wiped her eyes and looked for something under her bed. She pulled out a shoebox that was filled with candy and gum. "Do you want a piece of candy?"

"Sure, thank you. Where did you get all of this?"

"Halloween, Christmas, Birthdays, and when I go shopping with my friends. I like to have it under my bed so nobody can know where it is. Don't tell anyone, not even Dylan. If he knows I have it he'll eat it all. And, if my mom ever found out she'd kill me. I'd be grounded for like ever. So, how did you like Dylan's band?"

"They're okay. Your brother is really good."

"Yeah he is, but the rest of the band kinda sucks. Don't tell anyone I said that."

"I won't." We both ate a few pieces of candy and then she put the shoebox back in its secret hiding place. "I thought you had friends over?" I asked. I didn't want her to know I overheard their conversation on purpose.

"Yeah I did but they had to go home. Are you new?"

"Yes, Monday was my first day at this school. I'm living with Kira and Mark Warner. Dylan said you were friends with Kira?"

"Yeah," she said. She was now happier than she was earlier and I was happy we were getting to know each other. "I love babysitting for Bailey; he's so cute isn't he?"

"I know. I love him already."

"So why are you living with them?"

"My mom left us alone for a week and I told one of my teachers. He told some other people and now my sister and I are living with them until they find my mom."

"Oh. I'm sorry."

"That's okay. I like living with Kira and Mark and I like my new school and my new friends."

"Hey, do you want to go to the mall with a bunch of us tomorrow? We might go to a movie after too. If you want Lilly can come."

I couldn't believe what I heard. I thought it was a dream but I didn't want it to be at all. I was getting what I have always wanted throughout my life. My wish every time the digital clock struck 11:11 or 1:11 or 2:22 was to be a normal kid who people liked and who was invited places with friends, now it was becoming a reality. I answered quickly and maybe a little too excitedly, "Yes."

"Great." She smiled.

"Amber, what are you doing?" asked Lilly who must have remembered that I was with her and went looking. "Mrs. Warner's here to pick us up."

"Okay, bye Beckah, I'll see you tomorrow."

"Yeah, I'll call you. Tell Kira I said hi."

"I will." Lilly and I walked back downstairs. I hadn't thought I was gone for that long. When we got to the dining table the only band members left were Frankie, Greg and of course Dylan.

"Hey look who came back, what happened did you go for a swim in the toilet?" Dylan remarked.

"No, I was talking to Beckah."

"Totally whack man, leaving us all here wondering. Crispin thought that my dog, the lion had eaten you. Man that kid can be so strange sometimes." He brushed his hair back with his left hand the same way he had in the basement. I was beginning not to like him. He had that arrogant attitude that always had and always will turn me off. "Well see ya in school on Monday, Later."

"Bye," I said.

"Bye Dylan, I loved your songs, they were magical." She waved in a very flirtatious way and only got a slight nod of the head from her prince charming back.

"So, what did you and Beckah talk about?" Lilly asked as we walked to the car.

"Just stuff."

"Her friends were laughing so hard when they left; I wonder what was so funny."

"I don't know, I was in the bathroom." I didn't want her spreading Beckah's humiliation all over school so I kept my information to myself.

"Are you going somewhere with her tomorrow?"

"Yeah, we're going to the mall and maybe a movie. She said you could come if you want. Please come, I really want you to."

"Is Dylan going to go?"

"I'm not sure. She said 'a bunch of us are going' so I think he might."

"Okay," she smiled.

Kira dropped Lilly off at her house and then asked me if I had a good time. I told her about the band and how they were awful, how Dylan clearly liked me but I didn't like him, about the conversation between Beckah, Bridgid, and Beth, and about Beckah inviting me to the mall for the following day. I really loved it how Kira truly listened to me when I talked. She really cared about what I thought and what I had plans for. I had never had someone in my life that was as nice and loving as Kira was.

When we arrived back at the house Alicia was doing homework on the kitchen counter and Bailey was running around the house screaming. Mark had cooked dinner and was off on another adventure when we arrived. I told Alicia about my night and then headed to my room where I wrote in my journal.

Entry 34: <u>November 1991</u>

That Saturday morning came blustering in and I awoke to grey skies and deep white bolts of lightening cutting through the dark clouds. An hour later the clouds had opened up and let loose their wrath. Large thick raindrops fell from the sky hitting the ground with a splash. It was the kind of rain that you couldn't see two feet in front of you, the kind you definitely didn't want to go outside in. I was bumming, the mall was probably out of the question now. All morning we watched movies, ate popcorn and played board games. We were having a blast.

Beckah called me at noon and told me that the mall was not going to happen and they would probably go next weekend if I still wanted to go. I told her yes and then continued playing Twister. So far I was doing pretty well, I only had my right foot on blue, my left foot on green, and both my hands on red. Alicia on the other hand was twisted like a pretzel; and the fact that Bailey was crawling underneath her didn't help her situation. It was a sight to see, I was laughing so hard and that only made Bailey continue his escapades.

We sat down to lunch when a young man knocked on the door. Kira looked at us with confusion while she wiped her hands using a dishcloth. "I wonder who could be out in this storm," she said. We shrugged.

"Don't know momma, is raining ouside," said Bailey.

"I know it's raining sweetie, it's raining hard isn't it?"

"Yeah!" he smiled.

Kira walked to the door and peered in the peephole. Standing there was a soaking wet skinny guy with a briefcase in his hand. She opened the door and welcomed the stranger. Something about the guy made me nervous; his visit didn't seem to me to be anything that could result in our happiness. I was worried for not only myself but for my sister.

"Come in Sir, can I help you?"

"Yes ma'am, is there somewhere where we can talk alone?" the man asked.

"Sure, girls why don't you take Bailey upstairs and watch a movie in my room okay? Pick out a movie from the collection and then head upstairs."

Alicia went to the collection and chose a suitable movie for Bailey while I took him out of his high chair and carried him up to Kira's room. After getting him settled and putting the movie in I told Alicia I was going to go to the bathroom and for her to stay and watch Bailey. I didn't go to the bathroom however; I went to the bottom of the stairs and listened to their conversation. I was getting pretty good at spying and I had to admit, it was a little fun.

Crouching low, out of sight and still within earshot I listened to Kira and the mysterious man chat about my mother.

"I'm sorry to bother you this afternoon, but I wanted to tell you that we found Mrs. Jacobs." My mouth dropped and my eyes started watering.

"Oh my God, where was she?"

"Well we got a call from a twelve year old boy saying that he found a woman lying in an abandoned building and that she was dead."

Kira gasped and held her hand over her mouth while I sat there hoping she had and hoping she hadn't all at the same time. "Oh," Kira sighed.

"An ambulance was called and brought her to the nearest hospital. She is alive but barely. Turns out she had been staying there with some guy and had been using. Her arms aren't in good shape, track marks on both."

"Is she awake?"

"Yes, when she got to the hospital they set her up and started an IV. She woke up this morning and asked for her kids. We contacted her ex-husband and he didn't want to hear it. Does he know that his daughters are here with you?"

"Yes, the social worker told me that when Shelley left they had asked him to take in Amber and Alicia but he said he wouldn't. He's married again and they have a newborn now, he didn't want added responsibility. What a jerk."

So my father didn't want us. I knew it deep inside my heart but I had never heard anyone say it before. Truth hurts. Even when I had long ago stopped thinking of him as my father and forgot about him I still felt that familiar pang of disappointment.

"That's pretty much the impression I got from him. Now about the girls, Shelley has asked to see them..."

"I'm not going," I interrupted.

Kira got up and went to me. She held my shoulders and started to lead me back upstairs but I wasn't having any of it. "I don't want to see her, why are you going to make us?" I asked the stranger.

"You must be Amber, right?"

"Yes."

"Now Amber, I'm not making you go I'm just saying she wants to see you and your sister. You won't be able to go home with her when she leaves; she has a lot of recovery to go through so you both will stay here with Mrs. Warner."

"Sweetie, I think that you and Alicia should go see your mother. I think it's a good thing for both of you."

"But I like it here, I don't want to leave," I cried, embarrassing myself.

"Honey," she kneeled to my level. "You aren't going anywhere just yet. Your mom still has to go through a trial before she's able to go home and the judge won't let you go home to her unless she's not on drugs anymore. You and Alicia will be here for a while longer, I promise you."

I sniffled but she made me feel a tiny bit better. I hugged her and went back upstairs to watch the movie with my sister and Bailey. I told Alicia that our mother was found and was in the hospital but I neglected to tell her about how our father had moved on and had a new family, and had completely denied us the right of a dad.

Kira came upstairs after the detective left and sat on the bed next to me. Bailey had fallen asleep against Alicia's shoulders and Alicia herself was falling asleep fast. Kira put her arm around me and we watched the end of the movie together. The following day we would be traveling to the hospital to visit the woman who had caused Alicia and me so much pain and suffering.

Entry 34 part 2: <u>November 1991</u>

On that Sunday morning we went to the hospital. The drive was long and unusually boring. Alicia and I sat in as stony silence dreading the point of no return. I couldn't believe we were going to see her. After two weeks of no biological mother I began to wonder what it was like to have one. The music played and Kira watched the road in front of her. Beckah was babysitting for Bailey and Mark was off at work again. He worked a lot and I could tell that Kira missed him when he wasn't around. I began to resent him after a while.

I didn't concentrate on any of my surroundings on the way to the hospital. For all I knew we could be driving past hills, oceans or desert. Alicia played a video game that she borrowed from her friend Stephanie. All sounds were blocked from entering my ears and I was oblivious to the world.

"Amber, we're here," Kira's voice echoed. "Come on, let's go inside."

I slowly stepped out of the car and onto the cement of the parking lot. My legs were incapable of movement and my eyes void of emotion. I wasn't going to show my mother that she had hurt me. I knew just the way to make her tick, and boy was I going to use it to my advantage. I smiled a little.

The elevator opened and we stepped inside the motorized beast. Alicia had always been afraid of elevators so she clung to Kira. When the doors opened again and let us out near the nurse's station we were flooded with the smell of sterilization and sickness.

"Kira, I don't want to see her," I said. "I'm scared."

"I know you are sweetheart, but you have to remember she can't hurt you. I will be in there for a little while but then I have to go to the waiting room. You want to know a great trick?" she asked. I nodded. "Don't let her know that you are afraid. Show her that you are a strong person and that you and only you control your destiny."

"Okay, I'll try."

Alicia still hadn't said a word and I was worried about her. I didn't know what she would do when she saw our mother.

"Are you ready?" Kira asked us even though she knew the answer. Neither Alicia nor I said anything. The door creaked open and I immediately saw her. My body jerked back but Kira was holding my hand, and she dragged me in.

"Nurse?" said a meek voice. She didn't even sound like herself. She sounded weak and vulnerable. She needed something and she couldn't satisfy her wants. "Damn it, give me something please, I need something."

We finally reached the spot where my mother lay. She looked defenseless and emaciated. Her eyes were swollen and red and she had needles in her hands and monitors attached to her chest. Her wrists were bound by a tan strap that was attached to the hospital bed and were bleeding from her constantly trying to escape the clasps. She was moving around uncontrollably as if something was attacking her and she was trying very hard to fight it off. I looked at Alicia and she had tears running down her red cheeks. I looked up at Kira who had a look of worry in her eyes. I didn't know what was wrong with my mother but I did know that she deserved whatever it was.

"PLEASEEEEEEE GIVE ME SOMETHING!" She screamed in intense pain and started kicking the bed with great force. Her head lurched back and her hands clenched and for a second I believed she was dying. I must have been shaking because Kira wrapped her arms around me and held me, telling me that my mother was going through withdrawal.

The three of us watched and listened as the woman in the hospital bed thrashed about and screamed. Just then the social worker came into the room. He looked as if he had been running to the room.

"So sorry I'm late, traffic was horrendous. Kira, you should probably go to the waiting room if Shelley sees you in here there's no telling what she might do."

"Okay. Amber, I have to leave but you'll be fine. Just remember what I told you to do and take care of Alicia."

"I will."

Kira hugged me and then my sister before she left the room. We were left in there with two people who I didn't particularly like. Both Alicia and I stood there for a while before Chuck Diggins told us to go to her. I went first.

I stood by the bedside and stared at her without saying a word. She was staring at the ceiling and her body was violently shaking.

"Hi Amber," she said turning to look at me. "You have to do me a favor sweetie; you have to do it, please."

"What?" I said shortly.

"I need another blanket, I'm so cold. I need so many things Amber, so many things and nobody here will give them to me. Go find someone and ask them if they have a blanket, or a drink, or some drugs. Any of those and I will be happy. Don't you want me to be happy Amber? Don't you want your mama to be happy?"

She sounded so pathetic, and I had no pity for her and my answer was, "no, I don't want you to be happy."

Suddenly her face changed and she looked evil. I was afraid but I thought about what Kira had told me, 'don't let her see that you're afraid,' and I kept my fear inside. "You've always been a bitch Amber; I don't know why I even asked you to do me a favor. You have never wanted me to have anything, everything is always about you; and I am fucking sick of it. You need to know your place little girl, you don't talk to adults like that. It's rude. Now, where is your sister?"

"I'm here mama," she said in her quietest voice. "I'll get you a blanket."

"Now that's my girl, thank God you're not like your sister. If only she was more like you the world would be a better place." She looked at me with a grin on her face, mocking me. I could feel rage fill up my body and I just wanted to get out of that room. Chuck was staring at me so I just sat down on the chair as far away from her as I could get.

Five minutes later Alicia came back in the room with a blanket. She draped it over my mother's body and sat with her as she stroked her hair. They talked to each other, as best friends would talk. They whispered about what they would do when they were back home together again. I looked at the door and crossed my arms. I couldn't stand watching them it made me sick. My mother acted semi-normal and if anyone walked inside and saw her like this they would think she was the best mother in the world.

The hour we were there seemed like an eternity. The clock kept ticking but time didn't pass. After our little fight my mother didn't say one word to me until our goodbye.

"Okay Shelley, the girls have to go back now, you have to say goodbye."

"Go back where? We're going home, right 'Licia?"

"Right," my sister smiled.

"I'm sorry but I'm afraid that's not going to happen for a while. You won't be out of the hospital for a few days and then you have to go to trial for drug possession. Amber and Alicia will be staying with the Warner's for that time."

My mother looked confused and angry. I stayed far away from her, even though she was attached to the bed I was still worried about her turning into the incredible hulk and breaking free. Suddenly as if remembering that she hadn't had a drink or drugs in a long time she started panicking.

"Goodbye," I said and walked out of the room. I could hear Alicia screaming and my mother yelling for some type of sedative. The heavy wooden door opened and Chuck came out. He carried my screaming sister.

I had never seen her like this before; I didn't know why she was acting like this. What did our mother tell her that made her think that anything would be different if we went home with her?

We reached the waiting room and saw Kira pacing back and forth. I could tell she had been crying, her eyes were watering and her lip was bleeding from biting it. That was her nervous habit. I had seen her do it some nights when Mark was late from work. But when she saw us her face lit up with joy. Alicia was still crying but she had stopped a little when we got on the elevator. Kira held her tight rubbing her back trying to console her. Every once in a while she looked at me with a look trying to see if I was all right. I wouldn't look at her I was still livid at my mother.

Entry 35: <u>November 1991</u>

I remember that day as a turning point for me. I realized that my mother wasn't ever going to change and there was nothing I could do about it. I stopped caring about her and what happened to her. All the way back to Kira's house I was silent and my sister was asleep next to me. She tried to sleep on my shoulder but I was angry at her behavior with our mother so I pushed her away. When we arrived at the house I went to my room and shut the door, I didn't want to be around anyone at that time.

"Amber, are you okay?" Kira came into my room after putting Alicia in her bed. "I'm worried about you honey, you seem distant. Did your mom do something to you?"

"I don't want to talk about it, I just never want to go back and live with her. Please make sure you won't let them take me back."

"Well, I wish I could promise you that but she's your mother and I don't have the power or the authority to keep them from taking you. Believe me Amber, if I had a choice I would let you stay here forever.

"You know, at the beginning when they asked if I would take two sisters I was scared, I was scared that you and Alicia would be so incredibly close that you would shut me out and not care about me, Mark or Bailey. I wanted you to like me so much that I prayed every night. And when you two came my fear disappeared. I took one look at your beautiful faces and knew at once that we would become like family."

"I was scared to, I still am. Maybe if I pray every night God will let me be with you forever."

"I wish it were that easy. Why don't you get some rest? Write in your journal, I know that makes you feel better. If you need anything just come down and let me know okay?"

I nodded. She kissed me on the cheek and rubbed my back. When she left I cried into my pillow and fell asleep. My dreams were filled with thoughts about living with my mother again and her forbidding me to ever see Kira, Mark, or Bailey. I tossed and turned all night long and around 11:00 p.m. I needed a drink of water. I walked out of my room and heard Kira and Mark talking in their bedroom. I told myself not to listen and started to walk toward the stairs but I heard my name and was curious so I turned around and tiptoed to the closest place I could hide to listen. Alicia slept in the fetal position, holding her stuffed animal as tightly as she could. I shut her door quietly before returning to my quest.

Slumping close to the door I listened to my wished—for parents as they talked about my future. Kira was crying and distraught, I closed my eyes and pictured her in my mind. She was wearing her usual lavender silk nightgown and her hair was still damp from her shower. Her toenails were freshly painted a beautiful shade of maroon and her fingernails matched. Her brown eyes filled with brand new tears and her cheeks were stained with long streaks. Mark sat next to her, his arm around her broad shoulders, as he comforted his wife in her time of sadness. He was dressed in just a pair of pajama bottoms, exposing his muscular chest to the room around him. His hair was un-brushed from sleeping on it and his blue eyes showed sympathy.

"I can't believe it, I know they say not to get too attached to the foster kids but Mark, I just can't help it, I'm already in love with those two girls. I don't think I can face losing them. And Amber, I'm worried about her Mark; she is very fragile. I'm afraid that she'll break if something happens."

"From what I can tell she seems to be a very strong person, I wouldn't call her fragile. If she was fragile Kira, she wouldn't have made it this far."

"You should have seen her today; she didn't even shed a tear. Anger is a lot harsher on the soul than hurt."

"Why do you say that?"

"When people are angry they hold all of their emotions inside, they don't want anyone to know that they are hurt so they convince themselves that they aren't. Anger is a mask for all their feelings. If they are angry they can't be feeling anything."

"Sweetheart, just because your sister went through a terribly difficult time with your parents divorce doesn't mean everyone will act the same way."

"Kristin went through something more than a difficult time Mark, she killed herself. Great time to bring that up, thanks."

"I'm sorry, I didn't mean that. But I don't think you have to worry about Amber, she isn't Kristin. She seems to be having a wonderful time with us."

"She told me when we got home from the visit that she wanted to stay here forever and she was going to pray to God. If Shelley gets over this problem of hers the Judge is going to give her kids back. I don't want her to lose faith in God, or to think that I didn't want her or Alicia. And I don't want them to go back to their mother, she isn't a good person."

"I know this is hard for you, and I know you don't want to hear this but that isn't for you to decide. We are just here to make sure they are fed, clothed, and educated. You're not a psychologist, or a social worker. Maybe we should call up and have them placed in another home."

"WHAT?! Don't ever say that again, or think it for that matter. I can't just send them away. They don't deserve that."

"Okay I'm sorry. I don't want to see you get hurt when the Judge rules in Shelley's favor. I love you Kira."

I was crying because I didn't want to leave and I knew I probably should. I thought I would run away and take Alicia with me. I hated to make Kira sad; it killed me inside to hear her in so much pain because of us.

I got up from my crouching position and quietly packed a suitcase with a few belongings of mine and Alicia's. Alicia wasn't the happiest person when I woke her up but we had to go at night while Kira thought we were asleep.

"Leave me alone," she said to me before rolling over back to sleep.

"Alicia, we have to go. Mark doesn't want us here and Kira is upset, we have to leave."

"Where are we gonna go?"

"I don't know, just somewhere. Maybe we'll go to my friend Beckah's house. We have to go now Alicia, before Kira comes and checks on us."

"I don't want to leave."

"I know, but we have to. Come on."

Finally she got out of bed and we crept out of the house and we walked the five blocks to Beckah and Dylan's house. Both of us were exhausted and Alicia was dragging her feet and complaining the entire way there. I knew we shouldn't be doing this but I also knew we had to.

When we reached the house I found the window that led to Beckah's room and threw tiny stones at it. Five stones later the light flicked on and Beckah looked out. She opened the window and looked down confused.

"What are you guys doing here?" she asked in a quiet scream.

I signaled to her to let us in so she walked down and in minutes we were in her room getting ready to sleep.

Alicia was sleeping in a sleeping bag in between the wall and Beckah's double sized bed just in case her mom came in.

"So, what are you doing here?"

"Mark and Kira had a fight about me and I didn't want to cause any trouble so I decided to leave. Don't worry though, because tomorrow after school Alicia and I are going somewhere else."

"You can stay here if you want."

"I don't think that your mom or dad would like it, plus they might tell Kira where we are."

"Amber, don't worry about it, she'll never find out. Live on the edge see how far you can walk before you fall."

"I have never been sneaky in my life."

"Well now's your chance."

"Ok," I was excited to rebel for once. I was sick of being so good and was happy that Beckah was going to help me gain some self-confidence and a sense of self. However, later on in life I looked back on this day and wished I hadn't listened to her. I realized that no matter how cool you think a person is, you have to be okay with who you are in order to realize that that so called person is only a façade.

We stayed up late and read magazines and took the various sex quizzes that were found within the pages. I found out that Beckah was dating this boy Joel and they had gotten to second base already. I told her about Chris and how he had moved away.

We stayed up far past our bedtime and awoke the next morning to Beckah's mom shaking us enthusiastically. I was groggy from lack of sleep and confused as to where I was. Alicia was sitting on the floor looking lost and alone, as if she had been plucked from her home and plopped down in a forgotten country where the people are foreigners and the place unknown. I rubbed the sleep out of my eyes and faced the wrath that was Beckah's mom.

"Beckah, who is this? Who are you? Where have you come from?"

"Mom, calm down, this is my friend Amber. She's staying with Mr. and Mrs. Warner until her mom gets out of the hospital. Geez, take a chill pill."

"Do not talk back to me young lady; I am not here to help you out of tough situations. Hey, aren't you the girl who came over last weekend to hear Dylan play?"

I was scared. Beckah's mom looked like she was in a fury and nobody better cross her. I said in a meek voice barely audible, "yes ma'am."

"What are you doing here, and who is this other little girl on my floor!?"

Alicia started whimpering and stared at this stranger who was way beyond crazy.

Suddenly her voice got really deep, "I asked you a question, WHO ARE YOU and why are you here?"

"M-m-my name is A-a-alicia, and I am Amber's S-s-sister." She stuttered through tears. I felt the need to get off the bed and sit beside Alicia and comfort her. I now felt stupid for leaving Kira's house.

"I still haven't gotten an answer as to why you two are here without my knowledge. Is anyone going to answer me?"

Before we could open our mouths the phone rang. "Don't think I'm not coming back. Beckah get dressed it's time to go to church."

"Yes mom. Don't worry about her Amber; she's a little crazy in the mornings."

She got out of bed and started getting dressed. I had calmed down a little and told Beckah that we were going to go back to Kira's house. I didn't want to cause any more problems between Beckah and her mom.

"Come on Alicia, let's go."

"O-o-okay."

We just reached the staircase when Beckah's mom came out of her room with a stern look on her face. I guessed that the phone call was from Kira. "You have a phone call young lady." She then got right up in my face, so close that I could smell the Listerine on her breath. "If you ever make my house your hide-out again you will be sorry. The phone is on the nightstand. I'll assume you will be leaving after you talk."

"Yes, thanks Mrs. York. I'm real sorry about this I didn't want to cause you any trouble."

"Well you did, now go talk I have to be at church in twenty minutes." She started to walk away. "DYLAN-wake up."

I heard from behind a closed door, "okay mom." And Alicia and I went to answer the phone.

I knew it, it was Kira and her voice was shaky, filled with worry, anger, and sadness. I quietly said hello and the line was silent for a moment. All that was there was breathing. I was nervous.

Finally, "Amber, are you and Alicia all right?"

"Yes, Kira. I'm sorry we left last night."

"Why did you leave? I was worried sick when I went into your room this morning. I don't understand, I thought you wanted to stay here." Her voice caught in her throat and I felt intense guilt and sadness to put her through that.

"I heard you and Mark talking last night and how he said you should call that man and have him take us back. I know you said you didn't want to do that but I felt bad. I don't want you and Mark to fight over us. My dad left because we were too much for him, I don't want Mark to leave you because of us too."

"Oh, Amber, you weren't supposed to hear that conversation. I am so sorry. You don't have to worry about those things; you are only a little girl. You should worry about boys and homework and what clothes to wear not our problems. And Mark and I aren't going to split up. Why don't you two come home we all miss you. I'll pick you up in five minutes."

Five minutes later on the dot Kira drove up and jumped out of the car. Bailey was in the back seat chewing on a toy. She was still in her pajamas and her hair was un-brushed. She looked as if she had just gotten out of bed. As soon as she reached us she threw her arms around us and squeezed as tight as she could.

"Don't ever do that again." She was crying. We arrived back at the house in record time only to go straight to our rooms. I wrote in my journal as I listened to music. I could hear Alicia in her room talking to someone. I snuck into her room and she was on the phone.

"Who are you talking to?" I asked angrily.

"None of your business. I'm not talking to you Amber."

"Why not?"

"I'm in trouble because you forced me to leave last night. This is all your fault. I hate you. Leave me alone."

I stormed out of the room back to my room as quietly as I could. She had never told me that she hated me before and I was shocked. I sat on the bed and folded my hands around my chin. I contemplated those words and what they meant. I knew she was angry with me about this but she had been mad at me other times and not said it. I guess it was because she was getting older and her personality was changing. I hated, no strongly disliked change and wished everything could stay the same as it was then.

I picked up my open journal and wrote some more. Writing always helped me think rationally and get all my thoughts out on paper. I wrote,

"Today my sister told me she hated me. The words stung like a wasp that didn't stop at one. Buzzing around my ears like a bumblebee looking for a great place to build a nest that terrible word hate found the best place hanging from my earlobe. My best friend shot me through the heart with the devil's arrow piercing through my soul finding the bull's eye in only one second. The one blow from the tiniest fist caused a black and blue across my wounded face that an adult fist couldn't touch. How can one word be so destructive? How can *Hate* be so harmful that I could crumble into tiny pieces on the ground? Just one word caused more pain and hurt than a lifetime of abuse from the one person who is supposed to love me unconditionally. Life isn't fair and death is too definite and frightening.

"Living is tormenting me beyond my usual pain. Life is the Titanic, gliding through day by day waiting for that iceberg. Life is a volcano, lying dormant until the day it erupts. Life is a Looney Tunes show waiting for the Coyote to finally catch the Roadrunner. But unlike the Looney Tunes show in life the Roadrunner would always be caught and brought to its final judgment. Life is inevitable, death is inevitable. Between birth and death is the chance to grow and mature, and have fun. But what about those of us who hate the in between, just as my sister hates me? Where is the justice? What will happen when the volcano erupts, when the show ends, when the Titanic finally hits that iceberg? The answers are never there so I will keep on gliding through day by day trying to avoid the iceberg, keeping my burning lava dormant, keeping that Roadrunner running and keeping my hopes alive."

I had no more words left in my brain so I put my pen down and listened to the soothing music I had put on just a while ago. My eyes slowly shut and I was asleep in seconds. I dreamt that I was in a vast field in the middle of ten million sunflowers that towered over me with their beautiful yellow petals. All of a sudden an ugly caterpillar with round sunglasses and a wise English accent landed on my shoulder and told me that I was going to be okay. The caterpillar and I had a long conversation about life and then he became nervous and agitated. He said that in everyone's life change has to happen and it was his time. He rolled himself into a cocoon and emerged a beautiful monarch butterfly. "Change is good Amber," he said before he flew off into the sunflowers.

I awoke to darkness and quiet. The clock beside my bed flashed bright red, reading 12:56 a.m. I had already slept ten hours and my stomach was growling with hunger. I slowly crept out of the warm bed and was greeted with the fuzzy rug on my bare feet. I noticed that I was no longer in my clothes but in a long t-shirt and sweat pants, my feet left to bare the cold. I slowly tiptoed through the house toward the kitchen to get myself some food and my feet adjusted to the changing floor beneath them. The ocean blue tile in the kitchen was like walking on a frozen slip and slide and I cringed with the sensation my feet were feeling. Finally I arrived at the refrigerator and I opened it to see a dish covered in saran wrap with my name on it.

I grabbed the plate and brought it to the table but not before turning the light on. The food looked delicious, and with my hunger bursting through every part of me I reached for my fork and knife and took a dive into the filet mignon and mashed potatoes. Next I took a forkful of filet, potato and corn and stuffed it into my already full mouth. I felt as if I hadn't eaten in centuries and I was enjoying every last bit of it. I gulped down my glass of milk and quietly placed the licked clean plate and empty glass into the sink.

"Hey you," a voice echoed behind me. I almost jumped out of my skin. I turned and realized it was only Kira. "I was thirsty and noticed you weren't in your bed. I was worried you ran away again." She smiled.

"No, I'm just not tired, and I was hungry."

"I bet, on both accounts. I went in to tell you that the punishment was over and you were sound asleep, I actually believe you were talking."

"What was I saying?"

"Umm, something about the smell of flowers, I could be wrong you were mumbling." She grabbed a glass from the cupboard and poured herself some water. "So, got any plans?"

"No."

"Okay, how about you and I play a game?"

"Aren't you tired?"

"Tired? Me? Heck no! C'mon, let's play a rousing game of scrabble."

The two of us played three games of scrabble back to back at one-o-clock in the morning. I won all three of them. She accused me of cheating but in a joking way. We were laughing so hard we were afraid we would wake Bailey, Alicia and Mark up.

"Want to watch a movie?" I asked. I was still wide awake.

"Sure, I would love to."

We popped a video into the VCR and popcorn into the microwave. With two large glasses of ice water next to us, the popcorn in between us and a warm blanket covering us Kira and I watched the movie. Half way through Kira fell asleep, her head resting against my shoulder. When the movie ended I shut the television off and fell asleep myself.

Entry 36: <u>March 1992</u>

The next few months went by without consequence and Alicia and I thrived in our new environment. Every Saturday we headed up to the hospital and visited our mother. After the first visit she had escaped her captors and almost killed herself by injecting her arm with a syringe filled with nothing but air. She needed her fix and she would have done anything to get it, including death. The judge had granted Kira and Mark temporary custody of Alicia and I until our mother was fully off drugs and living on her own holding down a job. She wouldn't be able to get us back until she was off drugs and alcohol completely for one entire year after staying in a rehabilitation center for nine months.

I was ecstatic. The sixth grade was almost at an end and I would soon be attending the prestigious catholic school the next town over for middle school. Lilly was going to the school with me. Unfortunately Beckah and Dylan were going to continue to attend the public middle school where my life had changed just a while ago.

Bailey got cuter by the minute and already we were like brother and sister. Mark and Kira hadn't talked about sending us back since that dreadful night and I finally felt a sense of family living there. Every Friday night we would have game and pizza night. Bailey would stay at Kira's mother's house and we all would sit around the family room table playing cards, board games, or our own made up games while we ate pizza with everything on it, even anchovies! I looked forward to those Fridays more than I had ever looked forward to anything before. It was so much fun.

Alicia was now eleven years old and I was turning 13 in two months and I anxiously awaited my birthday for the first time since I turned three. Alicia had received a birthday card from our mother but I did not expect the same for me. On the Saturdays we visited she barely talked to me or looked at me. I hated those visits but Chuck told me it was not only my duty but my obligation to let my mother know I loved her and cared for her; which I didn't but was basically pulled by my hair to the hospital and rehab center.

On the weeknights Lilly and I hung out at either her house or my house and did our homework. Lilly and Dylan started dating, they'd go roller-skating, and to the movies and sometimes miniature golfing. Dylan informed me that he let Lilly win, which I sometimes doubted but I had to laugh at her.

Entry 37: <u>April 1992</u>

One week in the middle of April Kira pulled me aside to have a girl-to-girl chat. I had been in the middle of writing in my journal that was almost filled when she came into my room.

"Amber, I have something to tell you, will you come with me for a little ride?"

I was nervous, my insides trembled and my stomach felt as if it was coming out of my mouth. "Yeah, sure."

"Thanks."

I sat in the passenger's seat and wondered what she was going to tell me. Was my mother cured? Was she dead? Did she give up her parental rights? Had my father reclaimed us as his children? Had Alicia decided she wanted to live on her own? No, I thought, Alicia's too young. I sat in anticipation, worry and fear for twenty minutes.

Kira drove down to the ocean and parked overlooking the waves crashing against the rocks. We sat there in silence for a good minute, she smiled and looked utterly and magnificently happy. That gave me some relief.

"Okay, let's go for a walk on the beach."

"You're just going to keep me wondering for a while aren't you? Just tell me."

"No, I want to torture you a bit more. Didn't anyone ever teach you that suspense is the best part of news? Come on, let's go."

We got out of the car and walked on the smooth sand. My feet sunk low and I felt the water cover my ankles. It was cold but refreshing. I wore jean shorts and a purple tank top. "Okay Kira, I've been waiting in suspense long enough, tell me already!"

"All right, all right. Well, I hope you're happy about this…"

"You're adopting us!" I interrupted excitedly.

"No, you know that I can't do that."

"I know," my face fell in disappointment even though I knew the answer.

"Well, I found out a few months ago but I wanted to wait to tell you and Alicia because I wanted to be sure. You are the first person I've told, besides Mark," she paused for dramatic effect. "I'm pregnant."

My mouth went wide in surprise and happiness. "You are!"

"Yup. Are you excited?"

"YEAH!" I screamed. "When are you due? Is it a boy or a girl? What are you going to name it?"

"Calm down sweetie, I am four months pregnant which means the baby will be born in September. I'll find out if it's a boy or a girl in two weeks, and I don't know what I'm going to name it."

I looked away and thought about the baby and names flashed ferociously around in my brain. I didn't share them though, the name wasn't my decision. I just couldn't wait to have a baby around. "When are you going to tell Alicia?"

"I was thinking tonight. I wanted to tell you first though."

I felt special and loved whenever I was around Kira but this day was the most special day of my life. I had never been the first to know anything never mind something this big. We walked to the end of the beach and then back to the car. When we got back to the house Mark had prepared a huge turkey dinner. The table was set with their fine china and two white candles in the center. Mark glowed; he smiled at us both and then gave Kira a hug and a kiss. They stared at each other for what seemed like eternity and then he lowered himself to my level and asked what I thought.

"I'm really happy Mark, congratulations."

"Thank you Amber. Now we have one question that we want to ask you. Kira and I made a deal, she would tell you about the baby and I would ask you this very important question."

I nodded.

"Now, before I ask the question I want you to understand that this is a huge undertaking and you have to be willing and able to take it on. It's a huge responsibility but we think you'll be able to handle it."

"Oh my goodness, what is it with you people, I know suspense is the excitement of this game you play but seriously, just ask the question!"

We all laughed in unison.

"Okay, we would like you to help take care of Kira throughout the pregnancy, could you do that?"

The day had gone from great to fabulous. I jumped up and down, "YES!" I screamed for the second time. I don't think that I had ever raised my voice this much in my lifetime but here I was twice in one day.

Dinner was delicious, the turkey was moist, the mashed potatoes were buttery, the stuffing was the best I had ever had, and the cranberry sauce was to die for. Alicia was ecstatic to hear about the baby and wouldn't stop talking for three hours about what she was going to do with the baby. Bailey just said "baby" over and over again. He was still too young to understand, but he would find out soon enough.

That night I wrote down the happenings in my journal and went to sleep. I awoke to blood on the sheets and I screamed, for the third time.

"What's the matter??" Kira panted as she ran into my room and turned on the light. Mark was right behind her and Alicia behind him. Bailey was crying from his room. I sat on my bed and cried. When Kira saw what happened she told Mark to take care of Bailey and for Alicia to go back to bed.

"Sweetheart, don't worry, this happens to every girl when they become a woman."

"I don't like it. What happens."

Kira explained what was happening to my body and what I would need to do for seven days. I was terrified and horrified at what this so called "period" was all about. After she got me settled and changed the sheets she kissed me goodnight and went back to sleep. I fell asleep after a few pains. I don't know if I wanted to be older anymore.

Entry 38: <u>May 1992</u>

The next three weeks went by very slowly. I anticipated the doctor's appointment to find out the sex of the baby for a long time and finally it was here. Kira told me I could go into school late so I could go with her. I could not wait. Her belly was getting bigger and I loved talking to the baby.

The doctor's office was a fifteen-minute drive but seemed as if it was three days. When we arrived we had to wait in the waiting room for the doctor to finish up with his patient. Finally ten minutes later Dr. Robert Wynn received us in the office. Kira dressed in a gown and sat on the cushioned chair.

"Well good morning Kira, how is everything? How's the pregnancy? Any morning sickness, cravings?"

"Well the first two months I was so sick in the morning but it has passed. I have been craving banana ice cream with strawberries and blueberries on top, and a side order of pickles."

I cringed, that was disgusting. Dr. Wynn didn't seem to think it was that gross.

"Okay, we're here to find out if you're having a little girl or a little boy. Are you sure you want to know?"

"Yes I am. And Amber here wants to know too."

"Are you excited Amber?"

"Yes I am, very much."

"Well then, let's hurry this along."

"Finally, someone who speaks my language!"

Kira and I laughed but Dr. Wynn looked with just a smile on his face. He put some jelly on Kira's belly and turned on the monitor. He placed the camera device on the jelly and moved it around. His face got all serious and he was looking very closely.

"Hmm, seems we have a problem here."

"What is it?" Kira asked. I sensed the worry in her voice.

"I hope you don't mind a lot of work. We've got twins here Kira."

"Twins? Are you sure?"

"See here, here's one of the baby's heads, and right here is another one. Unless the baby has two heads I'd say I'm pretty sure."

"Wow, that's amazing. Would you look at that?"

"I can't see anything." I responded.

The doctor pointed out the little heads and I finally recognized the images. They were there all right. Two babies! I couldn't believe it. Twice the excitement, twice the fun! "Are they girls or boys?"

"Let's see." He moved the camera around to get a different angle. "What we have here are fraternal twins, one is a boy and one is a girl."

Kira was silent, a smile covered her face. I sat with my head leaning on my hands and stared at the monitor, looking at those two little people growing inside Kira's body. I thought about when they would arrive and what they would look like and if they would cry a lot or laugh all the time. I also wondered how Bailey would react to his new brother and sister. I hoped he would love them and care for them.

It was time for us to leave but not without a printout of the babies' first picture. I held it in my hands and looked at it the entire ride home while Kira stared out of the window thinking of her son and daughter inside of her. She dropped me off at school and I told everyone I came in contact with; Beckah, Dylan, Lilly, Rachel, and all my other friends. They were all so happy.

The school day went by quickly and I crossed off the day in my calendar. My life had taken a complete turnaround. I had gone from dreading every day to looking forward to the days ahead. My birthday was just around the corner and I could see it being the best birthday I had ever had. And until then all we would talk about were the babies.

Everyone at the house was ecstatic about the twins and partied it up. Kira's mom and dad were at the house as were Mark's sister, brother-in-law and nephew Nikolas. Bailey and Nik played in the playroom for hours while Alicia and I played a game of scrabble and the adults chatted.

I placed the final letter on the board forming the word 'love'.

"Okay, that's seven points. You're turn."

"Hey, I got your birthday present already."

"You did? What is it?"

"I'm not telling, then it wouldn't be a surprise!"

"You're a tease! Now make your move or I'll beat you."

We laughed and finished playing the game. For once in her life Alicia won. Her word, 'Zebra' put her ahead of me by 4 points. She would never let me live this down.

"Okay girls, it's time for you two to go get ready for bed. Alicia use my bathroom and Amber you use the hallway bathroom."

"Okay."

Entry 39: <u>May 1992</u>

It was finally Wednesday, May twelfth, my birthday. I put on my favorite new outfit that Kira had bought me for Christmas. It was a pair of pink cutoff pants with matching pink sandals and a white tank top and white short sleeve shirt over it. My hair was pulled back in a high ponytail and I put in a special pair of earrings Alicia had gotten me for my birthday this year. That was her surprise. They were beautiful silver hoops that she had hid under my pillow for when I awoke in the morning. With my toenails and fingernails painted pink, an ankle bracelet that matched my earrings and a pink bracelet my look was almost ready. I just had to put on a little makeup and I was all set. Kira had told me that my day was already planned and she wasn't telling me one detail.

I skipped downstairs and found Kira, Mark and Bailey sat on the couch and waited for Alicia and I. Alicia was still upstairs, probably perfecting her image. She was very image-conscious and always had to look absolutely beautiful, which wasn't a problem for her.

"HAPPY BIRTHDAY AMBER!" screamed Bailey as he wriggled out of Marks' arms and ran up to me. I picked him up and he gave me a tight squeeze and a kiss on the cheek. "I got you a toy, wanna see it?" He had an amazing vocabulary and I loved listening to his many conversations of the Teenage Mutant Ninja Turtles and the Power Rangers.

"Sure. Thank you Bailey."

He smiled and let out an excited grunt as he pulled me towards the family room.

"Bailey, why don't we wait until Alicia comes down until you give Amber her present?"

He scowled and closed his fists but then agreed. Five minutes later Alicia popped into the family room as if she was early.

"Hey guys! What are we waiting for? Let's go." As I had thought, Alicia looked as cool as she always does. She had French braided her hair in two braids, not one piece of a hair was out of place. Her makeup was flawless and her purple dress was wrinkle free. She certainly didn't look ten years old.

I opened up Bailey's present and it was a stuffed bear. "Do you like it?"

"Yes, thank you so much. Come here, I want to tell you a secret. But you have to promise you won't tell anyone."

"I promise!"

I whispered into his ear "it's my favorite present ever."

His smile grew and it was from ear to ear. He whispered, "I won't tell anyone."

"Okay, are we ready?"

"YAY!" Bailey screamed. "Babies, are you ready?" he asked Kira's belly. He put his tiny head against her belly trying to hear their responses. His face was intent and he tried as hard as he could to hear them.

"What did they say Bailey? Are they ready?" Kira asked him as she patted his soft brown hair.

"They're ready!"

"Okay! Then let's go!"

"Where are we going?" I asked.

"I told you, I'm not telling you anything. We're just going to go." She put her arm around my shoulder as we walked to the car.

With Bailey in his car seat and all four of us in seatbelts Kira put on Bailey's favorite CD—Raffi. He sang along in his highest voice and we all joined in.

Our first stop was the miniature golf course down the street. We minigolfed, went to the batting cages and raced on the track. Kira beat us all, except for Bailey and Mark, they watched as we passed by, each lap Bailey waved at us.

After we finished there we went out to lunch at a nice Italian restaurant, and for dessert a chocolate fudge brownie with vanilla ice cream, covered with caramel. So far this day was absolutely fabulous. Each day with Kira, Mark and Bailey proved to be the greatest day of my life. I never thought that I would feel like this but now all the best emotions were swirling through my body.

After the restaurant Mark dropped the three girls at the mall and him and Bailey went back home for naptime. We walked towards the center of the mall and I saw another surprise. Sitting on a park bench next to a water fountain were Lilly, Beckah and Alicia's friend Emily. I looked at her, my mouth agape.

"I figured you needed a girl's day shopping."

"Thank you so much." I hugged her and ran up to my friends.

"Hey Amber, happy birthday!" Beckah and Lilly said simultaneously. We were all jumping up and down excited for this day of luxury.

"Where should we go first?" Lilly asked.

"I say, why don't we go from the beginning of the mall to the end of the mall and then back again. We should hit every store!" Emily said.

"That would take forever Ems; I am not walking that far." Alicia responded.

"Okay girls, listen I have another surprise at 5:00 so if you could all meet me in the food court, I'll be reading a book." Kira gave us money and smiled as she walked towards the food court.

Beckah took me into this little store and told me to pick out something I thought was cute. I found a cute top that was yellow and had a yellow duck on the front of it. She bought it for me.

Next Lilly took me into a different store where I chose a box of stationary that I loved; it was purple with sunflowers on the top left corner and bottom right corner. It came in a box that matched along with a pencil and envelopes.

"Hey Amber, I know that I already got you the earrings but I thought that I'd get you something else."

"You don't have to."

"I know, but I want to, you're my sister after all."

"What is it?"

"Well, it's actually from all of us."

"And Dylan too," Beckah chimed in.

"Yeah, and him too. We know you like to read and write so we're starting a book club with you as the leader and every month we'll read a book and then come together and talk about it."

"Really?" I asked. "That would be so much fun! You guys are the best!"

We shopped around some more and then we passed a store with cute baby clothes in it. "Hey, I want to get something for Kira from here."

"But it's your birthday."

"I know, but I have my own money."

I bought the babies a beautiful soft blanket, one pink and one blue. I also bought them a little blue stuffed dog for the boy and pink rabbit for the girl. Five-o-clock rolled around faster than we thought possible so we met up with Kira and then she took us into the department store where her surprise was waiting. Each of us got a makeover from this nice lady named Beatrice.

When our makeovers were completed we all looked like movie stars, and decided that we should act like them too. Walking out of the mall we spoke in proper English, walked upright and talked like old women. Beckah, Lilly and Emily were picked up and Mark and Bailey met us outside and took us to dinner. I showed them what everyone bought for me and what I bought for the babies. Kira and Mark loved the blankets and stuffed animals and told me I shouldn't have. Dinner was great and I was stuffed to the brim with food.

We got back to the house and they had an ice cream cake just for me. On the top in purple frosting read "Happy 12th Birthday Amber." I didn't know how I could eat another bite but I managed two pieces. Bailey went down for bed around 8:00 and the four of us watched a movie and went to bed. All day I had waited for the bomb to drop and it hadn't. I fell asleep with a smile on my face.

Entry 40: <u>August 1992</u>

That summer flew by in a flash. Alicia and I went to pool parties, birthday par-ties, cookouts, the movies, and watched as Kira's belly grew larger by the minute. Every night before bed I talked to the two babies and told them how much I was looking forward for them to be born. Nobody had thought of any names for them yet but we were throwing out names left and right. Alicia would joke around and tell them Barney and Cornelia, Oscar and Flavia. One night Alicia made a suggestion of Jezebel and Lucius. Kira, jokingly, said yes to those names and Alicia's face dropped. For the next three days Alicia followed her around the house saying over and over "I was just kidding, please don't name them that."

Their room was almost ready, two cribs, a changing table, a closet full of baby clothes, a dresser also full, and the room painted a beautiful shade of light green. Each crib was decorated for that particular baby. The crib on the left was covered in blue sheets and the blanket I had bought on my birthday, the mobile had little blue dogs and bears on it and the toys around the crib were trains, planes and automobiles. The crib on the right was covered in pink sheets and the pink blanket I had bought her. The mobile featured pink balle-rina bears and on a shelf above her crib were little angels and dolls. A rocking chair sat in the corner of the room next to a tall lamp with a green-checkered lampshade.

The house was already baby proofed so that wasn't necessary to do again. Kira had her baby shower three weeks ago and it turned out to be a success. Baby clothes, two car seats, a high chair, a baby bathtub, shampoo, soap, wash-cloths, brushes, diapers, wipes, and everything else imaginable were given to her by family and friends. Bailey had turned three in July and he was starting to understand more and more each day that he wasn't going to be the baby in the family anymore. His brown hair had turned curly over the summer and he looked adorable, his big blue eyes always looked curious and thoughtful and his vocabulary was getting better as each day passed.

Entry 41: <u>September 1992</u>

School started last week and it was going well so far. I loved my classes and my friends and I was having the time of my life. My mother was still in rehab and had tried to escape more than once. One time during June she got out for a few hours and when they found her she was drunk and high. The judge sentenced her for another six months intense therapy. I had no problem with that.

On September 14th a Tuesday morning Kira went into labor. Alicia and I were allowed to skip school and go to the hospital. I was scared and excited. I wondered what they would look like, if they would look like Bailey at all or not at all. Bailey stayed with his grandmother and Alicia and I stayed in the waiting room with Jerry, Mark's brother. I had never been this nervous before in my life and I felt new emotions that I had no idea how to describe. I was pacing back and fourth in front of Jerry, which was aggravating him to no end. He had told me to sit down more than once.

Wasn't he nervous? He was the uncle, and godfather to the boy. What would they name them? I wondered that more than anything. Three hours later the doctor came out and told us that she was still in labor and that they were all doing well.

"How long is this going to take?" I asked.

"Well, it could take a few more hours."

"Ugh."

"I'll let you know first, I promise." He winked at me.

Five minutes later I was back to my pacing. By now I could feel the sweat beads dripping from my forehead and I wiped them away with my hand. Bailey came to visit for a little while and then his Grandma took him to a movie. Jerry took Alicia and I to the cafeteria and we ate some lunch and then back to the waiting room we went. I slept a bit on the chair and Alicia read a magazine.

At around 6:40 the doctor came out and told us that they were born, two healthy babies. He also told us we could go in and see them in a few minutes. I jumped up and down and screamed. I was so happy.

When we were escorted in to the room we were beyond happy. Jerry was the first one in followed by Alicia and myself. Kira was holding a little dumpling squeezed tight with a blanket and a little pink hat on her head while Mark was holding another little dumpling squeezed tight with a blanket and a little blue hat on his head. They were so adorable. They had blonde fuzz on their head and blue eyes just like Bailey.

"Wow," I said barely audible.

"Would you like to hold your new sister?"

"Really? Can I?"

"Of course you can, come here, sit next to me."

I sat next to her and she placed her in my lap. She was so beautiful. Her little hand popped out of the blanket and I put my finger in it. She closed her fist and I felt as if I was floating on thin air. "So, have you named them yet?"

"Yes we have actually. Once we saw them we knew. We actually knew the names we wanted for a few months; we just didn't want to let you know."

I looked at her pretending to be mad, when in reality I could never be mad at them.

Alicia was sitting on the chair holding the baby boy and she looked as if she were in another place in another time. She was just staring at the baby. Although they weren't identical twins at this point in their lives they looked exactly the same. "So, are you going to tell us?"

"Yeah, I guess we can tell you now. Alicia, you are holding the handsome Perry Graham Warner, he weighed in at 5 lbs. 1 oz. and Amber you are holding the gorgeous Brynne Courteney Warner, she weighed 4 lbs. 5 oz." she paused. "Do you like their names?"

"Yes. Hi Brynne, I'm Amber. I love you already. Hi Perry, you are beautiful too."

Kira and Mark were smiling at us and then Kira began to cry.

"What's the matter?" I asked worried.

"Nothing, I'm just so happy right now."

I knew there was more to that but I didn't pursue the matter. I just held Brynne and enjoyed myself.

That night when we got back to the house; Jerry was staying with us, we decorated wooden letters we had bought on the way home. Jerry helped us nail them to the wall. Above one crib we put Perry and above the other one we put Brynne. We also bought Bailey a huge stuffed dog which he loved when he got home the next day. Kira, Mark, Brynne and Perry would come home the next day and we made sure the house was perfect for its new members.

Entry 42: <u>September 1992</u>

From the moment they all arrived into their home, a mist of love and happiness drifted through the house. It was always there of course but now with the twins it grew thicker and stronger. I could almost see it, feel it. I smiled inwardly and prayed that I would enjoy this feeling for many more months. Alicia felt the same way about it as well, she went into the nursery every night after everyone was asleep and just stared at the sleeping beauties, and some nights I joined her. Bailey loved his new brother and sister but still at times he became overly jealous and began to whine whenever they were getting more attention than him. We all understood, being an only child and then all of a sudden two new babies are in the house stealing your mother and father away—it could be hard on a toddler.

The christening went well, the twins looked beautiful in their white garments and I was proud to be holding Brynne for Lucy, her Godmother until she took the baby up to the altar. Next to her was Jake, Kira's nephew who was the Godfather. Holding Perry was Mark's sister-in-law Isabella and his Godfather, Jake. The ceremony was very nice, along with the twins there were five other babies baptized the same day. Afterwards we all went back to the house and had a nice celebration.

The few weeks following the christening were filled with dirty diapers, baths, bottles, and lots of crying. One night when the twins were three months old I woke up in the middle of the night to get a glass of water. I noticed a silhouette of someone sitting on the white leather couch in the family room. The light of the moon was casting an eerie glow onto the large room and I imagined an award-winning photo coming out of it. I tiptoed through the kitchen and sat next to the figure on the couch.

It was Kira and she looked awful. She stared straight ahead as if focused on some invisible object that she feared. Her eyes were red and her hands shook. She blinked once and noticed me sitting there. Immediately she turned away and covered her face with her hand.

"Amber, I didn't see you there. Why are you up sweetie?" she said trying to sound cheerful, but I could hear the tremble in her voice.

"I was thirsty."

She still wasn't looking at me, trying as hard as she could to regain her composure she said, "Did you know I had a sister?"

"No," I responded even though I did. "I thought you just had brothers, Ben and Taylor."

"She was beautiful. I looked up to her, admired her; wanted to be just like her. When I was two years old my parents adopted her. Maybe that's why we were so close; we both had that in common. Ben and Taylor were the real kids but we were the chosen. The fact she was a girl didn't hurt either. She was three years old and we were inseparable.

"Her parents were abusive; they hit her and her brother all the time. When social services came they put Joshua into a foster home across town and Kristin in with us. My parents adopted both of us at the same time. We had a huge celebration and Kristin and I were thrilled."

She paused a second biting her lip, I had seen her do that on occasion. I wondered why she was telling me this story; a little worried a bad ending would come out of it. I felt important and loved and I was so happy to be here listening to her and being there for her when she needed me. Being needed was a great feeling, one I've very rarely felt before. But, now I felt bad that I had lied to her about knowing about Kristin.

"As I said, we were inseparable. We did everything, gymnastics, dance, cheerleading, volleyball. When we were in high school she auditioned for the school musical and she got the part. I was so proud of her. It was the first thing she did without me. I did feel a little left out but I decided to volunteer at the local children's hospital helping young kids with cancer. I would read them stories, tell jokes, give them parties. It was a fulfilling thing to do and I loved doing it, those kids made me happy." She smiled at me but it was a sad smile.

"Kristin's part in the musical was just awesome. I never realized how much talent she possessed. Her voice was beautiful and at the curtain call she received a standing ovation from the entire audience. I was at my happiest then.

"My world was great! I had loving parents, protective brothers and a best friend and sister all in one package. Life was good. You know what was funny about Kristin and me?"

"What?"

"We actually looked alike. People would always tell us that. She had brown hair like me, brown eyes, and she was a few inches taller than me. She did have more boyfriends than I did though, she was more popular, had more friends, more outside activities, and more interesting stories. She was very talkative, only I could get a word in edgewise. When we were young we made up our own language that used to drive Ben and Taylor crazy, we used to say random things just to bust them up. Laugh out loud funny!

"This one day when I was fifteen and she was sixteen, Kristin had just gotten her license and for her birthday our parents bought her a mustang convertible. She loved it, so we went out driving. We had the top down, radio blaring and we were both screaming the words to the songs. It's one of my favorite memories. We were stopped at a red light still singing at the top of our lungs when this car stopped alongside us. Three very good-looking guys were looking straight at us. Kristin and I both smiled and she said 'Brinkanoose, brambey belladoo brasabelle.'"

Kira started laughing and I laughed with her until we were both quiet again. I asked, "What did she say?"

"She said 'Hey Guys meet us at the soda shop.' You know that feeling you get when you're with your best friend having the time of your life?"

"I never knew that feeling until I came here."

She put her hand on my cheek and smiled. "It's one of the best feelings in the world isn't it?"

I nodded.

"When the light turned green she put her foot to the gas pedal and we zoomed off leaving the boys in the wind."

"But didn't you want to hang out with them since they were cute?"

"Nah, we were having too much fun with each other. That day we drove a few hundred miles just to drive. We went to the movies, got a couple of burgers at a local burger joint, went miniature golfing, bowling, and before we arrived back home we went to the ice cream shop down the street and ordered some sundaes. I remember I ordered a banana split and Kristin ordered a triple-decker vanilla ice cream sundae with hot fudge, caramel, walnuts, whip cream and three cherries. Neither of us thought she would finish it but she did. After we ate the delicious ice cream we blasted the stereo and danced in the parking lot. Everyone stared at us but we didn't care a bit, we were having way too much fun. Now that I look back on that I blush in embarrassment but don't regret it one bit.

"By the time we got back home our hair was a mess, a brush wouldn't go through it. When our parents saw us and asked us what we did for an entire day we just looked at each other and laughed hysterically. My father, in his low key way looked at us with a small grin and said 'girls, I'll never understand them.' I love to think of the good memories of Kristin. We always had a great time together."

A tear escaped her eye and rolled down her cheek. I already knew what happened but just kept quiet. I let her tell me when she was ready. A few minutes passed with her holding her head up and silently crying. She finally looked up at me and smiled the saddest smile I had ever seen in my life.

"When Kristin was a senior and I a junior in high school our parents started having marital problems. Everyone was taking it badly but Kristin was going through something I hadn't thought was possible for her. She was always so happy before, always upbeat and cheerful. My parents divorced and Kristin just went downhill. Every year in school was her year, honor roll, number one in her class and she was expected to be valedictorian on her graduation day. She was a shoe-in to become the lead in the new play and she and her boyfriend were becoming really close. After the divorce her grades dropped and she dropped out of the production. She went from number one in her class to number eighty-five. She broke up with John leaving him devastated and I don't think I saw her smile more than once a week. I stayed strong throughout all this because of her. I couldn't," her voice trembled and she cleared her throat before she began again. "I couldn't deal with my parents divorce because I was worried beyond belief about my sister, my best friend.

"I tried telling people about what I feared might happen to Kristin if she stayed on like the way she was but nobody would listen. They'd just say 'oh, she's just going through a tough time, we all are, she'll get through it don't worry Kira.' I hated when people said that. People who said things like that didn't know my sister very well. Then right around graduation day she started cheering up. She apologized to everyone for acting like a 'baby' she called it. She made up with John and she and I talked all night before the big day. She told me she was excited about graduating and going to college and getting married and giving me nieces and nephews. We talked about everything that night; well I thought we talked about everything, but I was so naive. I am kicking myself now for the mistakes I made. I could have helped her.

"The day after her graduation, the day after she stood up in front of everyone holding her diploma and smiling as if she was the happiest girl in the world, she took too many pills. I found her lying on her bed, looking so peaceful with a note on her night table. I screamed and called the ambulance but it was too late, she had died. I was…God, I could have saved her. If I had just gone into the room an hour earlier, if I had known that her happiness in her last few days was all fake."

"It's not your fault Kira." I said as I put my arm around her quaking shoulders.

"Oh my God Amber, I shouldn't have told you all this, it's too much and you're so young. I am so sorry."

"I'm not too young, you can talk to me and I can talk to you. That is what a mother daughter relationship is."

"You're so sweet. I don't know what is wrong with me. I think it's because of the twins here, and not getting enough sleep. I've been rather stretched to my limit. And just thinking of the kids not being able to know their Aunt, really gets to me.

Come on, let's get you back to bed, you must be exhausted. Look at the time, I've been talking for well over an hour."

"That's okay; I like hearing about your fun times with Kristin. She seems like she was a good person."

"She was. Maybe tomorrow I'll show you a picture of the two of us. But for now both of us need some well deserved sleep. And just remember Amber, always cherish and love Alicia because sisters are the greatest part of life."

"I will."

"I love you kiddo."

"Love you too Kira."

We embraced and Kira held on an extra few seconds. I wished with all my might that Alicia and I could stay here forever. I know it isn't a nice thing to think but I had also prayed that my mother would forget about us and leave the country. I had a gut feeling that my prayers wouldn't come true.

Entry 43: <u>September 1992</u>

The sun peeked into my window trying to catch a glimpse of me sleeping. When it noticed I was, it curled up beyond the sky and shed light into my room. With agony I growled at the beautiful sun and covered my face with the darkness of my blanket, I slept an extra two hours and then said my good morning. I went downstairs and noticed Kira was still in a gloom but putting on a happy face for the sake of Bailey, Brynne, Perry, Alicia and myself. Surprisingly Mark was there; I was only used to seeing him at night with the hours he worked.

I smiled at Kira and she smiled back. I felt a special bond between us at that moment and I filed it in my memory to look back on every time I felt down or lonely. I wanted to know why Kira had been and still was upset but didn't want to ask; I didn't feel it was my place. So, I sat down at the table and played peek-a-boo with Brynne.

"Hey Amber, guess what?" said Alicia with excitement in her eyes.

"What?"

"I got a letter from mom yesterday."

I shuddered and noticed Kira dropped a fork on the ground, apologizing for being so clumsy. But I knew Kira wasn't the least bit clumsy. What was going on in the world?

"Yeah? What did she say?" I asked even though I didn't care.

"She said that she's doing well and they're going to let her out! She said she's coming home soon and she's going to come and get us."

"Well if she does I'm not leaving. You can go if you want since you like her so much but I don't, I'm happy right where I am." I went back to canoodling Brynne.

"Ugh Amber, you can be such a jerk sometimes." Alicia got up from her seat and went to her room angry. I shrugged.

I wanted so badly to stay with the people I had grown to love and knew that no matter how much I fought and protested there was nothing I could do to stop her from taking me.

Trying not to think about the dread of going back to living in hell, I played with the twins and watched them laugh their little socks off. They were becoming their own people. Brynne and Perry had their own personalities. Brynne was outgoing and happy while Perry was quiet and aware of all his surroundings. Bailey was another story; he was just a ball of laughs. He was the clown in the family. Being almost four years old he was into everything and was in pre-school for half a day, which was his favorite thing to do.

"Kira, can Lilly and Beckah come over?" I asked.

She looked at me distractedly while washing a dish. "Of course," she answered before turning around getting back to her task at hand.

They both showed up an hour later and we all went to my room.

"So, I have an idea" Beckah said enthusiastically. "Let's prank-call people! Dylan and his friends were doing it last night and it was hilarious!"

"That's fun. What should we say?" Lilly piped in as I sat there getting more nervous by the minute.

"Won't we get in trouble?"

"Loosen up Amber, it's fun. Where's the portable?"

I handed her the phone and watched as Beckah dialed a number she made up. She put the phone on speaker so we could all hear the other end.

She changed her voice from normal to squeaky. She sounded as if she was eighty years old. "Good afternoon, my name is Esther and I want to see a movie with a few of my girlfriends. What do you suggest for an old lady?"

"Well, what type of movie do you usually enjoy?" asked the teenage boy on the other end.

"I like all kinds; I love romance, horror, mystery, comedy and old movies from my childhood. I don't like magicians; if you give me a movie about magic of any sort I will be very angry."

"Okay, how about 'Sylvia Rangley' it's a romantic comedy set in the 1900's."

"Does it have magic?"

"No ma'am."

"Don't call me ma'am; you're making me sound old."

"I'm very sorry. No it doesn't have any type of magic, wizards, or supernatural stuff in it."

"Okay good. Now, how much is the candy? I just love my sweets."

We all laughed hysterically, but the teenager was clearly annoyed.

"It depends on how much you get. If you buy from the candy shop it's by the pound but if you buy from the concession stand it ranges from two to three dollars."

"What are you trying to do? Rob me blind? That's crazy. Between the prices for these damn movies nowadays and then you charge customers heap loads of money just to fill their bellies. Okay, so you are very kind. I have another question. My granddaughter Molly is going to come with us, she's seventeen. Would she enjoy this movie?"

"I'm sure any moment spent with you would be fun, so yes."

"Oh you are so very sweet, even though I know you're lying young man. Is there any sexual content in the movie that would be inappropriate for her? You know, like kissing?"

"Yes, but it isn't bad, she's old enough."

"What about that movie 'Case by Case'?"

"That's a murder mystery, supposed to be very scary. If you want to jump in your seat you should definitely see that."

"Actually, I don't feel like seeing a movie anymore. But, thanks for all your kindness. Tell your manager I am a pleased customer. Good afternoon."

"Good afternoon to you too," he answered in a monotone voice signaling his aggravation for wasting his precious time.

Beckah hung up the phone and the three of us laughed so hard our stomachs started to hurt. Kira walked in on us and laughed herself.

"I don't know what is so funny but your laughter is addictive. I'm glad you girls are having a great time. Would you like anything? Cookies and milk?"

"No thanks Mrs. Warner, we're fine. Thinking about going to see a movie actually," Lilly said and started laughing harder. We all just rolled on the floor in hysterics.

"Okay, let me know what time and I'll give you a ride."

At 7:34 we went into the movie theater and we saw Case by Case, which turned out to be excellent. Afterwards Beckah and Lilly came back to Kira's house and we had a slumber party. We stayed up till midnight and watched movies while eating popcorn and drinking soda. At 2:00 a.m. we decided to make pancakes.

"Shhh, we have to be very quiet, if Kira catches us she'll be so mad." I whispered.

"Mkay," Lilly whispered back.

We turned on the kitchen lights and took out the ingredients. After whipping up the batter and making the mix we put the batter onto the steaming pan and watched as the watery cream-colored stuff turned brown and tasty. When the cakes were done we turned off the stove and started chowing down.

All of a sudden we all heard a noise coming down the stairs. We figured it was Kira or Mark so we had to make a plan happen and quickly so as to not get into trouble.

"Okay, so we have to turn off all the lights and move quietly and gently so we blend in with the darkness," Beckah said.

We all agreed just for the sake of agreement. Both Lilly and I thought it was a pretty dumb idea, but who were we to judge?

Well, Kira found us so obviously our plan didn't work and she laughed at us again. "Look, you burned your pancakes. Let me make you some. But after you eat them you have to go to bed right away. And no more cooking without parental supervision you hear me?"

"Yes," we agreed. "We understand. Thank you."

She made us the best pancakes we have ever eaten and obeying her we all went to bed. We however, didn't go to sleep. We stayed awake for another hour or so talking about our night. It was a fun night and we all promised to always be friends no matter what happened. I truly hoped that our promise would hold true forever. I knew I'd keep up my end of the bargain. Friends no matter what, that was our motto.

And with that, we all fell asleep until noon the next day.

Entry 44: <u>November 1992</u>

Six weeks after the night we called "pancake night", Alicia and I were watching television. Our mother was released the day after pancake night and ordered to find a job and a house for us to live in. I learned that our house had been sold to the highest bidder. I guessed Chuck didn't keep his promise, or my father refused to pay.

Kira was on the phone arguing with a caller, Mark was at work, Bailey played with his blocks and the twins napped when there was a knock on the door.

"Amber, can you get that?" Kira said to me.

"Sure," I answered while getting up. I walked slowly to the door because the show we were watching had gotten to a really good part. When I opened the large wooden door I wasn't expecting what I saw. Standing in front of me was a woman. She was dressed professionally, a beige colored suit on with her reddish blonde hair pulled back in a barrette. She had makeup on and she was wearing a perfume that smelled of lavender and lace.

"Hi there sweetheart, boy have I missed you!" my mother said to me as she embraced my stiff, shocked body. I didn't know what to do, I just stood there while she held me; I stood there with my mouth open not uttering one word. "Well, how are you? You have gotten so big," she said as she let me go. Her eyes teared. "I can't believe I am finally out. So, are you going to let me in?"

I moved over so she would come in. When she stepped into the kitchen and Alicia saw her she smiled broadly and ran towards our mother into her arms hugging her so tightly. I was still silent, and now Kira was too.

"Oh my baby girl, I've missed you so much." She kissed Alicia's face over and over. "I'm so happy, so very happy. Hi, you must be Mrs. Warner. I'm Shelley," she said as she extended her hand to Kira.

"Yes, hello," Kira said curtly. "You can call me Kira. I wasn't expecting you today. Why don't you have a seat?"

My mother sat down at the table with Alicia still grasped tightly to her neck. Kira sat across from them and I sat down in the family room and played blocks with Bailey. I kept my ears open to hear what they were all talking about.

"I want to thank you so much for taking care of my beautiful girls. It means so much to me that you would do that."

"They're great kids. I'm very happy I had a chance to meet them."

"I also wanted to apologize for any mean things I said to you when I was in the rehab center. I don't remember any of it but if I was harsh in any way I want you to know it was the drugs and not me. I know I've hurt Amber and 'Licia very much and I feel so horrible about that, but I have changed. I have been drug and alcohol free for over a year and plan on staying that way."

"Can I ask you a question?"

"Sure you can. You can ask me anything you want, don't be afraid."

"Well, I don't mind because you are their mother, but are you allowed to be here? Did the judge give you permission to come and see them?"

"Didn't you get the letter? Or a phone call?"

"No, I haven't received any mail or phone calls."

"Oh. I'm so sorry I didn't know that. I thought someone got in touch with you. I wouldn't have just shown up here like this if I had."

I sat there building a castle just so Bailey could knock it down and listened to the conversation. I thought that this was all a game to my mother. This person she pretended to be; responsible, respectful, kind and loving wasn't who she really was. What was going to happen? I also wondered if Kira believed anything Shelley was saying. I decided I wasn't going to refer to her as my mother anymore; from now on she was just Shelley. I was also frightened that she was going to take Alicia and me with her tonight. I didn't want to go and I wasn't going to.

"It's okay, you're here now and I see Alicia's happy to see you."

"Yes she is. And I'm happy to see both my girls."

Just then one of the twins started crying. I jumped up and volunteered to retrieve the baby. Bailey came with me.

"Baby crying! Baby crying!" he screamed as we ran up the stairs.

It was Perry who was crying. He was lying on his back looking at the door anticipating someone rescuing him from the prison of his crib. When he spotted Bailey and I he smiled and cooed. I lowered the crib railing and picked up the baby. I sat with him in my arms in the rocking chair. Bailey climbed up on my lap too and I rocked them both while watching Brynne sleep in her crib across the room. How she slept through Perry crying I don't understand, but she did. I hummed Bailey's favorite song to them and I cried because I didn't know how much longer I would have with my brothers and sister.

We stayed like that for ten minutes and then Brynne woke up, saw us and became extremely jealous. Bailey jumped off of me and I scooped my God-daughter into my arms and sat back down. Bailey had become preoccupied when he started playing with one of the baby's toys.

Twenty minutes later Kira came up with two bottles and looked into the room at me holding the twins and Bailey playing in Perry's crib. She stood in the doorway for what seemed like an eternity and then she left only to return with a camera. After taking four pictures she gave me one of the bottles and took Brynne away from me to change her diaper. I fed Perry and then Kira and I switched babies.

"Where's Shelley?" I asked.

"She's downstairs with Alicia. They're playing a game. How are you doing?"

"Is she telling the truth? Did the judge really say she could come here?"

Kira looked down at her feet and rubbed her forehead. "I called Mr. Diggins from social services and asked him that. I'm afraid it's true. She wasn't suppose to come here herself and Mr. Diggins mentioned that I could tell her to leave."

"Good, then we can go downstairs and play."

She looked at the ground trying not to look me in the eye. "Amber, I invited your mom to stay here for a few days so you and Alicia can get used to her again. She agreed. Amber, I am so sorry but she is going to take both you girls to your new home on Sunday."

I knew this day would come and I knew it would hurt but I hadn't realized just how much. My nearly healed heart felt as if it had just been crushed like a cracker in a toddler's hands. The walls that surrounded us were beginning to close in on us, and my breath caught in my throat; I didn't know what was happening. The angst I felt at that moment was nothing I had ever felt before. My chest clenched up and my airways failed to open. My eyes were hazy. I could see Bailey in his crib but couldn't understand why he looked as if he was on the spinning teacups at Disney. Kira wasn't there anymore, where did she go? Brynne and Perry were in their cribs, how did they get there?

"Amber, here, breathe into this." Kira said, handing me a brown paper bag. I didn't ask any questions and just took it. It helped. Suddenly Bailey was off the spinning teacups and I could see again. "You know, it seems to me that your mother has changed. She's stopped the drugs and alcohol and she sounds remorseful for what she has done to you and Alicia. Maybe if you forgive her your life will be what it's supposed to be?"

"She's acting. This isn't her and I don't want to go back with her. I like it here; I want you to be my mom. I'm not going to forgive Shelley. Ever." I broke down and Kira held me.

"I think we should go downstairs before they get worried. I want you to at least pretend to be civil toward her. Do it for Alicia because you don't want to lose her. She is very happy that Shelley is here and if she believes that you aren't she will be upset."

I agreed, with the knowledge that this was going to happen whether I liked it or not. I had to accept the inevitable and move on with my life. So with that thought in my mind I picked up Brynne while Kira held Perry and Bailey and we all went downstairs to join Alicia and Shelley.

Entry 45: <u>November 1992</u>

Three days later Kira and my mother sat in the backyard with a cup of tea and watched all of us play in the sandbox and on the swing-set. Mark pushed Bailey in his baby swing and he was having the time of his life. Brynne and Perry lay on a blanket kicking their chubby little legs and cooing while Alicia and I built a sandcastle waiting for Bailey to rejoin us. We were all having so much fun. While we were enjoying ourselves I listened to my mother and Kira talking. I couldn't help myself. I was still a little leery of my mother

"You have a lovely family Kira."

"Thank you Shelley. I think so too."

"How did you and Mark meet?"

"Well we were in college together when we first met and I wasn't interested in him. Every day he would come up to me and ask me for a date, and I refused every time. I don't know if it was because I wasn't ready for a relationship or I was afraid but it took him eight months to finally get me to agree."

"What did he say that finally made you change your mind?"

"Nothing special. It was actually pretty dull. He said 'Kira, this is your last chance, if you let me go now you will never see me again. You will regret it for the rest of your life; always thinking back to this day and hating yourself. I feel like you are the woman I'm meant to be with for eternity and please don't reject me again. Please go out with me.' I felt so bad for him that I just said yes."

"That's not dull, it's actually pretty romantic. When David asked me out I agreed immediately and we were married shortly thereafter. Amber was born and then Alicia and we were very happy. Amber was always 'Daddy's little girl' and Alicia was, well she cried a lot and David was always annoyed by it.

"He was never a romantic either. Not that I minded, I loved him and he was my world. And when he left I was devastated. I'm sure you know the rest."

They were silent for a minute and then Kira spoke.

"Would you mind if I took Amber and Alicia out for dinner and a movie tomorrow night to say goodbye to them? Just the three of us?"

"Of course you can. I have some errands to run before we leave, so while you girls are eating I'll do those."

"Thank you so much."

At that they were silent and watched over at us and laughed as Bailey screamed in joy "higher, higher."

❦   ❦   ❦

"What do you want?" I asked through the darkness. Someone pushed on my arm and ordered me to wake up. "Who are you and what do you want from me? I am sleeping, leave me alone." I turned onto my stomach and wrestled the comforter away from my nemesis. Pulling it over my head I began to fall back asleep.

"Come on Amber, wake up. I want to ask you something. Wake up, wake up, wake up," screamed the voice I didn't want to recognize.

And, as quickly as the voice came it was gone and I didn't care. I went back to sleep. Sleeping comfortably only lasted for a few minutes longer when the voice came back to haunt me ten fold. "You didn't listen to me the first time, so now I'm using extreme measures. You brought this on yourself Amber, and don't say I didn't warn you." All of a sudden, right in my ear, a whistle blew. It was the most horrendous noise I had ever heard in my life and I was furious.

"God Alicia, what do you want? This better be important."

"Hey, don't yell, I told you I wanted to ask you something. Anyway, be quiet everyone else is asleep and if they wake up this will be ruined."

"What will be ruined? A dumb secret you want to tell me about how you can't wait to go home with Shelley and how you wish that she and David would get back together? It's not going to happen so get over it. I'm going back to sleep. Goodnight."

"No, that's not what I want to say. You can be so mean sometimes."

"I'm sorry, but you woke me up out of a dead sleep. What's so important?"

Alicia was wearing a pair of pajamas I had never seen before and I looked at her with a weird expression. She rolled her eyes at me and climbed up on the bed. When she was finally sitting next to me with the covers on top her crossed legs she began her speech. "Well, you know how this is our last day with Kira, Mark, Bailey and the twins?"

"Yeah, don't remind me."

"I want to do something nice for them, as a going away present. I think they would really like that. But I don't want to buy them anything; that would just be dumb. So I was thinking we should make them something."

"You woke me up for that? Why couldn't we just discuss this in the morning?"

"Because I had the idea just now. You could write something and I could take a picture of you and me and frame it in a handmade frame made by the one and only," she made a gesture to herself, "me."

"Okay, that's a great idea. I'll dream about what I will write while you dream about what you are going to make the frame out of. Goodnight."

"No Amber, we have to do this now!"

"It's the middle of the night," I said getting aggravated. "We can do it tomorrow."

"Oh and why would we waste time away from them when we can do it now and spend all day with our new friends."

"They're not my friends, they're our family."

"Whatever. Come on, you write your poem or story and I'll go and look for frame supplies. We can have a sleepover," Alicia said excitedly as she jumped off the bed and ran out the door quietly.

I knew that there was nothing I could do to make her change her mind now so I got out my journal and wrote a story. It took almost two hours but it was finally perfect and I was actually very proud of it and I knew that Kira would cry when I read it aloud to her.

Alicia's frame was beautiful and she used colors that matched the family room. She found a 'make your own frame' package in one of the craft drawers in Kira's study. It was from Alicia's birthday party. She painted the frame itself maroon and put rainbow glitter on top of the maroon paint. She found beads shaped like hearts and glued one in each corner. A yellow heart in the top left corner for my favorite color, a purple heart in the top right corner for her favorite color, a blue heart in the bottom left corner for Bailey's favorite color and in the bottom right corner she placed a pink heart and a green heart for the twins. On the side she wrote in her best handwriting 'Alicia' and on the opposite side she wrote 'Amber.'

"Okay, now I have to take a picture of us. Hmm, how am I going to do this?" She looked around the room thoughtfully. "Should we have a picture of the two of us or wait until the morning and have the babies in it?"

"It's up to you, it's your present. My opinion is you should wait till morning."

"Yeah, I'll do that. Do you like the frame?"

"I love it, it's really pretty. Kira and Mark will be so happy."

We sat in silence for a few minutes. The sleep that I had abandoned had now left me and I was wide awake. "So," said Alicia. "What did you write?"

"I'm not telling, you have to wait until I read it to them tomorrow."

"Come on, I let you see my frame."

"I'm waiting."

"Okay fine. I'm going to bed now. Goodnight."

"Goodnight."

Entry 46: <u>November 1992</u>

The next morning the house smelled of pancakes, toast and corned beef hash. Our favorite breakfast! Immediately Alicia had Kira take a picture of the five kids to 'keep as a memento.' After breakfast we rode our bikes to the nearest store to get the pictures developed. I bought some nice decorated paper and then we played some video games at the arcade for an hour.

We arrived back home just as Brynne and Perry were going down for their nap.

"Amber, are you leaving tomorrow?" Bailey asked me.

"Yes, but I'll call and write to you all the time."

"I don't want you to go away." His lips quivered and I sensed a tantrum coming on.

"Bailey, why don't you and I go play on the swings for a little while."

"Okay," he said excitedly. Crisis averted. "Let's play under the falling bridge."

"Sure, I love that game."

"Me too."

Under the falling bridge was a game where I would push him high and then run under the swing before he came back. The goal was to get under without any part of the swing or him touching me. He thought it was hilarious, I thought it to be rather frightening. One time I ran a little too late and got the plastic swing right in my face. I had a bruise on my cheek and a huge bump on the side of my forehead. Bailey made me presents for two weeks following the incident.

"The swing is cold."

"It is? Well once you sit on it your bum will make it nice and warm."

"Ha, ha," he laughed. "You said bum."

Boy, was I going to miss his laugh and his smile. I was going to miss everything about this place. It had become my sanctuary and my favorite hideaway. I didn't have the normal fort; I had a family instead.

"Come on, push me. Really high."

"Okay, I was just getting ready. Are you ready?"

"Yes," he yelled.

"What? I can't hear you. Are you ready?"

"YES," he yelled at his loudest voice.

"Now, that was better." I pulled back his swing and held it there for a minute and then pushed as hard as I could. His little Nike covered feet whooshed into the air and returned back to me. I pushed a few more times and then said my ritual before I ran through; "Falling Bridge, falling bridge, please don't hit me like you did once before. Falling Bridge, falling bridge, stay high as a bird until I reach the other side."

I got to the other side safely and heard Bailey screech in delight. This was so much fun.

An hour later Bailey and I laughed our way back into the house where we started watching a movie. He fell asleep on the couch within ten minutes. I rubbed his back for a while and then left him with Kira and Shelley to go 'rest' in my room for a while. I didn't rest though. I transferred my story onto the decorated paper I had bought at the store.

All of a sudden I had a horrible thought, something I had totally forgotten about. I don't know how I could have forgotten something so important. I ran downstairs to ask Kira something. She answered me and I rushed to the phone. I dialed the number.

"Hey Lilly, do you want to come over? Please, it's really important."

Lilly said she would, and then I called Beckah, Dylan, Rachel and Alicia's friends Emily, Ariyanna, Krista, Mike and Tommy. How could we forget to say goodbye to them?

"Hey Amber, are you ready?"

"Not yet. I just invited our friends over for a little while. We forgot about them."

"I didn't. I called them on the phone and said bye. But that's wicked cool that they're coming over. I made stuff for them."

"Okay. We'll do the present thing after dinner," I whispered.

"That's a good idea," Alicia whispered back behind a cupped hand.

All of our friends came by a few minutes later. Alicia and her crew went up to her room and my posse and I went outside and had a picnic.

"Okay Amber, what is this about? Why are we all here? Party?" asked Lilly.

"Kind of."

"Hey girls, and boy," said Shelley. "Amber, are you going to introduce me to your friends?" She was wearing a yellow sundress with her hair combed nicely. You would never believe she was an alcoholic and drug abuser at any point during her life.

"I guess. This is Lilly, Beckah, Dylan and Rachel. This is Shelley." I said to them all.

"Hi," they all responded. They sounded quiet and confused.

"It's very nice to meet you. I'm Amber's mother."

My face was down, ashamed and I could feel it getting hotter and hotter. I didn't want anyone else to notice so I covered myself with my hands. Why did she have to come out here? She's not involved in this part of my life and I don't want her to be.

"Okay, I'll let you get back to your little get together."

"Thanks," I said shyly.

After the door shut behind her Beckah spoke up. "That is your mother? Wow, you don't look like her at all."

"I know."

"She's beautiful."

"Gee thanks Dylan, I don't look like her and she's beautiful."

"I didn't mean it like that. I just was expecting her to look different."

"She's tall. Alicia doesn't really look like her either. I mean; she looks more like her than you do. Weird," Rachel said.

Lilly sat there and looked at the ground. She did not say anything. I wondered what she thought. I saw that she was the only one who had actually acknowledged the fact that I would probably be leaving if my mother was there at the Warner house. Her eyebrows were furrowed and her eyes were sullen. She pulled grass out of the lawn and her lips were hidden under her teeth. She was trying to hold in her emotions.

"What's the matter Lilly?" asked Beckah.

Lilly didn't say anything. She was still pulling out grass.

"Lil, tell us, what's wrong?" Then as if suddenly a light bulb flashed over Beckah's head, "No way, no way."

"What?" asked both Rachel and Dylan.

"Her mom is coming to take her and Alicia back." Lilly suddenly screamed, ripping a chunk of grass out of the lawn revealing some earthworms and dirt. She ran through the house and Kira went after her.

"You're leaving?" Dylan asked me incredulously. "Now, who's going to be my number one fan? I can't believe it."

"Yeah," I answered. "I am. I don't want to, but she came back."

"Well at least she's sober," Rachel said.

"She's not going to stay that way. I know her; she'll go back to like before. The judge should have never let her out."

"Amber, if she does go back to drinking, you can always run away and live with us. Beckah told us about how you and Alicia ran to her house."

We all laughed. It was a relief to laugh. "Yeah I could do that. We can all be pen pals and I'll try to call when I can." The mention of pen pals made me think of Chris. Our letters had become few and far between, as I was so busy with my new life. I missed him.

"We could all kidnap you and hide you in the basement of the school. Nobody would know."

All of us turned around and Lilly stood there with Kira behind her.

"Look who I found wandering around my house. Now you aimless wanderer, go hang out with your friends." Kira's voice caught in her throat.

"Can I sit next to you?" Lilly asked me.

"Okay."

Two hours later we had talked, laughed and made a pact with each other to always stay in touch no matter what. Then we all huddled together and stood there for a few minutes.

"Friends forever," we all said.

After saying our millionth goodbye they all left. I remembered the day that Chris left and suddenly my whole body went into total emotional breakdown. I thought to myself that every good person in my life leaves in one shape or another and it is always at the fault of my mother. Well, Chris left because his mother got a job far away but I liked blaming Shelley.

"I'm going to get ready for tonight," I told Kira.

"Okay sweetheart. We're going to leave in about an hour."

I took a shower and put on the dress Kira bought me for my birthday. It was purple with a pink and yellow flower print. I put my hair in a high ponytail wrapped with a yellow ribbon. I put sandals on my feet and went downstairs.

Entry 47: <u>November 1992</u>

Julie Andrews waved at me; I can't believe it, she waved at me. She was sitting in the private room of the restaurant Kira took Alicia and me to. When I saw her I was so excited. I have loved her in every movie she made; in fact, "Mary Poppins" is my favorite movie of all time. I waved back ferociously and had a smile on my face that spread itself thin from ear to ear. This is going to be a great night. I forgot for a minute that tomorrow morning we would be on our way to a different house with the one person I couldn't stand to be around.

The atmosphere of the restaurant was very nice and Kira and Alicia both looked beautiful. Kira had her hair in barrettes and she wore a pair of black pants and a mauve v-neck cashmere sweater. Alicia wore a dress that was very similar to my own, with her blonde hair up half way in a butterfly barrette and curled the rest of the way down.

This was our favorite formal restaurant. We came here on the Friday of our first day at the Warner's. It was called Queen Isabella's, named after the former owner who had passed it on to her daughter Evie. Kira and Evie were good friends and she had come over to see how we were doing.

"So, I hear you two are here for a special occasion. I'll be sure you have the best night of your lives. You girls are so beautiful tonight; tell me what your secret is."

"You know the secret Evie. All women do," Kira winked. "Right girls."

"Right," Alicia and I said simultaneously.

"Okay, well I have to get back to work, enjoy your meal and if you need anything, anything at all, tell Matthew. He's your server tonight. I'll tell him you are royalty. Fair thee well my Queens." Evie left for the kitchen and we had a wonderful dinner. No one mentioned Shelley or our departure or anything depressing. We had a very nice night and delicious food to boot.

"Are you two ready for a surprise?"

"There's more?" Alicia asked.

"Of course there's more silly, just you wait to see what I've got planned for you."

Driving the scenic route was just breathtaking. I stared out the window at the spectacular view of the ocean waves crashing against the rocks that caused a roaring noise to warn all viewers it meant business. In the distance on a lonesome rock in the middle of the ocean four or five seals sat and looked around at their home. To the left was the bridge that connected to one of the state islands. The lights were shadowed in the glistening water below.

We turned into a park and there was a blanket on the ground. Mark, Bailey and the twins were there with ice cream.

"Oh my God, what are they doing here?" I asked.

"I told them to come. I called just as we were leaving the restaurant so Mark could get the ice cream without it melting. Are you happy?"

"Of course!"

Bailey ran up to us screaming something that was incomprehensible due to the chocolate ice cream in his mouth. I took him by the hand and we all sat on the checkered blanket and ate our favorite flavors. Then we walked to a tiny beach and we ran barefoot in the ocean screaming and laughing and having a blast. Kira chased the three of us while Mark sat with Brynne and Perry.

It was now 9:00 and it was past the twin's bedtime, but Mark had made an official decision that they would make an exception this one time. We were all now back at the blanket near the car and we had a light hovering above us.

"Okay Alicia, I think right now is the time we should, you know."

"What?"

"You know," I coughed trying to make her understand the presents.

"Oh, yeah. Good idea."

I turned around. It was a poignant sight. Kira was sitting next to Mark who held Bailey in his lap. The twins were both in their car seats fast asleep. The way the light fell on them was amazing. They looked so angelic and that picture stays in my mind always.

"Amber and I have something for you too."

"You do? You didn't have to do that. You're both so sweet."

"I made you this," she handed them a wrapped box. She did a pretty decent job for an eleven-year-old. "Do you like it?"

Kira unwrapped the paper slowly and opened the box. The frame was in there with the picture of all of us from that morning. She put a hand to her mouth and started tearing up. "I love it. Thank you so much Alicia. I will keep this next to my bed for eternity. Come here and give me a giant hug." Kira held Alicia close to her for a few minutes, running her fingers through her hair. "I love you Alicia." She kissed her forehead. "Always remember that okay."

"I will. I love you too." They hugged again. "Okay, Amber's turn. I don't know what she did."

"I'm excited."

"I am too. I've been waiting all day."

"Hey Bailey, do you want to know what Amber made for us?" asked Mark.

"Yeah!" he screamed, lifting his entire body up for a bounce.

"Okay Amber, we're all ready."

"I wrote a story for everyone. I called it 'A Beautiful Gift.'"

"Did we bring tissues?" asked Kira.

"Well my dear, I thought ahead and out of my magician's sack I give you my very own magic tissues that are guaranteed to heal and comfort in any time. I might need to use some myself."

"Mark, you are my savior, I love you." They kissed.

"Okay, now we're ready princess."

I loved her names for me. I could feel myself getting a little teary. I might have to invest in some of Mark's magic tissues.

Here goes. I read my story aloud.

"She was beautiful, he was handsome, the baby shy and curious. I stood scared to no end until the angel in front of me spoke words that only I could find comforting. With my best friend by my side and an obnoxious Santa Claus figure behind me,I knew I was finally safe.

"Her arms were a safe haven, her eyes warm and inviting. I knew from the moment I saw her that I would love her and think of her as the mother I had always wanted. Every day was once a day I didn't want to live through until I met the most wonderful family on earth and through the amount of time I spent with them each day became the best day of my short life. She opened her home, her mind, her thoughts and her heart to me and she will always be a very important part of me that nobody can take away.

"His strength and his love made me learn how to feel loved and love back. He is a wonderful husband and father and I only wish I were as lucky.

"The two beautiful souls merged to create three gorgeous children who I am proud to call my sister and brothers. Through blood makes them related but through love makes us all a family.

"I am blessed to have known them and spent time as their daughter but the time has come to move on and I will do that, for them. Kira, Mark, Bailey, Brynne and Perry you are all my life away from life; my home away from home; my true family including my blood sister Alicia. I will miss you so much and will always remember my time with you. No matter how far I am I will always be yours and I will always write to you. I love you and will keep you with me all the time."

Kira cried hysterically. I guess Mark's tissues didn't work as well as he would have liked. In fact, Mark and Alicia were also crying. Bailey had fallen asleep. I went into Kira's outstretched arms and let her hold me. Mark came closer to us and put his free arm around us. We all sat there for a long time crying, letting our emotions pour out of us.

"I'm going to miss you girls so much. You are both so beautiful and talented and smart. I am the luckiest woman in the world for having the opportunity to know you. I don't understand how your mom could have left you, she was wrong and I'm sure she regrets it. I want you both to know how much I love you. A piece of my heart has been broken and you girls are taking it with you. I am always with you. I'm only a phone call or letter away. You can always come to me if you need anything, you know that right?"

We nodded.

"I wanted you two to know," Mark started. "I love you girls as if you were my own flesh and blood. I don't love you any less than I love Bailey, Brynne and Perry. I know I'm not around as much as any of you would have liked. I will make absolute sure that Bailey and the twins will always remember you, and I'll send pictures all the time. Our house will be so different. You two have changed us completely, all for the good. I will miss you both so much. I love you."

"We love you too."

Entry 48: <u>November 1992</u>

It was the day, the day I had been dreading for a long time. I kept my eyes closed as long as possible hoping against all hope that if I stayed asleep I wouldn't have to leave. Then I thought that if I stayed in bed I would lose the precious moments I had left. So I rolled out of bed and began my day.

Downstairs my mother fed Brynne while Perry sat in his chair. Kira wasn't around and neither were Mark or Bailey. Alicia watched television in a trance.

"Hey Amber, good morning."

"Good morning, where is everyone?"

"Kira and Mark had to take Bailey to the doctor."

"Is he okay?"

"Yes, it's just his yearly checkup. They'll be back soon."

"Amber, come watch the movie with me."

I grabbed Perry from his chair and held him in my arms as we all watched the movie. I felt the oddest feeling at that moment. Everything seemed right in the world, and I don't know how it all happened. The house was peaceful and quiet, and our mother was happy feeding someone else's baby. She looked at Alicia and me with love and admiration, something she never had done since my father left. I noticed something shift within me. I experienced an emotion that was unfamiliar: forgiveness. But, I didn't want to forgive her! I wanted to shut her out of my life forever and never have to worry about her messing up our lives anymore.

How could I stop it? I turned away from her and continued to watch the movie. Perry reached up to my face and pulled on my ear. I looked down at him and he smiled; his blue eyes sparkled with joy. I smiled back at him and then gave him a raspberry on his belly; he laughed in excitement. All three of them loved when I did that to them, but Perry liked it the most. He would give me the most reaction when I puckered my lips to his belly and tickled him.

An hour later Kira, Mark and Bailey returned.

"Look what I got! A Lollipop!"

"Oooh, that's your favorite kind Bailey, red," I said to him. His face was red and he had a smiley face sticker on his arm.

"I had to get a shot."

"You did? Wow, you're brave."

"I'm superman."

"You sure are."

"Look Alicia!" he continued.

"Hi Amber, can you come here for a minute?" Kira asked.

"Sure." I put Perry back in his chair and pushed the lever for it to swing back and forth while the calming music played.

When I walked into the living room Kira and Mark were sitting on the couch with a big box between them.

"We got you a little something that both of us think you'll like."

"Thank you." I ripped open the paper and opened the box. Inside was another box. The box contained a word processor.

"This is so you don't have to write freehand anymore. You can type on pieces of paper. It will be faster and more fun."

"Wow, this is awesome. I love it! Thanks." I gave them both a huge hug.

"Keep going, you're not done yet," Mark said.

I took out the word processor box and found a large pile of paper. Underneath the paper was a smaller box. I opened it up and it was a fancy storage box. It was decorated in dried flowers and written on top in purple cursive writing it said "Amber's Journals: Private." Inside the fancy box was a new journal. It was leather just like the one Chris had bought me. It was light purple, and the pages were edged in gold. I opened it and read:

ॐ

"Amber,

The door opened up that day and two beautiful girls walked into my home. I was nervous, excited, anxious and most of all humbled. Mark and I couldn't believe that two extraordinary young girls had no place to live. We didn't understand how a woman who had the privilege of being the mother of these children could abandon them. But with every tragedy comes something good. And the good from this is that I could help these children.

There is a reason for everything and I believe with all my heart that God put you and Alicia into our lives for a purpose. There was some greater force behind it all. Mark and I had almost changed our mind about being foster parents when Bailey was born, but then we went through with it anyway. My heart yearned to reach out to children less fortunate than others. I know that the two of you lived in such a neglectful environment and to be with us would be a relief and a vacation. I hope with all of my soul that you are now able to look at your lives and are grateful for all of the good things you do have. Alicia is such a wonderful sister and friend and the relationship you have with her will always be strong no matter what happens. You now have five new "family" members who love you dearly.

Bailey will always remember you and will always consider you his sister. Brynne will always love you for who you are. Perry will also be reminded on a daily basis of your kindness and of your love for him.

We will always there for you whenever you need someone to talk to. Although you are in a different home far away from here, we will always there with you, in your heart and your memories. Remember the great times we had together and you will be happy. Memories will always make your day shine brightly.

You are beautiful Amber and we will miss you terribly. Keep us in your heart. You will be in ours forever.

Love always,

Kira, Mark, Bailey, Brynne and Perry Warner

Entry 49: <u>November 1992</u>

First a knock on the door and Shelley and Alicia walked in with the twins.

"We have to head out now, our new home is a few hours away and I want to beat the traffic. Are you ready Amber?"

"Okay."

Shelley handed Brynne over to Kira and Alicia handed Perry over to Mark. When we all moved into the kitchen area the twins were placed in their chairs and I kissed them goodbye, as did Alicia. They just cooed.

"Are you leaving now?" Bailey asked.

"Sweetheart, Amber and Alicia have to go home to their mommy now."

"But Mama, why can't they stay here?"

"Because their mama wants them to go with her, she misses them."

"I don't want them to go." He started crying.

"I know you don't, but they have to, so why don't you give them a big huge special Bailey hug? I think they'd like that."

"Okay," he said through sobs. He gave each of us a giant hug, even Shelley. I was going to miss him. Then he went to play with his toys in the corner.

"I'll go put your stuff in the car. I'll meet you all outside." Shelley said nicely.

After she left Mark gave both of us a big hug and kiss on the cheek and then brought Bailey and the twins outside.

"Well, Alicia, give me a hug! I'll miss you, but I know you'll be happy. Right?"

"Yeah, but I'll miss you too. Thank you for taking care of us while she was away."

"It was my pleasure. You take care of your sister okay?"

"I will. I love you."

They hugged. "I love you too." Tears brimmed her eyes.

"I'll help mom with our stuff."

Both Kira and I just stood there opposite each other and said nothing. Her jaw was clenched and her eyes showed deep pain. The forgiveness I felt towards Shelley disappeared. The truth seeped into my brain, the truth that Shelley cared for nobody but herself. If she had thought of me, or Kira she would have had more compassion and let me live with the Warners.

"Well, this is it."

"This is goodbye."

She knelt to my level. "This is not goodbye Amber; this is see you later. I am always here for you. You can call me or write to me any time. And we'll see each other again."

"I don't want to leave." I cried uncontrollably at this point and I didn't anticipate it stopping any time soon.

"I know you don't, but your mom is back and we talked about this happening. You know, I had a long talk with Shelley last night and she is so remorseful about leaving you two alone. She understands that what she did was wrong and horrible and she wants to make amends. She loves you so much Amber. She lost her way and she's on the path to finding it. Coming back to you girls is her first step. Do you think you can forgive her?"

"I don't know. I don't want to."

"I know it's difficult after everything you've been through but forgiving her will make you feel better. Your life will be happier. It's going to be a tough road but I know you can do it. You are so strong, so brave and so talented. Just write to let things off of your mind. And when you are done writing, write some more. Can you promise me that you'll try to forgive her? Let her in? Let her know you, the real you?"

"I promise I'll try, for you."

"You are so beautiful. I am the happiest woman in the world to have known you. Don't forget to write to me."

"I won't. I love you Kira." I melted into her arms for the last time and stayed there for a while. We walked out hand in hand and met up with the rest of the clan.

I walked over to Shelley and hugged her. It felt weird, forced but it was also a relief. Immediately I felt somewhat better. When we released the hug Shelley had tears in her eyes. I hadn't seen her have a true emotion in so long I had forgotten what it looked like.

Shelley thanked Mark and Kira again and got into the driver's seat. Alicia and I sat in the back. As we drove away from the most caring people in the world my heart broke again. Alicia and I waved until we were out of sight and we noticed Mark holding Kira tightly while they both waved back. The entire ride to our new home I just stared out the window while Alicia and my mother sang traveling songs. I hoped and prayed that this new part of my life wouldn't turn into the past. I looked at my mother, who seemed happy and took a snapshot in my mind. Just in case my prayers didn't come true.

I fell asleep in the car after a half hour of travel and awoke to an empty car. I immediately panicked and looked around. The car was parked at a rest stop and sitting at the picnic table right outside of McDonald's was my mother and Alicia eating burgers and fries. I opened the door and walked over to them.

"Well Good Morning sleepy head!"

"Where are we?"

"We have about another hour before we reach our new home, but Alicia was hungry so we had to stop. You looked so peaceful we didn't want to wake you up. Do you want anything?"

Shelley gave me some money and I went inside to get myself some food. When I got back to the picnic table they were just finishing, but they stayed and waited for me to finish. Alicia was telling our mother everything that happened while we were at the Warner's. She told her about the time we ran away and stayed with Beckah, the birthday fun at the mall, the day the twins were born, the christening, and more.

"It sounds like you two had fun. I'm glad. Did they take good care of you?"

"Yes, they are very nice people. Kira liked Amber better though."

"No she didn't."

"Don't worry Amber, I don't care. She totally did."

I smiled inwardly, I knew that Alicia was right, and I knew that she didn't mind that Kira and I had a special bond that was between just the two of us.

"You girls are very special, how could anyone not love you?"

I wanted to ask her that question but I didn't want to ruin the mood, so I just smiled and took another bite from my burger.

We were on the road again within minutes and they were back to singing. I had to admit, the singing was making the time go by faster so I joined in, quietly. After singing fourteen songs we arrived in front of a cute little house. It was white with green shutters and a white picket fence hugging the yard. There was a well out front and a stone walkway. The front door was bright red with a shiny gold knocker. I smiled. This house looked like a normal family house where a normal family lived. I pictured the three of us living there happy and healthy, drug free, alcohol free and friends over all the time. I pictured our mother inviting Kira, Mark, Bailey and the twins over for Christmas dinner and I pictured Alicia and I having a good time in this house.

"So, what do you think?"

"I love it!" I exclaimed, surprising even myself. "Do we get our own rooms?"

"Of course you do. Why don't you two go inside and look around and I'll start bringing in your suitcases." Shelley smiled and I could see in her eyes love and happiness. A flood of memories rushed to me from when I was four and she and my father had a romantic dinner in the kitchen late at night. I had snuck out of bed to watch them.

The rooms were dark except for a glimmer in the kitchen where there were two white candles lit on the table. The smoke glided off the tips of the flames and curled into the air evaporating into the room. My mother wore a beautiful black evening gown with her hair curled and my father was in his best suit, cleanly shaven. They sat, side by side and my father had his arm around my mother. She was looking into his eyes with such admiration and love. They had finished their dinner and were eating homemade apple pie. My great-grand-mother's recipe. He fed her a piece of pie topped with vanilla ice cream and caramel and she returned the favor. They both shared a kiss mouthful with apple.

With the candlelight and soft music my adoring parents danced in the middle of the kitchen as if they were in the middle of a ballroom. It was a magnificent sight and I am so happy I was there to experience that. Two months later he left.

"What are you looking at?" my mother asked me.

I caught myself and just smiled. "Nothing." I ran after my sister and we both explored our new house.

Entry 50: <u>November 1992</u>

The house itself was small and bare, but otherwise a nice place. I had imagined a dump. I didn't realize she had actually taken the time to make sure that it had enough bedrooms in it so Alicia and I could have our own room. I ran to the end of the hallway and found the perfect room. I decided then and there that this was my new room.

"Amber, look at my new room!"

I walked to the door next to the room I had chosen and saw my sister sitting on the window seat in the spacious room she had chosen for her own. "Wow, that's really cool. Want to see my room?"

"Yeah."

We walked into my room and looked around. The walls were still naked and unloved and the floor yearning for furniture but it was a great room. There were two windows on one wall and another large window on the adjacent wall. I also had a window seat. "I can't wait to decorate it!"

"I know; I can't wait until my room is done either. It's going to be so rad!"

"What are you doing?"

"I'm not telling, it's going to be a surprise. I have to go draw a design right now." Alicia ran in her room and shut the door. A second later she slowly made her way back to my room. "I don't have pen or paper."

I just laughed. "Okay, help me decide what I'm going to do. I want my bed over by those windows with a night table on each side. In the drawers is where I'll keep all my writing. I want pink lamps on each table. On this big wall I'll paint a mural of my favorite authors with quotes all over it. Over on the window seat I'm going to have a pink cushion with pink curtains and purple, green, pink, yellow and white throw pillows. That's where I'm going to do all my writing. So, if you see the curtains shut you know not to bother me. I want a fluffy rug in the middle of the room and a desk right against my mural wall. That's where I'm going to put my word processor from Kira and Mark." I was so excited. In my mind it signified a brand new beginning, a chance to start over and maybe begin to trust my mother again. Although that would take a little longer than a few days.

"It's going to be an awesome room Amber! I can't wait until it's finished. How are you going to paint the mural?"

"Well, I'm a pretty good artist. I've been hiding my abilities. It'll be fun, can you help me?"

"Really? You want me to help?"

"Yeah, it will be fun."

"I'll tell you what, I'll help you paint your mural if you help me paint mine."

"You want a mural? I thought you weren't telling me what you wanted because it was a surprise?"

"Well, I'll keep it a surprise from mom."

"Okay, I'll help you then. Do you think she'll buy us the paint?"

"I don't know. MOM!"

"Geez, you don't have to scream! We don't live in a mansion."

"Ha ha, sorry."

We talked to Shelley and she took us immediately to the paint shop. We started our "surprise rooms" the next morning. Because we didn't have any furniture yet we slept in the family room on the floor in brand new sleeping bags. Alicia's had a Cinderella theme and mine was pink. I had to admit, she was doing well so far.

At the crack of dawn Alicia and I woke and ran into my room and began drawing out the room in the new sketchbook we bought. Then we painted the wall white. While waiting for that to dry, we plugged in a brand new stereo and painted the remaining three walls a pale pink.

"This is a lot of fun Amber; thanks for letting me help you."

"You're welcome."

"Hey, I have an idea! How about for the windows and the door we paint it the dark purple you bought."

"Yeah, that will look pretty."

We continued painting and after an hour the walls were painted and the white wall was almost dry. "Let's get a drink and a snack."

We went to the kitchen and grabbed a soda and a bag of chips.

"Hi girls, how's the surprise going?"

"Good," we said and then giggled all the way back to my masterpiece.

"Okay, now after we finish snacking let's draw the authors on the wall and then I'll start painting them while you start writing the quotes around them."

"That sounds good. What authors are you going to put up there?"

"Jane Austen, Emily Bronte, and Alexander Dumas."

"Oh." She said stuffing chips in her mouth.

Two and a half hours later Jane Austen and Alexander Dumas were done, and all of the quotes were written on the wall.

"Wow, this is going to take longer than I thought." It seemed I was talking to myself because Alicia was sound asleep on the floor with the pencil in her hand and drool dripping from her mouth. A slight noise made its way through her nose and mouth. She looked so cute. I had to admit, she had the right idea, so I fell asleep on the floor next to her.

All of a sudden I felt a tiny tug on my shoulder.

"Amber, wake up. Amber, Amber? Are you awake?"

"What time is it?"

"It's two o'clock, you've been asleep for three hours."

"Where's Alicia?"

"She's still asleep. But I want to talk to you for a minute, just the two of us."

"Okay." At that moment I couldn't understand why in the world she woke me up to talk to me. Why couldn't she have waited until I woke up myself?

We walked into the family room and sat on the floor opposite each other.

"Don't you think it's weird we're talking on the floor? Shouldn't we buy some furniture?"

"We will, I promise. As soon as you and your sister finish your rooms we'll go to the store and get everything we need. No need to do something twice when you can get it in one fell swoop."

"Good idea." I yawned.

"I'm sorry I woke you up. I just really wanted to talk to you alone. I'll talk to Alicia another time. Did you enjoy yourself with the Warners?"

"Yes, they are very nice people. I hope you don't mind if I write to them a lot."

"Oh, no, not at all. I know you became close with Kira and I don't blame you. From our conversation she seemed like a very likable person. I just wanted to make sure they took care of you."

"Yes, they did. They loved us." I looked away feeling a rush of pain. I could sense a crying spell coming on and I didn't want to cry.

"Amber, I know you felt as though I stopped loving you when your father left us. I want you to understand that I never stopped loving you. I was a mess when he left, I still feel the hurt and the pain from that but I am able to deal with it in a much better way than I was before.

"When he left I was already in bad shape. I don't know what was happening to me. I had two young children, Alicia never stopped crying, and your father was always away on business trips. I was left alone and I didn't know what to do. I felt incompetent as a mother and I took out my frustration on your father. That final night he couldn't take it anymore so he walked out the door. He left a crumbled woman with two beautiful but young children who wanted and wanted and wanted. It isn't your fault or Alicia's fault that he left; it was mine. He wanted to be there Amber, I wouldn't allow him to be happy."

"But why did he leave us?" The question just popped out. I didn't expect myself to ask it.

"I asked him that in one of my therapy sessions. He said he didn't want to leave you, he just knew that if he had come back I would have coerced him into staying. He knew he would have listened to me and ended up miserable.

He did come back though. Do you remember the birthday party when he came to visit for the first time since he left?"

"Yes, he wanted to take us with him but you wouldn't let him. Then he left without fighting for us."

"I'm going to be honest with you Amber, because if I'm not than my recovery wouldn't work. He did fight. When we went into the kitchen, he said there was nothing I could do to stop him. He said that he was taking you two with him and his new fiancé to live across the country. At the time I was only thinking of not losing you but him raising you. It was stupid; I know that now. Hell, I knew that then too but I didn't care."

"Why did you start drinking?"

"I fell into a deep depression that no one could get me out of. I chose the wrong path. I should have gotten help; I should have listened to my mother and went to see a therapist instead of turning to the bottle to cheer me up. I told myself that one night would bring me up from the depths of hell. But one night wasn't enough. The next morning I was even farther down, so I went out again, and again the next night. It became a pattern, as you know. Then one night a friend; or should I say someone I thought of as a friend, told me to try this new drug he had. I did and that's when it happened.

None of this was because of you or Alicia. I want to keep telling you that so you don't think it's your fault. Every time I left the house and looked at your face, saw your disappointment, your hurt I would cry until I got to the bar. Alicia was always fine with any situation. She was too young to realize the severity of my problems so she would adapt to anything; the babysitter every night, grandma over a lot, grandma not there for a while, grandma back, grandma gone forever. You on the other hand, you knew everything that was happening and that was the thing that got me every night."

"So, why didn't you stop then?"

"It wasn't that easy. I was in too deep and I didn't want to hear anything about getting help. I wasn't ready to admit I had a problem. Even now it's so difficult for me to admit to you, my daughter that I had one. It is still with me, that problem but every day I work to overcome it. For you and for Alicia, you are the only two I have left in the world."

"Where did you go for that week? Why did you leave us alone? Why didn't you leave a note? I was so scared, I didn't know what to do."

"Well, from what I hear you did the right thing. You told a teacher and got help. I am so proud of you. You are so strong and so brave. That is why I treated you the way I did when I was high or drunk. I know I wasn't nice to you when I was that way. I am so sorry for that. I was jealous of you. I saw you as this strong, courageous kid who had the ability to find a different and better way to deal with things in her life. You reminded me so much of your father. You still do. You were the complete opposite of me and Alicia was my mirror image.

That week I went to the bar and left Marissa with you two. I got really drunk and agreed to go to Jamaica with Jon Luc." That name made me cringe. "The next morning we partied on the beach, a margarita in one hand and a cigarette in the other. We came back from Jamaica about eight days later and partied some more. Jon Luc had this studio apartment so we hung out there. When they found me in the alley that day I was at my all time low. I had overdosed again on drugs and had been drunk for four days straight. In the hospital two days later they told me you two were in a foster home and I wasn't allowed to see you for a while. My mind was messed up from not having drugs or alcohol in my system for a few days. I was not with it, my body was there but I wasn't.

If I could take back those years I would. I am so sorry for all the pain and suffering I caused you. It tears me up inside thinking of you watching your mother spiraling out of control and then to all of a sudden be home by yourself not knowing if I was alive or dead."

She stopped, clenched her jaw and covered her face with her hands. Her shoulders sharply moved up and down and her chest heaved. She made a tiny sniffle noise and instinctively I moved over to her and wrapped my arms around her. My face was wet and I shook slightly. I hadn't realized I was crying. I held her trembling body for a minute and then she grabbed me and pulled me on her lap holding me tightly, her face buried in the nape of my neck. She whispered over and over again, "I'm sorry."

Entry 51: <u>November 1992</u>

The next day Alicia and I finished painting my mural and I had to admit, it was very cool. We moved on to Alicia's room and had a blast as well. We painted a mural of all the celebrities she loved; Mary-Kate and Ashley Olsen, Joey, Matt and Andrew Lawrence, Nancy Kerrigan, and of course her favorite of all time, John Stamos. When we finished the mural we painted the walls a light yellow color. The entire time it took us to paint her room we sang songs by New Kids on the Block at the top of our lungs. A few times we could hear our mother, who giggled by the door.

Later that afternoon, we went to the furniture store and picked out a brand new sofa set, coffee table, television stand, new beds, desks, bureaus, a new kitchen table and a beautiful wall clock. After furniture shopping we went to the electronics store and picked up a new television, stereo, some movies and alarm clocks. Our last stop found us at a home design store where we all went crazy. We bought lamps, area rugs, artwork, frames, and plants. I couldn't wait to get home and start decorating until the furniture arrived the next day.

When both of our rooms were painted and decorated and ready for their occupants we danced to the music until we passed out on the floor again. The next morning found us too quickly but we both awoke with huge smiles on our faces. We ran out to the family room to where our mother was, but she wasn't there. Immediately my heart skipped a beat and sunk into my stomach. I couldn't believe that I had begun to forgive her and trust her again. Just as I was about to break down Alicia found the note on the fridge.

"Hey, Amber. Mom went to get us breakfast."

"Let me see the note." I read it out loud. "Dear girls, if you are reading this I am not here. Don't worry, I just went out to get breakfast. I really wanted to make you my specialty but we have no ingredients in the house. So, stay in your pajamas and I'll be back in a few. Love you, xoxo Mom."

"See I knew she wouldn't leave us again."

"I knew that too."

"No you didn't, I could tell what you were thinking, I am physic."

"You mean psychic."

"Yeah, that's what I meant, psychic. So, let's clean up mom's sleeping bag so that when the couches come the guys can put it in the right room."

We grabbed the sleeping bag and rolled it up and put it in the hall closet; then we did the same with our sleeping bags. "I'm so excited for my room to be completely finished."

"Me too, it's going to be so rad."

Just then the door opened and in popped our mother. She was still in her pajamas with the bunny rabbits on them, she had no makeup on and her hair was a mess. Alicia and I looked at each other and laughed out loud. I wished I had a camera.

"What? Did I forget to brush my hair again? Silly me."

All three of us just continued laughing. She put down the food on the floor and waved us over. Alicia and I joined her and completed the circle formation she wanted with the food in the middle.

"Okay, what we have here is the breakfast of angels, for you see, we three girls are angels and we deserve the best food there is. But first, each of us must say one thing that means absolutely nothing."

"What?" I asked confused.

"Well Amber, you're the writer why don't you go first? Just say any word that pops into your head. It doesn't have to make any sense."

I tapped my forefinger against my chin and my eyes went to the sky. As if the sky would have my word.

"Don't think, just say it. Thinking takes away from the creativity of the word."

"Okay, Balooba."

"Good one! Now what is the definition of balooba?"

"We have to think of a definition too?"

"But of course my dear one."

"Balooba is a new species of an octopus, instead of eight legs it has forty-three. It lives in the deepest part of the ocean and is feared by all that are smaller and loved by all those who are larger than it. It has one pink colored eye and one turquoise colored eye. It has a nose that can smell for ten miles and ears that can hear enemies coming fifteen miles away. The mouth of the balooba is located in the center of the forty-three legs. Every twenty years this animal grows a new leg. The life span is fifty years. The balooba has one unique feature that nothing on earth has. This feature is a tiny hole in the back of its head. This hole is used for eating tiny fish who try to hide in back of him."

"Very interesting. I wouldn't want to be caught in the clutches of the balooba, would you Alicia?"

"No way José!" Alicia said shaking her head and her eyes bugging out. "My turn. Wipper. The wipper is a type of wave that all surfers love. It is so big that every time it happens all the birds fly to land."

"How big is it?"

"It's fifty feet high and ninety feet wide. And, it comes so fast and so strong that it can push four blue whales a mile away from the beach."

"Wow, that's a very large and fast wave. Excellent word and definition."

"Thank you. Okay mom, it's your turn."

"Well my word is sundalil. A sundalil is a flower that is a mixture of a sunflower, daisy and lily. It is the rarest, most beautiful flower on the face of the earth. It is so rare actually that there is only one known in the United States. It is so tall that it makes the Chrysler Building look miniscule. And, if it is chopped down bad luck will follow the person who cut it down for thirty years. The only way someone can view the sundalil is by airplane or helicopter."

"Wow, good one mom!" said Alicia.

"Yeah, that was a really good one." I agreed.

"Thanks, it wasn't nearly as good as either of yours but I'll take it. Now, let's eat."

Entry 52: <u>August 1996</u>

A doctor once told me, to get better you have to get worse first. It didn't make sense at the time; what was the point of feeling horrible just to get well? I looked at him funny and he responded, "you'll know what I'm talking about when you're older." I was about seven at the time. Now that I'm sixteen I finally understand. I went through eight years of watching my family fall apart to be at this point in my life. I am going into my junior year of high school and have made some great friends. Alicia is a sophomore and is the most popular girl in our school. Shelley; Mom, has been sober and drug free for four years and we have been happy.

About a year ago my father contacted us, he wanted to see us. I agreed but Alicia didn't. I wanted to confront him about what he has done to us, but Alicia wanted nothing to do with him or his new family. I understood completely where she was coming from. A week after his phone call I met him at the ice cream shop. He was not alone.

"Hi Amber, I'd like you to meet my daughter Ella. Ella, this is your sister Amber."

My sister was beautiful. She was four years old and looked like her mother I guessed. Her hair was long and blonde, her eyes blue as the ocean. Her thin frame was covered in a green sundress and her tiny feet hidden by matching sandals. Her toenails and her fingernails were painted pink and her hair was tied back with a pink ribbon. A silver locket graced her neck. "Hi Ella," I said kindly. No need to punish her with my anger, it wasn't her fault for her father's mistakes.

"Hi," she said quietly as she cowered behind the man I hadn't seen in over nine years, her hand clasped in his afraid to let go. I thought to myself, you shouldn't let go of him or he might vanish right in front of your eyes.

"So, Amber how have you been?"

A furnace inside my belly lit up and I could feel the heat rise up my throat and out of my mouth. "Why do you care?" I said without even thinking. His face looked hurt and I didn't move an inch. I felt my own face red and hot, my hands clenched to my side and my head starting to hurt. "You think that after all of this time, after refusing to take Alicia and I into your home when we were abandoned, after pushing mom into a deep depression and ultimately to drink and abuse drugs you can come into our lives and become a father again? You think that you have the right and that you would just come here and convince me that you have changed and just like that," I snap my fingers, "I would forgive you?" I could feel myself shaking uncontrollably.

"I'm sorry Amber, I didn't mean for you to be hurt. I didn't want you and Alicia to go through any pain."

"You didn't mean it? You didn't want us to go through any pain? Then why the hell didn't you come and take us? Why did you let us go live with strangers instead of with you?"

"I heard you had a great time and became really close with the family?"

"I did, I love the Warners so much, they are my second family. Mark is more of a father to me than you will ever be. But that's not the point." I was screaming now, everyone was staring at me and Ella was now fully behind our shared father and I could see her cowering. "it would have been nice to know that our father loved us."

"I do love you Amber, you and Alicia."

"Bullshit." And with that I walked away from him. I had to admit, it felt great.

Entry 53: <u>September 1996</u>

The halls were the same as the year before except this year they were green. Green was what we all had strived for ever since the first day of school last year. Green marked our junior year of high school.

"Hey Amber; can you believe it? We made it to another year in high school. It's a crazy awesome feeling isn't it?" Madison was my best friend at school. When I first came back she befriended me without question. She and I were inseparable since our first meeting. "Oh, so guess where I'm going after school today?" Her bright smile showed all of her teeth and her grey eyes expressed the world.

"Umm…home?"

"Very funny. No. My dad's getting me a car! Can you believe it? I can't wait. We're going to some small car dealerships to find a really great one." Isn't it exciting?"

"It certainly is. Which means you know that you have to drive me everywhere and anywhere I want."

"Whatever. Why doesn't your mom get you a car? You've been sixteen for over a half a year now."

"She said she's waiting for Alicia to turn sixteen then she's going to buy us a joint car."

"That sucks you have to share with your sister."

"Nah, it's okay. We get along so it's all good, plus I have you to chauffeur me around the world and back again."

"Hey Amber."

"Hi Matt."

"Oooh, Amber's got a boyfriend! Why didn't you tell me?" she gushed after Matt walked away. I had to admit to myself that Matt was gorgeous; he had the most intoxicating brown eyes and a magnificent black mane of hair. When he smiled he smiled big, his mouth bragging its pearly whites. His body was muscular and his ass was very nice to watch.

"Shut up. We're not dating. We're just friends."

"Oh my God, you're blushing."

"Am not. Look, we're here. Darn." I smiled.

"Don't think you're getting out of discussing this. We, my friend, are not finished yet. Oh it's going to be so much fun this year especially that Alicia is at this school now."

"Oh great, I can just imagine what a fun year this is going to be."

I was very excited about English class this year. Another perk about being a junior was that we had the coolest teacher in the school. She was young and hip and actually understood her students. She had long brown hair, brown eyes and she was rather tall and thin. All the guy looked forward to her classes for according to them she was "hot and sexy."

"Good morning everyone. As most of you know my name is Ms. Trotty, but I hate that name so please call me Ava. The administration does not like the fact that I have students call me by my first name, and that is why I'm not one of them. This class is meant to be fun but we are also here to learn. I may be fun but I am not afraid of any of you, do you understand? Do not, I repeat, do not disrespect me in any way or you will regret it. So, are there any questions?"

A boy in the front row raised his hand. "Ms. Trotty?"

"What did I say to call me?"

He hesitated, "Ava?"

"Yes."

"What books do we need?"

"You should have bought your books before class. I see you have some right there on your desk. Those are the books that you need."

"No, not our school books. What I mean is, what novels will we read this year?"

"Our first book will be Wicked by Gregory Maguire. But we won't be starting it right now so you don't have to worry about it until the time comes. Thank you for being so interested. What's your name?"

"Brian."

"Thank you Brian."

She then started the class with a game of introduction. It was a fun beginning to a new year. And with everything that is fun and exciting it must end. As I left the classroom, Ava stopped me.

"You're Amber right?"

"Yes, how did you know?"

"I'm all knowing." She smiled at me. "I read one of the stories that you wrote last year for the school literary journal."

"Oh that. It wasn't anything big, just a little something I wrote one night. It wasn't even good, I don't know why they printed it."

"It wasn't good? Amber, it was amazing. When I finished reading, I swore I was going to find that a senior who was taking AP English classes wrote it. When I saw that it was a sophomore I was shocked. You have a rare talent."

"Thank you."

"Have you been writing for a long time?"

"Ever since I learned how. Yes."

"Listen, I wanted to talk to you because I teach a writing class at the Hark Center for budding authors such as myself. I would absolutely love it if you would come. It's just a few people."

"Really? Oh my God, I would love to. I'd have to ask my mom though, but she'll probably say yes." I was grinning ear to ear by now.

"Excellent. Let me know. Here's a flyer to bring home to your mom. It covers the basics; time, day, place, and what you need. It's a fun time. I know you don't have this class tomorrow but if you could stop by when you have a free period to let me know?"

"I will. Thanks."

"You're very welcome." Her smile held until I left the room.

"What was that all about?" Madison asked me.

"Oh, she teaches a writing class after school and she asked me to join them."

"Wow, that's big Amber."

"What is? Why?"

"Because, she holds that class each year and it's for the really good writers. She doesn't accept people who just write and think they're good. You actually have to submit a writing sample and if she doesn't think it can be published, she won't let you in. For her to actually ASK you to join that is just plain awesome! Can I have your autograph?"

I didn't know what to say. I was asked by the coolest teacher in the school to join her super exclusive writing class. My heart skipped a beat, someone who knows what they're talking about, someone who knows the writing industry thinks I'm a good writer.

"Um, hello, earth to Amber. Geez, five minutes of stardom and it's already gotten to your head."

"Sorry."

"Oh, so you are not going to believe what I heard from Jesse this morning. He was telling me that the reason Megan isn't back in school this year is because she got pregnant and her parents forced her to stay home until she gives birth."

"What? You can't believe everything you hear Madison." I had known for a fact that the reason why Megan wasn't re-joining our school was that she had been arrested over the summer and her parents immediately transferred her to an all-girl private school. Megan had actually started the rumor about being pregnant because she thought that being pregnant was less embarrassing than being arrested.

"Jesse's the one who told me."

"Oh right, Jesse! Silly me, I didn't realize you were talking about the King of the Paparazzi. My mistake."

"Shut up Amber. But anyways, I hope she's okay, I've always liked Megan."

"Yeah, me too. Ugh, math class."

"C'mon, I love math." As we walked into the room I noticed Matt sitting in the front row. Right in front of him was Deana, the most popular girl in the school. She was blonde, thin and beautiful. There was never a day where she wasn't made up and dressed to perfection. Today she wore a red halter-top that slanted down covering the waistline of a white-layered skirt and a pair of red strappy sandals. Both her toes and fingernails were decorated with red nail polish. Around her waist a decorative belt gently rested upon her hipbones and each piece of jewelry; rings, earrings, necklace and bracelets matched perfectly with the belt. Her hair was in curls today, which hung loosely on her back with wisps framing her face. "Look at her," Madison said. "She is all over him!"

I did notice how her stunningly blue eyes were staring deep into his matching brown ones and how her full lips turned into a smile letting out a sound of teasing laughter. Her nail polished hands gently caressed his hand as she turned back around with one last flirty look his way. I felt a pang of jealousy rise up my spine. Why did I feel like this? We were just friends; I didn't like him, not in that way. Or, did I?

"Amber, are you okay?"

"Yeah, why?" I snapped, coming out of my stupor.

"I don't know, you just lost yourself for a minute. You looked like you were going to kill someone."

"Nope, I'm fine. Let's sit over here."

"Hey, don't let Deana bother you. She's got nothing on you. I could tell when he said hi to you this morning that he really likes you. He had that look."

"What look?"

"The look of looove."

"Whatever. The teacher is here. Matt and I are just friends, he can date Deana if he wants to. I mean look at her, why wouldn't he?"

She rolled her eyes and opened her notebook and the class began. I remember staring at Deana with contempt the entire class while I tried to read Matt's face whenever she would turn around. It's not like Deana was a typical popular girl who was mean and snotty. She was actually rather nice, she always made time to say hi to me. But this was war. Wait, what was I thinking?

The air was warm and clean and to be back outside instead of in the stuffy school building was a relief. Madison left with her boyfriend Andrew and I walked back with Alicia. Suddenly Matt came by and walked next to us.

"Hey Amber," he said with the most gorgeous smile I had ever seen. Alicia nudged me.

"Hi Matt. How are you? What did you think of math class? Pretty boring huh?"

"It was okay I guess. It's school, what else can I say? Do you mind if I walk with you?"

"Yeah sure. This is my sister Alicia."

"Hey Matt. It's nice to meet such a handsome guy on such a fantastic day."

"Ha, thanks. It's nice to meet you too."

"Hey guys, wait up. Matt, are you going to the school mixer Friday night? Hey Amber." Deana said as she casually walked up to us.

"Yeah I guess. Are you?"

"Of course I am, with you."

"Well then why did you ask if I was going when you already knew that I was going with you?"

She turned her head toward me, "Amber, are you going? You should really go, it is a lot of fun. And, oh my God, you can go with Austin, he is definitely your type."

"I don't know."

"Oh come on, we'll go shopping for an amazing outfit for you and I'll do your hair and make-up. It'll be fun, what do you say? Please."

I had to think about it. I really wanted to go with Matt but he was already going with Deana. And what did I have to lose than to say, "okay."

"Great! So, tomorrow night we'll go to the mall. Tell Madi if she wants to come she can. Okay, have to get going. I'll talk to you guys later. Kisses." And with that she hopped into her silver convertible and drove off with a wave.

Entry 54: <u>October 1996</u>

Friday night came fast and furious and Deana and Madison were over to my house, Deana decided that we would all get ready together. I had to admit, she did have excellent taste. While at the mall, she commented on whether or not each dress was flattering and appropriate for the dance. After I tried on like ninety separate outfits we found the one that I would wear along with all the appropriate accessories.

As I sat on my bed and watched Deana gently make-up Madison's face, I wondered if Matt would notice me even though he's going with the most beautiful girl in the school.

"Now, go like this," Deana said making her lips turn up like a kiss. She proceeded to paint the lipstick onto Madison's lips. "Perfection. You know, if you looked like this every day you'd have to throw the men off of you."

"Wow Madi, you look so pretty," I said as I admired the amazing job Deana had accomplished. Now it was my turn. I was nervous and excited as I sat on the stool in my room and gave my face to Deana. "Be kind."

"You've got nothing to worry about Amber, even if I put too much on, you would have absolutely no problem. Austin is going to fall madly in love with you."

She put some eye shadow on and eye liner, mascara, cover up, blush and a magnificent shade of dark red lipstick. Then she used her blow dryer to dry my hair and then straightened it and pulled it back into half a ponytail and when she finished she let me look in the mirror. I couldn't believe the transformation; I didn't look like myself at all.

"I see you love it." She said noticing the grin open up on the finished canvas. "Okay, now get off of the stool and go put on your ensemble while I do my own make-up."

I went into the bathroom and put on the pair of white fitted pants and dark blue tank top on and finished it off with a matching pair of shoes. Madison chose the matching bracelet, necklace and earring set. I was done. I smiled because I now looked the part of popular girl off to the dance with the man of her dreams. Well, with the man of Deana's dreams for her. And who knew, maybe Matt would see her and ditch Deana at the dance.

Andrew, Austin and Matt showed up at my house ten minutes before we had to leave. The dance was crowded and I received more compliments than I had ever in my life. I saw that Matt glanced over at me every once in a while.

"Hey Amber, don't you look amazing." Ava said to me at the drink table. "I see you're here with Austin Grady? I thought you had a thing for Matt?"

"How do you know I like Matt?"

"It is kind of obvious the way you look at him. And he does look at you that way too. Don't worry, I won't tell anyone. So, why is he here with Deana?"

"Well she asked him first and he said yes. Actually she just told him they were going together and then left."

"I'm sorry. But I'm sure you will get together with him sooner or later. Austin is a great guy too, enjoy yourself tonight okay?"

"I will thanks." She smiled at me and continued walking around the gym.

After a few more slow dances with Matt and I giving each other flirtatious looks the dance ended. I was exhausted. Austin drove me home and walked me to the front door.

"I had a great time tonight, maybe we can go grab dinner and a movie some time soon?"

"I had fun too, thank you. Dinner and a movie sounds good," I semi lied.

"I'll give you a call then."

"Great." There was an awkward silence as we both stood on my doorstep and then he shyly waved at me and walked halfway down the walk. Then he turned around and briskly walked up and kissed me. I expected it and at the same time was taken aback by the kiss. It was my first real kiss and although awkward it was great.

That night I dreamt of Matt kissing me like that.

Entry 55: <u>December 1996</u>

Two and a half months later I was still dating Austin while I watched Matt and Deana fall deeper in love. Ava's writing class proved to be a great experience and I enjoyed every minute of it. The group of people enrolled in the class was amazing and unique in their own special way.

Georgia was a feisty fifty-five year old artist who was looking to publish a book on her artistic influences as well as a how-to in painting. She was clearly a child of the sixties; her hair was long and wavy. Her arms displayed an array of bracelets, which performed a song every time she moved an inch. Every week she came in wearing a long colorful skirt with a matching tank top. Her stories always told of love and peace. My favorite one was an autobiographical piece where she told of how she met her husband Larry. They were at a gathering one weekend and she was singing one of her own songs and he noticed her right away. She had noticed him in the crowd staring at her and as their eyes met they fell instantly in love.

Shannon was in his late thirties with flaming red hair and ghost white skin. He spent his first twelve years living in Ireland with his parents and brother Liam until his father lost his job and had to find one in the states. He still had a little bit of his Irish brogue, which I found to be a huge distraction. Whenever he spoke I got lost in his accent. He was an accountant for a law firm and in his spare time he enjoyed writing mystery novels. He already had two novels published and another close to finished. I read his first book "Wooded Hills" and was currently reading his second one "The Journey of Grayden Lafayette." He was an excellent writer and I couldn't wait until his third novel would be finished.

Jenn was one of my closest friends in the class. She was twenty-five and worked as a receptionist, which she hated. She was definitely one of the coolest people I had ever met. In her spare time she would use her video camera and computer to make fantastic short films, which she would only show me and a few of her other friends. She actually asked me to be one of the actors in her latest film, "Thanksgiving in the Summer." I played Rachel de Love, an eighteen-year-old runaway who found her way to a nice family in the south. Her boyfriend Curtis was the older brother in the family who fell in love with my character. They kept their love a secret and came up with a plan to run off together. It was so much fun hanging out with Jenn and her friends, and when the project was completed it was a huge success. As a matter of fact, Jenn loved it so much that for the first time she decided that she would make her movie debut one night during writing class.

Peter and Seth were identical twins, both with a head of dark curly hair. They were in their mid thirties and on occasion dressed the same so no one could tell them apart. Seth worked as a principal at a nearby elementary school and Peter was a lawyer. Seth was more laid back but could be aggressive if pushed hard enough, while Peter was often strung out and worried about what tomorrow would bring. On the days where they weren't dressed alike Seth wore jeans and a shirt with a Boston Red Sox hat, while Peter dressed in a three-piece suit and carried a black briefcase. Peter was never seen without his Apple PowerBook and Seth without a yellow legal pad. As much as they looked alike, their personalities were very different. Whenever we critiqued each other's writing, Seth thought of ways to compliment the author, while Peter argued his way so that everyone turned their views into his. I didn't like Peter at all.

The last person in the class was Cassie. She was 23 years old and so quiet. Jenn often asked her if she spoke at all. As Cassie and Jenn were so close in age, I assumed that they would be best friends by the end of the first class, but with four classes over they did not even speak to each other. Cassie sat towards the back of the room and kept to herself. She responded to Ava when spoken to and critiqued work if she had a good point to present. She was blonde and overweight. I never once saw her wear anything that flattered her body shape. She always wore sweatpants and either a baggy shirt or an oversized sweatshirt. Her grey eyes held in deep emotions and pain that only she knew about. I could tell because I was in the same boat. I tried to talk to her a few times but each time she would give me straightforward one-word answers, so I stopped. She wasn't going to open up to me any time soon. so I decided that if this is what she wanted, I would not bother her anymore. If she wanted to talk she knew I was there.

After class one night Ava called me up to her desk. Everyone had gone home so it was just the two of us. I was afraid I was going to be kicked out of the class, because the last couple of weeks I hadn't handed in any of her assignments.

"Are you doing all right? I'm worried about you."

"I'm fine," I lied. I didn't want to tell her what was really going on.

"Amber, you don't have to lie to me. You know I'm always here for you to talk to. Please talk to me."

I knew I could trust Ava and was confident that she wouldn't let anything I said to her become public knowledge. She also knew all about my childhood and everything Alicia and I went through. So I told her.

"My mom has a new boyfriend. His name is Derek and he has four kids. His oldest son Brad is almost sixteen, his daughter Sarah is twelve, his other daughter Maya is eleven and his youngest son Gregory is five. I'm afraid that now that she has a new guy in her life who has all this baggage that she is going to get overwhelmed and think that by having just one drink it will soothe her. I'm scared that one day Derek will walk out and he will break her heart, therefore breaking Alicia's and mine. Just like my father. If she goes back to drugs and alcohol our lives will become hell. Again."

"Have you talked to your mom about how you're feeling?"

"No, I haven't talked to anyone, not even Alicia. She's having the time of her life. You see, that's another thing. Alicia and Brad started dating. They are really into each other and she's so young and he's older, plus Brad is not one of the best kids."

"What do you mean?"

"I'm not trying to be mean or anything, it's just that he hangs out with all these druggies and he's a troublemaker. He's been arrested twice for burglary. Once I heard him telling Alicia this story of how he got away with getting paid $20.00 for almost stealing a car."

"How did he get paid for almost stealing a car? How do you almost steal a car?"

"Well he and his friend saw this car outside a hair salon and decided they wanted to go for a joy ride. They got into the car and put it into reverse. They backed it out and the owner ran out with her hair still in curlers. She screamed at them, so Brad and his friend got out of the car and convinced the woman that they actually noticed the car rolling backwards. They were afraid the car would get swiped if it rolled into the street, so they got into it before it backed up into another car. She was so relieved she gave them reward money and they left smiling. I don't want them to be together for long. Alicia's going to get in trouble dating him."

"You know, you should really take it one day at a time. Who knows, maybe your mom has really changed and she is a stronger person than she was before. If she and Derek don't make it or if she gets stressed hopefully she'll be able to deal with the pain in another way than drinking and doing drugs. And maybe Brad isn't as bad as you think he is. Get to know him a little better and then make a judgment. If he is part of the bad crowd talk to Alicia about how you feel about her dating him. But just remember that what you say may make Alicia angry with you so talk to her as a friend instead of as a dictator. Don't push her away. If she disagrees with you and continues to see him it's okay. If you are keeping an eye out for her and making sure he doesn't hurt her or she doesn't start hurting herself then everything will work out for the best. You also have to think that they are only fourteen and most relationships at that age don't last."

I nodded. Everything she said made sense, I just hoped she was right about my mom being a stronger person than before. "Thank you Ava."

"You're welcome. I hope I helped. See you tomorrow in class." She smiled and we went our separate ways.

Entry 56: <u>February 1997</u>

It was three weeks after Alicia's fifteenth birthday. I was home with her while my mom and Derek were out. We had fun; watched movies, ate popcorn, joked around. There was a knock on the door and it was Brad.

"Hey baby, happy birthday!" He handed over a dozen pink tulips and she squealed and leapt into his arms. "Want to go for a ride?"

"Yes. Amber, do you mind if I go out for a while? I'll be back before mom gets home, I promise. Please," she begged.

"You do know that her birthday was three weeks ago right? And, that you already bought her a present."

"I know. It's an inside joke."

"C'mon Amber, please." She put on her pouty face and put her hands together in prayer.

"Fine, but if mom comes home and you're not here I'm going to kill you."

"Thanks. I totally owe you!"

They left me there on the couch with a bowl of popcorn watching "The First Wives Club."

Two hours later the door opened and there she was. She seemed very relaxed and spacey and when she smiled at me and walked into her room closing the door behind her, I knew something was up. I couldn't believe this was happening while I watched her.

I stormed into her room. "Dammit Alicia, what the fuck are you thinking?"

"What?"

"You had sex with him."

She looked taken aback, surprised and angry. She stuttered, "No I didn't."

"Don't lie to me. I can't believe you."

"Why are you mad at me? You're not my mother."

"No I'm not but I have had to act like it practically our whole lives and, ugh nevermind. It's your life."

"That's right, it's my life Amber. So you can get off of your high horse and stop treating me like your kid. I never asked you to be my mother and I don't want you to be. I can do whatever I want and there's nothing you can do about it. If I want to have friends over I will, If I want to stay up all night I will, and if I want to fucking have sex with my boyfriend you can't stop me."

"Fine. Destroy your life, what the hell do I care."

We were both fuming when she slammed the door in my face. I turned around so fast I practically ran over my mother.

"What's the matter? What happened?"

"Oh nothing," I answered as I in turn slammed my bedroom door.

I called Madison and we talked about what happened. I cried to her about having lost my best friend and my sister. By the time I finished talking to Madi it was three in the morning and we were both exhausted.

"How am I ever going to wake up tomorrow morning? I feel so drained from crying and talking for so long." I said to Madison right before I fell asleep. As soon as my eyes closed my alarm blasted. I threw the phone across the room, which was still off the hook and beeping uncontrollably. I grunted while falling back onto my pillow.

The entire day at school I dragged my body to each class not paying attention to anything or anyone. Madison actually fell asleep during math, which caused the teacher to yell at her in his squirrelly voice and the entire class, including myself,to laugh. Needless to say by the end of the day both Madison and I had Saturday detention.

Every time Alicia passed me in the halls she ignored me. I tried to get her attention to apologize but she turned and walked away without even a glance. This went on for weeks and it didn't help to know that my mom and Derek were more involved with each other every day. He pretty much lived at our house, ate our food and used our car for everything. His kids were always over, which meant that Brad was always in Alicia's room playing his guitar and making Alicia fall in love with him faster and harder. She was young and very willing to believe anything he told her. He could tell her he had just murdered a few people and she'd probably shrug it off like it was nothing.

My mom was clueless about everything. She was drunk in love with Derek and didn't see anything that was going on with her kids. Since Alicia and I fought, she hadn't spoken about it and hadn't realized that we're not on speaking terms. She started to go back to old routines and I felt more and more alienated from the family. Alicia had Brad, my mom had Derek, and Sarah had Maya as her best friend. The only one who was left was Gregory and he was too young and we didn't get along anyway. In my opinion he was a spoiled rotten miniature devil, in disguise as a cute child with an aptitude for baseball.

I was glad to have Madison and Austin to talk to, and of course Ava. Letters from Kira and Chris also kept me sane. If things got really bad I knew of a place I could go.

Entry 57: <u>April 1997</u>

It happened six weeks after the fight with Alicia. It was about one month before I turned seventeen. It was a Friday night. Austin and I watched a movie at my house while Alicia and Brad were out at some party.

My mom came in without Derek. At once I knew something had happened. She hadn't come in looking down and out since the dark period in my life.

"What's the matter? Where's Derek?" I asked.

"Not here."

"Well obviously. Where is he? Did he take his kids to their mother's house?"

"Nope." She walked into the kitchen so I followed her.

"Is he coming later?"

"No."

"Throw me a freakin' bone here mom, I am not going to play Twenty Questions with you to try to figure out why he isn't here."

"He left me. Okay? Is that good enough for you? No? He took me out to dinner and told me that he couldn't see me anymore. He said he wasn't looking for a major commitment and he didn't want any more kids, his four were enough. And as if that wasn't bad enough he turned around and proceeded to leave. Just like that. To make it even worse he made me pay for the dinner. As I left, I saw him sitting at the table near the window," she paused and turned her head away. "He was with another woman, or should I say girl. She was in her late twenties. Does that make you happy? I know you didn't like him, didn't like his kids. I don't know how Alicia's going to take this, you know how close she and Brad are."

"How about how I feel? I liked him, I didn't love him but I didn't hate him. And you're doing well, I don't want anything to happen that would make you fall off the wagon as they say."

"I'm not going to fall off the fucking wagon Amber, I might just have one glass of wine to calm me down a bit but the wagon is steady and strong under my feet."

"You can't have just one glass of wine mom. If you have one glass you'll have two and then two will turn into three and then you'll be drunk and won't be able to quit again."

"I know you went through hell when I was drinking and drugging, but I'm not doing that anymore and you have nothing to worry about. I'm okay now. I'll only have one glass, I promise."

"No you won't." I began to cry. What would I do if she went back to the way she was? I didn't have Alicia to confide in anymore.

"Amber, it's okay. Just one glass, I promise you."

"Well if you want to have one glass I can't stop you but I am asking you to not have a drink."

She looked at me sympathetically and went into the cupboard and grabbed a wine glass and popped the cork from a bottle of wine she had just purchased. "I'm sorry, but I really need to have a glass."

"Fine, but if you're going to do this I need to go out, can I use the car?"

"Sure."

She handed me the keys and I grabbed an overnight bag and stuffed it with clothes and necessities and stormed out of the house. "Don't wait up for me, I won't be home for a couple of days," I yelled, completely forgetting about Austin who sat on the couch in total shock.

The road to Kira's house seemed longer than I remembered. When I pulled into the driveway I noticed all the lights were off. It was midnight and I kicked myself for not having considered the time before I decided to go. I debated on whether or not to leave and go to Madison's house when I thought, well I was here and I needed Kira more than I had ever needed her before. It was all starting again but this time I didn't have Alicia by my side. So I got out of the car and rang the doorbell and prayed that I didn't wake up the kids.

The door opened slowly and Kira stood there in her white silk pajamas and her hair perfect. She looked the same as the last time I saw her and at the sight of her I broke down. She grabbed hold of me and held me in a comforting and safe hug. She whispered in my ear that everything would be alright.

Ten minutes later we sat in the family room just like the night she told me about her sister Kristin. The room seemed to be frozen in time. Everything was the same, toys all over the floor; the TV sat in the same corner. The only thing that was different was the people and the pictures over the fireplace. Instead of just a picture of Bailey there was a large portrait of Bailey, Brynne & Perry. They were beautiful.

"So, what's the matter? What happened that made you come here and fall apart in my arms?"

"Derek broke up with my mom tonight and then she found him with another woman."

"Oh. Well I'm sure she's learned from her mistakes and is now strong enough to deal with them without drinking."

"I thought so too. But she came home and promised me she would only have one glass of wine to calm her down. You know how that is. If she has one glass she'll have the whole bottle."

"Oh my God Amber I'm so sorry. No wonder you're so upset. How's Alicia handling it?"

"I don't know. She's not talking to me, hasn't been for almost two months now."

"Why?"

"Well, I yelled at her for something and she accused me of trying to be her mother when she already has a mother and she doesn't want me to be her mother figure."

"What was it that you yelled at her for sweetie?"

I turned away. I didn't know if I wanted Kira to know about what Alicia had done. She thought of us as her daughters and if she knew what happened she would think less of Alicia. As mad as I was at her I still felt the need to protect her.

"Amber, you can tell me anything. I promise I won't be mad."

"I'm not afraid of you being mad."

"What are you afraid of then?"

"I found out that she…"

"That she? Tell me. Please."

"That she had sex."

"What? With who?"

"Well her boyfriend Brad, he is Derek's son. I let her go out with him while we were home alone. I shouldn't have let her go. We were having fun and he showed up and gave her flowers for her birthday and she begged to go out with him that night and she'd be back before mom got home. When she came home she looked different so I confronted her. I asked her if she had sex and she said no, but she hesitated and then got defensive about it after I accused her of lying. Ever since then she has banished me from her life. She hasn't looked at or spoken to me since".

"And now you have no one to talk to about your mom, and that's why you're here."

"Well I have Madison and Austin to talk to but you're the first person I thought of and I really needed you. Do you mind if I stay here for a few days?"

"Does your mom know where you are?"

"No. I just told her that I'd be gone a few days, plus she has my cell number, if she wants me she'll call."

"Of course you can stay here as long as you like, but I have to call your mom and let her know."

"Okay."

"Why don't you go to your old room and stay there. I'll come and say good-night in a little while."

I walked upstairs and went into the room that was mine so long ago. It was funny to me to think of how natural this felt, to come here and talk to Kira and find my room and unpack. I felt like this was and always had been my real home. I sat on the bed and wrote in my journal and fell asleep quickly. I don't remember Kira tucking me in, shutting off the light and saying "I love you" in my ear. Just like she used to.

The next morning I woke up to three little heads peeking at me. I smiled. "Good Morning."

"Good morning Amber." Brynne and Perry said in their quiet little voices.

Bailey jumped on my bed and threw his arms around me. "I miss you."

"Aww, I miss you too Bailey. I'm very happy that you remember me. I miss you too Perry & Brynne."

"You know I love all three of you very much."

"We know, mom tells us that every day." Brynne told me. "Come on, mom made your favorite breakfast."

"Oooh, blueberry pancakes?"

"Yup, with corn beef hash too," Bailey said.

The twins looked at each other and replied, "ewwww."

After breakfast I played with the kids out in the backyard and then we watched their favorite movie, 'The Lion King.' Mark took Bailey and Perry to soccer practice and Brynne to gymnastics while Kira and I took a walk around the neighborhood. It was a beautiful day outside and walking was part of her daily ritual.

"I've missed you so much Amber. The house seems empty without you and Alicia. I know; I have three young kids how can the house feel empty? I couldn't answer that but it does. How are things going, not including the set-back?"

"It has been good up until six weeks ago. My mom has been happy and we've been having great conversations, and she knows how much she hurt me when she was drinking so she has been trying to make it up to me since she got us back. I saw my dad a while ago and told him off, which felt so good. I have great friends and am dating Austin, who I've told you about. There's this really great writing program I'm in after school once a week and my teacher is great.

Her name is Ava and she knows about everything that has happened to me so if I need anyone to talk to she's there too."

"Oh, so I've been replaced. That cuts real deep."

We both laughed. "You could never be replaced Kira."

Entry 58: <u>April 1997</u>

I was there a week when Alicia came and surprised us all. I was writing a story in anticipation of my return to Ava's class and it was coming along well. Kira read a book on the couch, Mark was at work and the kids were all at school. There was a knock on the door and I went to get it.

"Hi Amber."

"Oh, so you're talking to me now."

"Well, mom's driving me nuts and I can't keep not talking to you. Can I come in or are we going to talk in the doorway?"

"Yeah fine, it's not my house but I guess."

"Hey Kira," Alicia said.

"Alicia?! I have both girls here at one time. This is such a great day." She gave Alicia a hug. "We need to talk, come with me."

They went into the den and talked. I didn't listen. I did hear Kira telling Alicia that she was too young to have sex and that she had made a mistake but that she still loved her. I was worried that Alicia would forget that she wanted to start talking to me again and get so mad at me for telling Kira. But when they came out she did the opposite of walk away, she hugged me and told me she was sorry.

"I'm sorry too Alicia. I just don't want to see you hurt or in pain. You're my sister and if mom isn't going to look out for you someone has to."

"I know. I was emotional that night and was aggravated that you weren't being nice to me. I wanted to talk to you and you just yelled at me about it. I know how I acted was dumb and I lost a sister and a best friend because of it."

"You didn't lose me. I thought I lost you. I tried to apologize to you the next day but you wouldn't even look at me. These past two months have been hell without you there to talk to."

"Tell me about it."

"So, is mom drinking?"

She abruptly looked at me startled, "How did you know? You've been gone for a week."

"Why do you think I left?"

"I thought you left because you hated me."

"I don't hate you. I never have. She came home telling me about how Derek dumped her and how she was going to have a glass of wine. I told her she couldn't have just one glass so I left. How much is she drinking now?"

"It's awful. I guess that one glass was Mary Poppins' glass because it never ended. She isn't drinking wine though; vodka is her alcohol. They're best friends by now. She told me where you were and to come get you."

"She just told you where I was? I've been gone a week."

"She didn't seem to think it mattered whether or not I knew."

"Are you still dating Brad? Mom didn't think you would take her breakup with Derek very well because you're dating his son."

"Yes, I'm still dating him. She's pissed about that too, which causes her to drink more. So, it's partly my fault she's gone back to the bottle."

"No it's not. It's her fault. She can't get it into her head that she doesn't need alcohol to be happy. Feeling no pain is worse than feeling it. Until she realizes that she's not going to get better."

"You know, before you girls go, why don't you stay for dinner? I know the kids would love to see you Alicia." Kira said.

"We can do that, but then we have to leave. Amber, can I talk to you in the other room?"

"Sure"

We went into the den and she told me why we had to leave right after dinner. "Mom said that if we're not back before ten she would call the police and have Kira and Mark arrested for kidnapping."

"What? Has she lost her mind?"

"You know how she is when she's drinking. She gets all possessive and jealous. She can be a bitch."

"You never thought that before. You always thought she could do no wrong."

"Yeah I was a stupid, naive little girl with all the hopes that her mother would love her one day. I'm not that same little girl now."

"She always loved you. It was me she didn't like. But what happened?"

"Well she found out that Brad and I are having sex and she flipped out. She went crazy. Threw him out of the house and vowed she'd never let me out of the house again unless it was for something she needed. Then when I yelled at her for going back to drinking she hit me."

"She hit you?" I asked exasperated.

"She threw me against the wall Amber. She's become an abusive drunk. She was never like that before."

"Probably because she didn't want to get arrested for murdering two little kids. Now that we're older and stronger she doesn't think that she can hurt us enough. Or she just went insane. Don't worry though, I'll come back and we can both take her down."

"We'll come up with something."

The departure from Kira's house went a little better than the last time. This time I knew that she was just a car ride away.

"Remember Amber, you can come here any time any day if you need absolutely anything. You remember that too Alicia. You two are my daughters even if you aren't blood related, or live with me. Just don't let your mother know, she'd have my neck."

"You have nothing to worry about Kira," I said. "I wouldn't allow her to do anything bad to you. We have to head back though, I'll call when we get to the witch's den."

"Okay, drive safely and buckle up! I love you girls." She gave us each a hug and stood at the doorway waving goodbye as we drove away.

The drive home was too short, but luckily we made it back before 10:00. Not that it mattered because when we walked in the door we saw that our mother was lying on the couch passed out. In her hand was an empty vodka bottle.

"Don't wake her up, whatever you do just don't do that."

"Why not? If she thinks we're still at Kira's she's going to call the police."

"Believe me, I'd rather her call the police because if they do come we'll be here and she'll have no ground to stand on. Now, if you wake her up, well I don't want you to know what will happen."

"She can't be that bad. People don't just turn into abusive people."

"You wouldn't think so would you? Go for it."

I went to go wake her up but then got scared. "Okay fine, I'll listen to you. I have to go finish the story I was writing earlier for Ava's class tomorrow."

"Good thinking. I'm going to call Kira and tell her we're home, unless you want to."

"That's okay, you can call her. I spent a few days with all of them so you can have some time talking with her. She misses us very much you know."

"I know. I miss them too. If only life were uncomplicated with family issues."

"If only is right. It's so good to have you back," I said grabbing her in a sisterly hug. It had been so long and it made every disappointment go away for a couple of seconds.

"I missed you sis. Love you much!"

"I love you too. Let's never go through this separation anymore."

She smiled and nodded and we went in our respective rooms. I could hear her in the other room as she spoke with Kira. At around midnight I heard my mom get up and she started to turn the knob of my door. I considered faking sleep but thought better of it. She'd probably only wake me up anyways.

"Oh you're back. Good, didn't want to cause any problems."

"Sure you didn't." I said coldly.

"Don't talk to me like that Amber; it was your choice to leave and I wanted you back here."

"Just because you want me to do something mom, doesn't mean I have to listen."

"Like hell it doesn't, I'm still your mother."

"Don't use the mom card; not now and not ever again. You promised you'd only have one glass of wine and I come home to find you with an empty bottle of vodka, and from what I've heard it's not you're only one. Not that I'm one bit surprised so it doesn't hurt as much as it would have."

"So, Alicia's been telling lies? Saying I'm an alcoholic again? Don't listen to her Amber; she just doesn't want us to have a good relationship. Yeah I admit I drank this bottle of vodka because I was upset about you not being here."

"Don't blame me for your problems." I got up from my bed and walked over to her. "I didn't want you to start drinking again, you knew that. If you hadn't taken the wine I wouldn't have left and then you're little fucking excuse of drinking one bottle because I wasn't here would be obsolete. I'm not a little kid anymore, you can't push me around." Right then she slapped me across the face with all of the force she carried in her scrawny right arm. I knew it was coming and yet it still stung and surprised me, the impact of her hand left a bright red mark on my cheek. With that she looked at me with accomplishment, as if she had defeated her enemy. I brought my hand away from my face and gave her a look that was meant to let her know that it was war. I shut the door in her face and locked it.

Entry 59: <u>April 1997</u>

"Hey, where the hell have you been? I've been worried sick about you." Madison screamed at me when she saw me walk into school. "I even put out a missing persons report, they only came back to me saying they found an Amber rock outside the quarry. That wasn't what I was looking for."

"You are funny," I laughed. "I needed to get away for a while so I drove up to Kira and Mark's house. You remember me telling you about them."

"Oh right. Hope you had fun; some of us here didn't though. I heard your mom started drinking?"

"Did Alicia tell you?"

"Nope, Austin did. The day you went missing he came to school and was extremely upset that you just left and he didn't know why."

"Oh my God! Austin." I said stopping in my tracks. "I totally forgot he was there that night. He must hate me."

"Well hate is a strong word. He just thinks you died or fell off the face of the planet. I don't think he's gotten the concept of gravity or that the earth is round yet. That boy needs some learnin' or else people are going to think he's dumb."

"Madi, you always know how to make me laugh. I'm sorry you all thought I died. I'm okay I guess." I turned to her.

"Geez, what happened to your face?"

"Oh that? Well it turns out my mom's an angry drunk now."

"She hit you?"

"Yeah, and Alicia said that she's hit her too."

"Oh, you and Alicia are talking again?"

"Yeah."

"Thank God!"

"Well, I didn't think you had such an investment in my relationship with my sister."

"I don't, it's just that you and Alicia not talking is like me not wearing make-up."

"I wouldn't go that far."

"Amber! Are you okay? Where have you been? What happened to you?" Austin asked as he ran towards us.

"I'll take this as my cue to leave now. I'll see the two of you in class. Peace out motha fuckas!"

"Well I see Madi hasn't changed since I left."

"Nope, but would you want her to?"

"Absolutely not."

"Hey, so what happened?"

"You don't know how sorry I am that this happened and that you had to be at my house to witness that scene. I'm so sorry I didn't tell you where I was going, I lost myself in what was happening that I kind of forgot you were there."

"I understand and I forgive you for making me believe you died."

"Don't be so dramatic. I'm here now and that's all that matters right?" I smiled as he leaned down and kissed me.

"This conversation isn't over you know, you need to tell me everything that's been going on. I care about you and I don't want to see you hurt."

"You are just the sweetest guy ever. You mean a lot to me too. Now, come on, let's go to class so I can have the entire student body staring at me and talking about me. It'll be fun."

That day at school I was brought straight back to childhood with only a few minor differences. Everybody stared, everyone talked about me behind my back and everyone knew about my mother's problem. The difference this time around was that I had friends by my side to stick up for me, and a boyfriend who gave me confidence. I didn't need everyone to like me; I had the most important people in the world there to help me through it all. I had Alicia, Madison, Austin, Deana, Matt, and Andrew. I also had Kira and Chris. To me my life was great, if you take my home out of the equation.

When it came time for English class I was excited. I looked forward to drowning myself in writing and reading. And of course I planned to apologize to Ava for having disappeared. As I walked into the classroom, something seemed different. I was nervous and scared. I had promised Ava that I would talk to her if I had any problems. I had broken that promise and thought that perhaps she would be angry with me.

It had to be done though, so one step at a time I walked into the room. There was a note on the board. It was an assignment to do in class. I took my seat and in walked this older woman whom I had never seen before.

"What's going on," I asked Austin.

"I don't know. She was in yesterday."

Just then the faux teacher started speaking. "Good Afternoon class, my name is Mrs. Cherrywood and I'll be your sub for the next two days. Ms. Trotty is out sick. But don't worry she'll be back on Monday."

"Oh no, I hope she's okay," I whispered. Austin nodded in agreement.

The class went by slowly, but I was happy because our assignment was to write about a recent event that happened to us that was either painful or happy. I chose to write about my last few weeks. In my mind I knew that she specified this topic for me, to help me. She wasn't here in person but she was here for me still.

At the end of the day the "group" went to the local hangout and ate some nice juicy burgers and talked as if nothing had ever happened. We stayed there for two hours and then called it a night. Austin walked Alicia and I home and then gave me a goodnight kiss. I went inside and he went to his safe loving home. It was a good day.

Entry 60: <u>April 1997</u>

The first writing class back with Ava was amazing. When I walked in she immediately came over to me and gave me a nice comforting hug and smile, she didn't say a word. I was relieved.

"Okay, we'll start off today with some great news."

Everyone in the room was smiling like children at Christmas. I was completely lost and confused. Whatever was going to happen it was going to be big.

"As you all know we are here for one reason, and one reason only. We are here to learn how to write to be published. Well, one of our writers in this room is now not only a writer but an author. I want to congratulate Cassie on getting her novel published!" Ava said smiling brightly and clapping. "Come one everyone, give her a standing ovation."

I was stunned. I had only heard Cassie talk once or twice and only for a few minutes. I hadn't ever had a real conversation with her. I didn't even know she was writing a novel. I stood there and clapped for Cassie and watched the reactions of everyone else. They all smiled brightly and they were so happy you could feel that energy. Jenn screamed at the top of her lungs and cheered. Peter patted Cassie on the back while Seth made a whooping noise in the air. Georgia and Shannon did some sort of high school cheer. While all this was happening Cassie herself sat down smiling, her face bright red. There was a feeling of comradery and celebration in that room.

After everyone settled down some Ava had more news. "You think that's all isn't it?"

"That wasn't the news?" questioned Georgia. "You are just full of surprises this past week Ava, aren't you?"

Ava gave her a little secretive smirk before continuing. I missed a lot being away, I thought to myself.

"Well, that was a piece of the news but there's more. I know how writers take inspiration from exploring far away lands and exotic forests in their imaginations. These experiences take them to some place in their mind where their immense creativity shines through in the stories they write. At least I know that's what I do. So, I've been working on this for a few months now and it has FINALLY been approved."

"What is it?" Jenn said a little too enthusiastically.

"Patience is a virtue my love. Do you want to know?"

"YES" we all screamed.

"Okay, fine I'll tell you, but you have to promise me one thing. You have to promise that you will all be excited. You will be thrilled. You will act like you have front row tickets to an Aerosmith concert. You will love me more than you already do. Do you promise?" During this speech she was pounding her fists together, pacing back and forth and speaking in a passionate, thunderous voice.

"We promise," we all screamed back. The hype that Ava was giving out got us all riled up and we didn't even know what we were excited about.

"Okay, well I got us all approved to go on a little road trip over the summer."

"What kind of road trip? For how long?" Shannon asked. He didn't look at all interested in it. He was excited and then once she said road trip his face dropped six degrees of Kevin Bacon.

"Well Ally McBeal, I rented a mini-van and all of us will be traveling by this mini-van to the Grand Canyon!"

"A mini-van?" Jenn asked. "I am so not going in a granny car."

"Hey!" Georgia said. Being the oldest at fifty-five she didn't like to consider herself a granny, and having a mini-van herself didn't help the matter.

"Oh not you darlin,' you're not a granny. You're as young as you feel sweet pea."

"Come on guys, you promised if I told you what it was you were going to be so excited you would practically jump on top of me with joy. You are really depressing me."

As Ava faked a cry, Jenn jumped up and ran to her and practically knocked her over. "I am so excited, I can't wait. OH MY GOD, we're going on a fucking road trip! AHHHHH! I can't believe it. I think I just fell in love with you Ava! How can this be happening? I have been waiting my whole life to go on the road with seven GREAT amazing people and now my dream is happening. I think I'm going to faint!" She fanned her face with her hands as we all laughed hysterically. "I would like to thank the Academy for this great achievement. And I would like to thank my agent, Miss Amber Jacobs, my publicist, Miss Cassie Chiqita, my dog jessibel, my cat lola, the snail I found as a child, ummm...my parents, my family, my friends. And to God, without you this wouldn't be possible." Jenn then turned around and pulled an Adrien Brody, kissing Ava hard on the lips. She began to walk away and then returned. "Oh and I forgot to thank my husband, Bob. THANK YOU EVERYBODY AND GOOD NIGHT!"

We all laughed so hard our mouths hurt, Ava was practically on the floor in hysterics. Jenn, on the other hand, acted as if nothing happened. That was Jenn for you, the comedian, the actress, the entertainer. What just happened was why I loved her so much. She was one of my best friends.

After class had ended I went up to Ava to let her know I was okay.

"That Jenn, she's one funny girl." I said.

"That's the understatement of the year," Ava laughed. "I missed you last week. I had some big news and you were one of the people I wanted to tell the most and you were gone. I heard about your mom, are you okay?"

"Yeah I'm okay I guess. It sucks that she went back to drinking but there's nothing I can do about it. I tried to stop her when she came home after breaking up with Derek but she wouldn't listen to me so I needed to get out of there."

"You could have come to me you know."

"I know, and I'm sorry. I just needed to talk to Kira. She was my foster mother when my mom went missing for a while. She went through that time with me, when my mom was drinking and drugging and she was taking care of me like her own daughter. I really needed her at that moment. I'm sorry I didn't come to you."

"Don't ever be sorry for doing something you feel is the right thing to do. I totally understand what must have been going through your mind when your mom started drinking again."

"It was hard and it still is but now that I'm older and wiser it doesn't hurt as much as it did when I was younger. I knew it was destined to happen sooner or later, I just wish it was later or never at all. There's really nothing I can do to help her. She has to want help and she has to get it herself. Alicia is on my side this time, which makes it easier to go through. And also this time I have friends and you and Kira and this class to help me."

"Good to hear. Kira must be a great woman for you to be so close to her."

"She is. You actually remind me of her a little bit. That's why I feel so comfortable talking to you. And you are always right about things. I should have listened to you about not confronting Alicia about her and Brad, but what do I do, I confront her. If I had listened to you we wouldn't have been on non-speaking terms for so long of a time."

"What's in the past is in the past. You're talking now so that's all that matters. So, are you excited for the road trip?"

"Yes, I'm very excited. I really can't wait. I've never been to the Grand Canyon and I know it'll be a fun time driving there with everyone. And if we ever get bored we can always have Jenn entertain us." We both laughed.

"I'm happy you're happy. It'll be good hanging out together."

"It will be a lot of fun. So, what's this big news you shared with everyone BUT me?"

"Oh, well. I found out two months ago that I am pregnant." A huge smile crossed her face and I could tell it from her eyes how extremely happy she was. "My husband and I have been trying for a year and it just wasn't happening. I got pregnant once but I miscarried. That's why I didn't want to tell everyone right away. But the doctors all say that this baby is doing well so far. Knock on wood! We're so excited about it."

"Oh my God, congratulations! You are going to be an amazing mother. Just promise me you'll never let your son or daughter down like my mother. And no drinking!"

"I promise. I'll do my best. And I don't know about the best mother but I've been wanting a child for so long now I think I'll make a pretty decent one."

"Don't sell yourself short Ava. You're an excellent teacher and friend. Your baby is one lucky kid."

"You're too sweet Amber, now get the hell out of here and go hang out with Austin and your friends."

"Okay. See you tomorrow?"

"Not if I see you first. Bye."

"Bye."

Entry 61: <u>May 1997</u>

The end of the year crept up fast and we were all antsy for summer break. I was leaving to go on the road trip with the writers group in the middle of June and would be gone for at least a month. We were going to drive across country and stop in each state where we would spend that particular night and do a few days of sight seeing. The place I looked looking forward to the most was the Rocky Mountains in Colorado. I heard great things about them. Their beauty and grace beckoned me. I couldn't wait. Austin was spending his summer bumming out on the beach with Deana, Matt, Madison and Andrew. I could only imagine how Alicia was spending her break.

I saw it now, her and Brad going to parties and using their fake ID's to get into the local clubs. Alicia had found this particular karaoke place where she loved to get up there and belt out the popular songs of the moment. Very rarely was she booed off the stage. She had acquired the good voice in the family. I had gone with her one night to watch her "perform." It was a fun night. She had no problem getting up there in front of all of these people who she didn't know as she sang her heart out. I was a very proud sister and friend. I was also jealous of her talent. I always wanted to be able to sing, but I am pretty much tone deaf.

When the last day of school finally came we were all so ecstatic we could hardly pay attention to what we were doing. It was very hot outside and there was a plan to go to the beach after classes ended as a celebration. We wanted to celebrate the end of classes with everyone before we had to cram.

The bell rang and we all jolted out of our seats and practically ran to our lockers and threw our belongings into backpacks and sped out of the building. It was a whirlwind and I was surprised that we all didn't get caught up in the twister being swept away into the inner realms of the school. But it was finally time for the beach and we were happy to be celebrating another year gone.

"Can you believe we're finally seniors?" Madi asked.

"Not yet. We still have to pass our exams. Plus, it's not like once we graduate that we never have school again. There's college."

"College is great Amber. College is like a free for all. My sister Elise goes to UCLA and she loves it. I even went to visit her once and I totally got into a frat party without them saying a word. I mean, I was only 15 when I went. It was amazing. There aren't any parents and all anyone ever does is party. I'm surprised that Elise is passing her classes. I was there for a week and when she got back to her dorm she would check with all her friends and then we'd be partying all night and then she'd go to bed. I don't think I ever saw her do homework. I can't wait. I am going so far away from this shithole."

"You are?" Matt asked. "I thought we were going to stay close together?"

"We are. You're coming to UCLA with me, remember?"

"I never agreed to that. I was planning on going to NYU. I thought you wanted to go to some place in Rhode Island, URI?"

"Yeah, that was so yesterday. I went to look at it and realized I don't want to live in a fucking four by four foot state. What's there to do? So I checked out UCLA and loved it. I think I want to go into film. I would love to be a director or producer or something."

"Okay Stephanie Spielberg."

"Who's that?"

"It was a joke Deana, Steven Spielberg is a famous director and you're a girl so I feminized his first name." Looking at her puzzled face Matt just rolled his eyes and said, "never mind." He was clearly aggravated and upset at the college situation.

"You two are being stupid. There is still over a year to talk about this. Let's enjoy the beach."

"Thank you Amber, I thought we were going to have to listen to these two go at it all night. You are seriously a life saver," Madison said.

We all agreed to drop the subject and just have fun. Austin found a nice empty spot on the beach right near the water, but not too close. Immediately Matt and Andrew started building a "majorly cool" sand castle. Madison and Deana stripped down to their bikinis and fell asleep listening to their CD players.

"So, we never got to talk about your mom." Austin said to me after we got settled on our towels. I wore a black one piece and he wore his favorite bathing suit. It was blue and red. Surprisingly, I found myself missing Chris. I hadn't seen him in a very long time, but our infrequent letters kept us connected. I felt guilty as I thought of Chris. I hoped Austin hadn't caught my thoughts.

"And, there's a reason why. I don't want to talk about her, especially not now when we're having fun."

"Is she getting better?"

I laughed out loud when he asked that. "Getting better? Not at all, she's actually worse than before. She's getting so possessive, I don't know why. She was like that a long time ago when we were with Kira and Mark but not as bad as she is now. She doesn't want me to go on the road trip with Ava and everyone because she thinks that Ava is trying to take over my mind or something. It's ridiculous. And she's been so aggressive towards Alicia."

"What do you mean?"

"For no reason at all sometimes she hits her across the face, pushes her across the room, grabs her arm and twists it around."

"That is terrible. Do you want me to come over and kick her ass?"

"No, it would be pointless. She would knock you down in a heartbeat. Plus I don't want her to take you away from me."

"How is Alicia handling it all?"

"She's not handling it at all. She's never home, and when she is she's locked in her room or in my room. I try to talk to her about it all but she just shrugs it off as if it was nothing. I don't think she wants to admit that our mother is a mean drunk. It's hard to accept because she wasn't like this when we were kids. I mean she was a neglectful mean bitch, but not physically. I don't really want to talk about her though. Look at the castle? That is coming along great." I clapped for Matt and Andrew trying to get off the topic of my mother.

Austin was quiet, so I assumed he sensed I was done with that topic and he respected my wishes. We joined Matt and Andrew in their quest to build the best sand castle ever. I built the castle gates while Austin started in on the moat.

"Hey Deana, come join us, it's fun." I called to them.

"Are you crazy? I do not want to be washing sand off of me for months, I am happy staying right where I am thank you very much." She put her sunglasses back on and turned over to start cooking her back.

Two hours later we were done and it was gorgeous. The castle wall and gate that I had built was sturdy and high and circled the castle perfectly, even on all sides. The moat was wide and deep and had about four inches of water that floated through it. Austin was a genius. The castle itself was magnificent. It was huge with seven towers. It was in all, three feet high, two feet wide and five feet across. Everyone who was at the beach came over and admired the architecture and stamina of this castle built of only sand.

After two and half hours at the beach and twelve pictures of the sand castle, it was time to go home. While Madison, Deana and I packed up, the three boys stood about three feet away from the castle and made a plan to run and jump on it. All of the convincing in the world for them not to do it was a waste of speech and time. We all watched in horror as they ran full speed into the castle and screamed. Two hours to build it and four seconds to destroy it.

"That was awesome." They all screamed in unison.

"You are all brutes," I said as we walked away from them.

"Aww, but you love us anyway." Austin said draping is arm around my shoulder. A fun day at the beach and now home to study for our last four days of being juniors.

Entry 62: <u>June 1997</u>

June rolled around and it was time for the road trip. I had packed a week ago and I couldn't wait to head out the door. I had passed all my classes so I was officially a senior and what was more exiting than that? One more year of staying here in this hell I had to call home. Or so I thought.

I was packed and ready to go. They would be at my house in ten minutes to pick me up when my mother came into my room.

"Amber, you need to do something for me."

"I can't do anything for you even if I wanted to. I'm leaving in five minutes."

"Where the hell are you going?" She asked furiously.

"Don't tell me you forgot. I've been telling you this for the past four days. You even signed a consent form. I'm going with Ms. Trotty and the writing class on a road trip across country." I knew to call her Ms. Trotty in front of my mother because she didn't approve of students calling teachers by their first name.

"You can't go Amber. I need you here."

"I'm going mom, and you don't need me."

"Yes I do."

"What do you need from me?" I asked, anger rising in my voice.

"You need to take care of Alicia. I have something important to do for a few days and you need to stay with her."

"Ugh, mom she's fifteen and a half, she can stay home alone. Or have her stay at her friend's house. I'm sure she'll be absolutely fine with it. Hell, she'll probably be thrilled."

"I don't know any of her friend's names. Or the names of their parents either. I want you to stay."

"I'm not staying."

"Don't tell me you're not doing something. I'm your mother and you will do what I tell you."

"Oh will I?" I asked getting angrier by the second. There was no way she was going to stop me from doing this. "If you don't let me go I'll go live with Dad and take Alicia with me. I know he'll be happy to have us and he'll probably never let you see us again." I knew this would get her; she couldn't stand to have something happen that would affect her. Even though she hated being a mother she hated even more for someone to do something that would make her a bad one. I also knew that our father wouldn't take us, not that we would go anyway but she didn't need to know that.

"Fine Amber. You go on your little trip with your stupid friends and when you get back, well I'll see you when you get back. And if you want Alicia to stay at her friends house you call whoever her friend's mother is and ask her."

She walked away just as the mini-van pulled up and Ava beeped. I grabbed the phone quickly and called Alicia's friend Suzanna's mother and got the approval. I then ran out of the house as quickly as I could and hopped into the van in the middle of Jenn and Cassie.

"Let's go before my mom changes he mind about letting me go. Metal to the Pedal Ava!"

"All right Miss Jacobs. Where are you headed?"

"To the Grand Canyon or BUST!" we all yelled loudly.

Ava was driving and Georgia got shotgun. In the middle was Jenn, Me and Cassie and in the back were Peter and Seth. "Hey, where's Shannon?" I asked.

"Oh, he had to fly back to Ireland. His sister was in a car accident and she wanted him there with her." Ava answered.

"Oh, is she okay?"

"She's fine. It wasn't a huge accident but I guess she's a drama queen and needs her baby brother to help her. I think she broke her leg and a couple of fingers. What a good brother."

"Hey everyone, look what I brought!" Jenn said with a huge smile on her face.

"It better not be alcohol young lady." Ava joked.

"Nope, it's better, Ta-da." She pulled out her video camera and we all laughed. "What's better on a road trip than my directorial skills?" She turned on the camera, "Say something Amber."

In my best British accent I said, "Welcome to Masterpiece Theater with the writers guild of Ava. Here you will learn what it's like to drive across country with seven unique individuals, each with their own personality. Will they survive? Only time will tell."

"Classic Amber. That is perfect."

"Cassandra my love, what would you like to say to the world out there watching this film of our road trip?"

"Jenn, my name is just Cassie."

"For the sake of the movie it's going to be Cassandra whenever we are filming. I am the director I say what goes."

"Well Jennifer, I would like to say that this is a truly remarkable trip we are taking and I am looking forward to spending it with all truly amazing people and writers and I feel it will be an awakening for me."

"Truly." Jenn laughed. "Beautifully said." Jenn turned around. "Now you two twinnies, what is your favorite piece of clothing that you brought?"

Peter and Seth turned to each other. "Well my favorite piece of clothing is a Red Sox sweatshirt. It's comfortable and appropriate." Seth said.

"Me, my favorite piece of clothing I brought is a Yankees sweatshirt."

Seth looked at Peter appalled and hit him. "How dare you? A Yankee fan? What were you thinking all of these years?"

"Not about what you would think," he said hitting his brother back. They were just playing around and going back and forth and I could see Jenn was loving it. She had a smile from ear to ear and she had the camera focused in on their fight.

"This is great," she mouthed to me before going back to staring through the lens of the camera.

"Now, Georgia like the state, what is your feeling on broccoli?"

"Broccoli is a peaceful food my love. It is green and looks like a tree. Trees comfort people and broccoli comforts me." She gave the camera a peace sign and a smile.

"Okay then. Now Miss Trotty, do you like to trot? No, I'm just kidding with you. When you realized what you were getting yourself into, what were your thoughts?"

"I thought, am I crazy? Taking Jenn on a road trip? I knew everyone else was fun and normal but I kept asking myself if Jenn was going to be okay in a mini-van when I know how much she despises them." Ava laughed and Jenn feigned shock and hurt.

Turning the camera on herself she spoke into it. "I am here for your enjoyment. This film will keep you interested because I am the star. And all of these little people are my minions. I will take over the world if it's the last thing I do. Goodbye for now." She shut the camera and put it back in her bag. "I'm going to take a nap now." And with that said she was out like a light in 2 seconds.

We listened to the radio and talked and sang songs and had so much fun. It was five hours until our first destination, Ohio. We got there in a flash. Ohio wasn't anything special. It was the same views of buildings and trees where we were from. We stayed in a cute little campground. After stretching out we all took a walk around and then set up our tents and cooked some mac and cheese. That night at the campfire we toasted marshmallows and told scary stories. It was like we were in elementary school.

The next morning we were on our way. There was really nothing to do in Ohio so we checked out a local Topiary Garden in Columbus on our way to our next stop. This specific Topiary garden had an array of shrubs and bushes designed as a re-creation of Georges Deurat's impressionist painting, *A Sunday Afternoon On The Island of La Grande Jatte.* Georgia, being the artist in the bunch provided us with an entire history. It was one of her favorite pieces and she was in her glory as she walked around the shrubs that were so lifelike. She was happy up until Jenn stuck a large stick in the lower area of the man lying down with a pipe.

"Look what we have here, he needs a woman!" Jenn said laughing.

Immediately Georgia grabbed the stick and threw it the other way with an angry look on her face. "Don't disgrace great art Jenn, it took a long time for them to do this and to have you doing obscene things to the work these people have so painstakingly created."

"Loosen up Georgia, life's a ball, you have to throw it once in a while." After saying this Jenn walked up to a shrubbery shaped like a woman and a man walking in the rain. She pretended to walk with them, every now and then saying something to the green object.

For the hour we were there we took several pictures of Jenn, who posed with the French bushes. It was a sight to see. She spoke in a very bad French accent, which she continued to do up until we reached our next destination; Indiana.

We ate at a Big Boy and had the best burgers ever. After lunch we drove to another campsite and set up our tents again. We checked out our Indiana location, only to find little to see. We went to a movie and then crashed in our tents.

The next morning we hopped into the granny van and headed on to our next destination. We all had a blast the entire time in the car because we had Jenn to keep us laughing and of course Ava joked back with her.

We drove through Missouri and continued on the road. It was pretty boring driving to our campsite in Kansas. We passed fourteen farms, one thousand cows, telephone poles galore and fields beyond belief. There were miles and miles of fields and every once in a while there was a house thrown in the middle of nowhere.

The heat killed us and we were thrilled to find that the next campsite was equipped with a swimming pool. Immediately we took over the place and jumped into the refreshingly cold water. It felt so good to get the sweat off of our bodies and relax in a pool of water as we looked up at the vast blue sky and thought of absolutely nothing.

Our next stop was Colorado and I was so excited. When we crossed the border of Kansas entering Colorado a joy flooded me and a smile crossed my face.

I had always wanted to be free on the top of the Rocky Mountains. Up ahead we saw the outline of the mountains and we thought to ourselves: we were almost there. Four hours later we were still about three hours away from reaching our destination.

"This is crazy, are we ever going to get there?" Peter asked aggravated. "The mountains were right there two hours ago."

"The mountains are big Peter," Ava responded. "Once we get to the mountains we still have an hour until we reach the hotel."

"We're staying in a hotel? Thank God! A real bed."

"Jenn, don't be so overdramatic, we're here to have a good time not to worry about your comfort. Now switch off with me and drive the rest of the way."

Jenn and Ava switched positions and Jenn drove the remainder of the way and finally we reached the hotel. I had never been so happy in my life as I was at that moment when we walked into the room and I just flew onto the bed.

"Hey guys, come here and look at this, but be very quiet," Seth said.

We walked out the door frowning at Seth for making us get up. Outside the hotel about four hundred feet away from us were two doe. They were beautiful. Jenn ran back into the room only to appear a second later with her video camera. We inched closer to them and they both lifted their heads toward us but didn't move. When we were two hundred feet away the deer got startled and ran away.

"That was amazing, I shall name them Mickey and Minnie."

"Jenn, they were both female," I said while we all laughed.

"Oh yeah, then Minnie and Daisy. Right. Perfect. Now, let's go for a walk."

We all walked to the local gift shop and bought some bumper stickers and magnets and postcards. Then we walked around grabbed a bite to eat and sat outside the hotel for a few hours and chatted before we crashed.

The next day we took a drive to the top of the highest peak of the Rockies. It took us two hours to get up there but it was worth it. It was hot outside so we were all wearing shorts, t-shirts and sandals. On the way up Ava's bag of chips blew up like a balloon and almost popped. The altitude was immense and our ears continued to pop. As we drove up and around the sides of the roads changed from green to white and by the time we reached the top, the snow was 10 feet high. It was extraordinary.

Getting out of the van at the top was like stepping into an icebox. We were not dressed appropriately. It was freezing but the sight we looked at was breathtaking. The expanse of the mountains was amazing; really no words can ever describe it. It was white for miles and miles away.

"Okay people of the GranVan we have come to our first writing experience. You have a half hour to sit on the bench and write a story based on your feelings and incorporate these beautiful mountains and the flat fields of Kansas. Once we get to the Grand Canyon you will write another. Go to it!"

While we wrote our stories Ava met up with a friend of hers from College. She had planned on getting together with Rachel here from the beginning so they went to the next bench and caught up with everything. Ava was about three months pregnant now and she had a small bump. It was very cute.

The half hour was over and although I was glad to get back into the van and back into the warmth I was sad to have to leave this. It was one of the best experiences I had had so far in life. I couldn't be more thankful for this month. We drove back to the hotel and had some hot chocolate even though we were back in the heat. The next day we headed to Utah and then to Arizona to our destination, the Grand Canyon.

The drive through the mountains to get out of Colorado took us five hours and as soon as we hit the bottom we were in Canyonland. It was so immediate I almost didn't' believe it. How could the largest mountains just stop and become the deepest canyons? It blew my mind. I would definitely use this in my writing.

Four days later we arrived in Arizona and set up camp in one of the campsites located in the Grand Canyon park. We saw an IMAX show on the Grand Canyon and then went to sleep in our tents. The next day we would be traveling to see the Canyon itself.

We drove to a look over place and it was thrilling. We were amazed that something unexplainable happened and caused something so beautiful. The rivets in the canyon walls and the beautiful orange color of the rock made this formation just fascinating.

After we looked over the wall we went on a helicopter ride over the Grand Canyon and got to see from a bird's eye view exactly what it looked like and it was incredible. There are no words to describe just how beautiful it truly is.

Entry 62: <u>June 1997</u>

It took us nine days to drive back and when we arrived I wished it had been longer. My mother was outside on the stoop smoking a cigarette with a glass of vodka in her hand.

Ava looked at me. "Are you okay?"

"Yeah I'm fine, at least it's not the entire bottle this time. Don't know where the cigarette came from though."

"If you need anything please call me okay?"

"I will. Thank you for a wonderful trip Ava. I really appreciate it."

"You're welcome. I'm glad you had fun." She smiled and waved goodbye before I stepped out of safety and into the war zone.

As the van drove away I braced myself for what was to come. My mother stood up, threw the cigarette on the ground, stomped it out and walked toward me. I could tell she was drunk from the drips of vodka spilling out of the top of the glass with every wobble she took. This was not good.

"Hey mom, I'm back. Did you miss me?"

She didn't say anything just walked right up to me stared me down for a few seconds and slapped me in the face hard.

"What was that for?" I asked angrily, tears already beginning.

"Where have you been Amber? I have been looking everywhere for you for the past month and I get no phone call."

"Oh, you didn't call the police?"

"Yes, but they don't do shit. They told me some story about how you were on a trip across country."

"I was."

"Don't lie to me. You left a month ago and never came back. You never told me where you were going. And who were those people in the van?"

"Those are my friends. Ava is my writing teacher and the rest of the group are the other writers in the class. We went on a trip across country, which I told you three months before we left, and the day I left."

"I don't want you ever to go to that writing class again or see any of those people again. I forbid it."

I laughed in her face. "If you think I'm going to quit the one thing that makes me happy you've got another thing coming." I started to walk away.

She turned around and said in the deepest calmest voice, which was scarier than her yelling, "if I hear or see you go near that Ava again I will throw everything in your room away, including your computer and journals."

"You wouldn't!"

"If you want to test me then go speak to Ava. Go on." She stepped aside to let me know that she wasn't kidding. I was furious.

"Fine." I yelled and ran into my room slamming the door.

"What's the matter Amber?" Alicia asked walking into the room.

"Mom just forbid me to go to writing class anymore or talk to Ava again."

"What a bitch. Don't listen to her, just don't let her find out."

"But she told me that she'd throw away everything in my room, including my writing supplies. She used the voice."

"Oh, the voice." Alicia said pondering. "Well I'll put them in my room. She said she'd throw away everything in your room not mine. And just don't let her know you're going."

"Sounds like a plan."

I was still upset but I told Alicia all about my trip and just talking about it made me happier. I couldn't' wait to get the pictures developed and start a photo album. I knew that I had to write everything in my journal soon before I forgot, so after Alicia went out with Brad I grabbed the newest journal that had never been written in and I christened it with a blue pen. It took me forty pages to describe everything but it was great. I sent a copy of the entry to Kira and Chris.

Madison called me that night and invited me to her house. Deana, Matt, Andrew and Austin were over and they wanted to hear all about my trip. I hurried over and they had pizza waiting for me. It was a great night. I told them everything that happened the month I was gone and what happened when I got home. They smiled when I was told them about Jenn and the topiary garden. But when I told them about how my mother had forbidden me to ever go to writing class or go near Ava again they were shocked and appalled. They all agreed with my plan.

We played some games and ate too much pizza and then I went home and went to sleep.

Entry 63: <u>January 1998</u>

Months of drinking, smoking, arguing and sneaking around passed and by January both Alicia and I were so unhappy at home we spent most of our time out with friends and frequenting bars using fake ID's that Alicia had acquired for us. Her name was Traci Markowicz and mine was Angelica Canide.

Austin and I had broken up a few weeks ago but we had left on good terms so we were still best friends. He just wasn't Chris. He would never be Chris. I hadn't seen Chris in such a long time. Perhaps I romanticized us…. Deana and Matt were practically engaged; they never spent one minute without the other. Madison and Andrew were on again off again and Alicia and Brad were still hot and heavy for each other. I still didn't really understand what she saw in him.

Jenn had previewed the film she made from our trip to the writing class a month ago and it was fantastic. We all sat back and watched it as we laughed and smiled at the antics Jenn threw at us throughout the journey. The entire topiary garden had us all on the floor in hysterics. Intertwined throughout the movie were quotes from the papers we had written as well as small interviews from everyone, including Shannon who had sent his interview to Jenn from Ireland. It was put together professionally and I couldn't understand why Jenn wasn't in Hollywood at the moment instead of the writing class.

I found it easy to sneak around and attend writing class. My mom was incognizant of anything that was going on around her. The only person she truly cared about was herself. That is what alcohol does to her. We were always out so when I actually went to the writing class she thought I was out with my friends. The only adult who knew what I was doing was Kira and although she didn't approve she promised not to tell anyone. There were many nights when I went to bed and wished that she was my mother instead of Shelley. I wished with all of my heart and soul that God had sent me to Kira. I didn't understand what his agenda was in sending me to this life. I was convinced that somehow the stork was dyslexic and messed up the mothers. But here I was and it wasn't going to change so I had to deal with it.

Senior year went well. I hoped to get a scholarship to go to a local state college because I knew that without the scholarship I wouldn't be able to afford a college education. Ava had set me up with this particular scholarship. I had to submit a short story, 30-50 pages long. I wrote it in a month and sent it in to the address in December. I waited for a response and didn't know what to do with myself. Every day I'd run to the mailbox but there would be nothing.

Deana and Matt had applied to UCLA and both had been accepted. They had already begun planning courses to take and dorms to live in. Madison was going to Fordham University while Andrew was going to Brown. Austin wanted to get out of the cold weather so he was going to Lynn University in Florida. He wanted to be a funeral director like his uncles. I personally thought it was a rather depressing occupation but he found it intriguing so more power to him.

It was Alicia's birthday the following week, so we decided to take her out to her favorite bar where she could sing. Neither she nor I drank but it was still fun to hang out with our friends and just have a good time. The eight of us went and it was a blast. Alicia sang a few songs on the Karaoke machine while everyone else listened and talked and pretended not to notice Brad as he talked to the bartender, Melissa.

"He is such an ass Amber, why is Alicia dating him?" Deana asked me.

"I have no idea, she's so infatuated with him that if I even mention it she'll snap at me and we'll have a fight. I can't afford to fight with her, especially now that my mom is crazy. Did I tell you guys that she has a new man in her life?"

"What?" Austin asked practically spitting his coke all over himself.

"Yup, his name is Jon Luc and he's an artist," I said like a prissy Frenchman. "He's always over to our house and he's so annoying. They were friends back when we were little and he'd always hang out at our house but then once my mom got clean he stopped coming around. I guess he found out she's off the wagon so he's been clinging. If you just hear him talk you'd think he's the best thing since sliced bread. He's not going to make her stop drinking either so it makes him that much worse."

"Fuck 'em Amber. Don't even let them enter your mind. They aren't worthy of your thoughts. Only we are."

"Thanks Madi, you always know what to say to make a girl smile."

"Hey all, what are you talking about?" Alicia asked coming back from the stage.

"Oh just telling them about Jon Luc."

"Oh that prick? Did you tell them how annoying he is?"

"Yes I did." I straightened my back and lifted up my chin and began to speak like Jon Luc. "Did you know that Madagascar is an island located southeast of Africa? I bet you did not. I can teach you girls all I know and then you'd have colleges fighting for you left and right and maybe even off center as well. Ha Ha Ha." Everyone laughed except for Alicia who looked straight at the bar and at Brad and Melissa.

"Look at him flirting with Missy. He told me that he was done with her. That is it, it's final. I am SO breaking up with him."

We all cheered so loudly everyone in the bar stared at us; however, Alicia did not get up.

"So, go do it." I said.

"What? NOW?"

"Yes, now. If you don't do it now you'll never do it. Go!"

"Fine." Alicia got up and we all stared at her. Brad got pissed off and Alicia yelled. He stormed out of the bar and Melissa gave Alicia a glass of sprite. "So, are you all happy?"

"Yes," we said in unison.

We finished off the night with one more song from Alicia and the bar closed.

Entry 64: <u>February 1998</u>

During that February my mother started acting strange, even for her. She always asked us questions, wanting to know where we went and whom we were with. It also seemed suspicious that she took an interest in Ava and the writing class.

I had no idea where this was coming from until the day I went to the class and found the classroom empty except for Ava, who sat at her desk, head in hand.

"What's wrong?" I asked. "Ava, are you all right?"

She picked up her head and I noticed she had been crying. She looked right at me and there was this immense sadness in her eyes.

"What's the matter, is it the baby? Did something happen to her?"

"No, Emily is fine. She's doing so great. You should see her."

I was worried. "Then, what's the matter?"

"Well, you're mother came in about an hour ago."

My face dropped and my body tensed. I hadn't given Alicia my stuff and now I was afraid that all of my writing supplies would have a new home in the garbage. "Oh no." I looked away. "I'm sorry I didn't tell you that she had forbidden me to come to the classes anymore. But don't worry, she won't do anything to you. It is me she is after. She's will throw my journals away and everything that I value in life." Tears came to my eyes. I thought that I'd be immune to crying by now.

"That's just it Amber, she can do something to me and she threatened it. I can't believe I'm saying this but, I can't keep you in this class anymore sweetie."

"What?" I asked. My mind spun out of control.

"This is killing me that you can't take this class anymore. You don't understand. You are one of the most talented kids I've ever met and you make this class a pleasure to teach. But your mom told me that if I let you back in that she would tell everyone that I was sleeping with a student."

"But you're not and there's no way she could prove it."

"I know I'm not, but she has a student who is willing to lie and we all know that there is no way that people are going to believe me over a student even if it is a lie. By the time they find out it's all a lie my reputation will be ruined and I'll never be able to teach again. Amber, I am so sorry." She started to cry again.

I bowed my head and then looked up at her through the tears that streamed down my face. There was extreme rage that boiled in the pit of my stomach.

"It's okay Ava, it's not your fault my mom is a fucking crazy woman. I understand. Thank you for all that you've done for me. I really appreciate it."

She nodded and got up and gave me a hug. I returned the hug even if it was a little stiff from the anger that bubbled up in my throat. When we released the hug, Ava immediately turned away and very softly said, "Goodbye Amber."

"Bye Ava." I responded and then turned and walked out of the room. Outside the air was warm and my surroundings blurred into nothing. I walked home in a steady stride. My mind had gone red. I couldn't think of anything but going home and going nuts on Shelley. How dare she do the unthinkable? This was the last straw and I was enraged. Stepping one foot in front of the other on the silver concrete, getting closer and closer to my house just infuriated me more. As I inched closer and opened the white picket fence gate I stopped. I felt my face distorted in anger and wet from tears and both my fists were by my sides clenched as I breathed, deep and slow.

I lifted my head and walked to the front door. Before I turned the knob I took a deep breath to calm myself but it didn't work. As I walked into the house, it seemed very familiar yet so different. I saw my home through eyes of hate. It seemed the earth stopped rotating and sound had ceased to exist. I felt as if I was in a sound barrier as I saw my mother lying on the couch sleeping with a bottle of vodka resting on the floor. The mouth of the bottle was leaning gently against the palm of her open hand; her arm hung loosely over the side of the couch. I screamed but I could hear no sound. I grabbed the bottle and threw it against the wall.

Shelley woke up abruptly and was startled to see me in this state. Inside I was breaking so I decided to break things that represented everything that she stood for. I raged against everything in the room, threw picture frames across the room, knocked everything off of the coffee table, sent chairs flying and kicked flower pots which spilled potting soil all over the floor. I ripped a picture of France off of the wall that Jon Luc painted himself and slammed it over the remaining standing chair. With nothing else to throw or break, I collapsed on the ground and screamed, pulling at my hair.

Shelley walked right up to me as I knelt on the floor rocking back and forth. I stopped, looked up at her and sound finally reappeared in my world, "How could you?" I asked.

She just looked down on me coldly and smiled as if she had won World War III. Then she turned her back and walked away. Just then I noticed Alicia who stood at the doorway and watched the scene. I broke down in tears. I stood up and walked into my room. I just wanted to be alone.

I collapsed on my bed and stared at the ceiling for what seemed like forever. My body was drained and I had nothing left inside of me. Twenty minutes later my mother walked into my room as if nothing had happened. I didn't even look at her. I was surprised that the wall didn't have a hole in it from the way my eyes burned through to the outside.

"You deserve everything you've got coming Amber. I pulled you from that fucking class and away from that bitch for a reason."

"Yeah, what reason was that? You don't want me to be happy?"

"You went behind my back and lied to me especially when I told you not to go to that class anymore. You applied to college."

"Oh, college, what a crime. It's a shame I want a higher education than you did so that I can actually do something with my life. It's every parent's nightmare to have their children go to college. I knew that and thought I'd make your life a living hell for once."

"I got this letter in the mail. It seems you were approved for a scholarship. Congratulations are in order I suppose."

"I got accepted?" I asked excitedly.

"You did. It's too bad you won't be going."

"What?"

"I won't let you leave here."

"You can't stop me. I'll be eighteen and I have a scholarship. There's nothing you can do."

"Wrong again sweetheart. The scholarship is only for half of the money needed to go to the school. I did my research. And I'm not paying for the other half. So unless you have some money hidden in your shoe you can't afford to go."

"I'll ask dad."

She laughed. "Good luck with that one. He moved last month and I have no way of getting in touch with him and I assume neither do you."

"Have I ever told you that you are honestly the worst mother on the face of the planet?"

"Oh, so you have experience with other mothers?"

"Yes, I do. I've had the happiness and joy of being loved and treated like a good person and daughter by Kira. She is a thousand times better than you can ever live be."

"Listen to me young lady. That little goody-two-shoes whore is a fraud. She lives in this dollhouse world where everything and everyone is plastic with unbendable arms and legs. She doesn't know what real parenting is because of this fucking bubble she lives under. She's got those kids trained like monkeys and they just learn to sit down and shut up. Me, I'm a great mother. You two have everything you need; you have a roof over your heads, you have food in your bellies and you go to a great school. Everything else is just useless shit."

I was stunned at the nonsense coming out of her mouth and didn't know how to respond. "Get out of my room. And before you call anybody else a whore why don't you look in the mirror."

"You can call me any name in the book, I don't care. But while you're doing it you better start looking for a job because after graduation you're going to want to start saving for when you move out." She said while walking out of the room. "Don't worry about slamming the door, I'll do it for you." She did just as she promised.

Entry 65: <u>April 1998</u>

My ears rang; the noise from the stereo vibrated throughout the entire house. How could any one sleep through this? After all of my life living in screaming, yelling, and loud noises one would think I'd be used to sleeping through anything, but I couldn't. The last four months flew by too quickly. It was a Sunday night and work approached rapidly. I lay in bed with my eyes wide open and stared at the ceiling and wondered where my sister was. She usually came home late but tonight she was later than usual. Three a.m. was coming up fast and the sound of her car hadn't yet filled the neighborhood.

Where the hell was she I thought to myself, and hoped she arrived soon, so I wouldn't be bored staring at the ceiling, which I knew already, had 478 small holes. I stayed awake until she arrived around four thirty. She walked into the room, her head down, and closed the door behind her. She wasn't acting like herself, something was definitely wrong.

"What's the matter?" I asked, worried.

She still hadn't turned to face me; she was looking at the door. I could hear her sobbing and saw her tremble.

"Alicia, talk to me. You can tell me anything. I'll take it to the grave," I reassured her, hoping she'd open up to me. She knelt to the floor, and held onto the door as if the floor were about to collapse into oblivion. I went to her and put my hand on her shoulder. I knelt down beside her as she cried and I wrapped my arm around my younger sister. Alicia turned around and we embraced. I held her as she cried.

She still wouldn't tell me what was the matter and I was extremely anxious and concerned for her well-being. There were no visible bruises on her body and she hadn't had an argument with our mother. I let her cry for what seemed like forever and finally an hour after her return home she calmed down a little.

"Alicia, please just tell me what happened."

"I can't, it's too hard."

"I'm your sister, I love you, please tell me."

"I can't because I love you. I don't want you to think less of me; well less of me than you already do."

"I don't think anything but good about you Alicia!"

"Oh come on, we all know you're the perfect one, the one with the talent and I'm the fucked up kid who is good for nothing."

"I do not think that at all. You are the perfect one; you are the one who has all the friends and beauty. I understand that you've been through a lot, the same as me. We don't exactly have a fairy tale life, and I'm sure people know that. I was always jealous of you when we were growing up, I still am."

"Why?"

"Because you were the one mom and dad loved. You were the 'cool' one, and I was just the kid who liked to write. 'What a waste,' isn't that what mom said when I was eight? You were the popular one in school, the one with all the friends."

We were both silent for a while, and cried silent tears. "You know," I said. "You are the greatest person I know. The one person I can confide in whenever I want, without you thinking I'm stupid. You will just listen to me because we have gone through all our troubles together. There wasn't one time, well okay—maybe twice, that you weren't there for me, truly and honestly. I want you to know that I will always be there for you no matter what, and whatever you have to tell me, I will love you for who you are."

We both cried aloud at this point. The sadness and love overflowed in our room. The music blared as loud as possible outside where my mother partied with her friends. It was now almost five in the morning and we were both exhausted.

"Well, Brad," she said choking back tears.

"Did he do something to you?"

"We were at Heather's party about two months ago, drinking and having a good time. I was hanging out in the living room with Missy, Ali, Eric, and Jason. We were all talking, enjoying the conversation; Brad came over to us and told me he had to tell me something."

She held on to me tighter, I returned the squeeze.

She paused for a second gaining her momentum back. "I went with him, even though I was mad. I let him know it too, you know my temper." I nodded. "He took me up to Heather's little brother's room and he locked the door, said we needed to talk without people coming in. I told him I didn't want the door locked, but he didn't listen. He kept coming toward me, he had this look in his eyes. I don't know how to explain it, and I was a little scared. I asked him what he was doing, what he wanted to tell me, but he wouldn't answer.

"He told me that he needed me, he wanted me. I didn't want to; I wanted to hang out with my friends that night, why couldn't he have let me? He started kissing me but I was pushing him off, I was saying no. I said no," she cried. I was crying, holding her tight. How dare he do that!

"We have to go to the cops."

"NO! I can't. He'll kill me. Why would the police believe me anyway? We were dating, I was his girlfriend and we had done it before. Plus, it's been two months, it's too late."

"Why are you telling me now, why didn't you tell me then?"

"I wanted to forget it ever happened then. I wanted to put it all behind me and move on with my life. I broke up with him the next day, and he won't stop harassing me about stuff. We both promised we wouldn't mention that he raped me."

"So if you wanted it all over with, why bring it up now? Why, after two months are you upset about it again?"

"Because I have had to relive it."

"He raped you again?" I said bewildered.

"No," she said. She stopped crying by now and she was curled up against me while I held her. My sixteen-year-old sister shook, she was emotionally unstable at this point and she told me with hurt and regret, "I'm pregnant."

Entry 66: <u>April 1998</u>

The words hit me like no other. She was pregnant, at sixteen. I wanted to kill Brad for doing this to her, nobody messed with my sister. We stayed awake for the rest of the night and sat on the floor holding each other and rocking back and forth, thinking about what was said over the past few hours. Just a little while ago I was annoyed about the noise and now I was deaf to it, all thoughts drowned out the rest of the world.

Morning came and we decided to call out sick. I called the movie theater where I worked, and James, one of my co-workers covered for me. I called the principal, and pretended to be my mother. The principal answered her usual "Mrs. Kificia here, how may I help you?"

"Hi Mrs. Kificia, this is Shelley Martin, Alicia's mother. I was just calling because she's sick."

"Well Mrs. Martin, Alicia hasn't been to school lately. She has been skipping more than she should. She is having problems in her classes, and may I add if she plans to graduate this year she will need serious help in both Math and English."

"It's MS. MARTIN, if you've forgotten my husband left me for another woman when Alicia was two. Yeah, I'll get her help, in fact while she's in bed throwing up I'll get right on that. Thanks for your time," I said as I hung up the phone with authority.

"Wow Amber, you sounded just like her. That's kind of scary you know."

"I know, but let's go. We'll have bonding time today."

The entire day was perfect, except for the reason of why we spent a day of quality time together. We went to the mall and did some shopping, I bought her a purse she had been eyeing and then we bought a pregnancy test, just in case the first one she took was wrong. We ate lunch at a local restaurant and then went to a movie. Following the movie we went back home for a while so she could take the test. Positive.

I called the doctor and made an appointment for Alicia for the following day, which meant she would have to miss school again. I didn't work on Tuesdays so that wasn't a problem. We decided during our lunch that we wouldn't tell our mother until absolutely necessary.

We both flopped onto our beds, the exhaustion taking over our bodies.

"So have you thought at all about what you're going to do?"

"I don't need to think about it. I want to keep it."

"Are you sure? You are only sixteen; you have your whole life ahead of you."

"I'm sure Amber; I don't want to be like dad, I don't want to abandon my baby before it has a chance to live. I want to give my child everything in the world, everything we never had."

"The baby won't have a father."

"No, but it will have a mother who will love it and the best aunt in the world. He or she will be happy, no worries, no sadness. This baby will always have someone there in case anything happens.

I couldn't believe how grown up my sister had become. She was a very responsible person and I respected her more than ever. She was the rebellious one out of us but she had a sense of future, a love of children, and the knowledge that everyone deserves the best. She wasn't one to repeat the mistakes of her parents. I cried as I watched her talk about the child growing inside of her. I knew she would be a great mother, and I would be right by her side helping her in every step of the way.

"I want to give this one a chance, a chance we never had. I do know that I'm young and I need to find my place, somewhere I belong. I think I can do it even if I have a baby. I can do anything, as long as you are there with me."

I climbed into her bed with her and kissed her forehead. "So, have you thought of any names?"

"No, not yet, what do you think?"

"Well, if it's a boy you should name him Oliver Jack Jacobs. Like our play-acting when we were kids, remember? Sir Oliver, we had a lot of fun."

"Sir Oliver of Montigne, the leader of all who conquer their adversities," we laughed about our early adventures when we'd be saved by a knight in shining armor.

"I don't know about a girl, that's tough."

"No it's not. If it's a girl I will name her Katia Amber Jacobs, after her aunt."

I felt something deep inside me tighten, a muscle I never knew still worked, my heart. I was speechless. She reached inside my soul and discovered a secret cavern, one that hadn't been found since its desertion; inside a pot filled with hope and trust.

"I love you Alicia."

"I love you too Amber." We embraced and then we talked to her belly. This was one of the happiest moments disguised as a horrible monster waiting to pounce. If only it would have happened to me. I would have done anything to take away her pain of being raped, being pregnant by her attacker. I would have traded spaces with her in a heartbeat. Tears called my eyes their permanent home, and embedded themselves on the cusp of my lids, threatening to jump to their evaporation.

I drove Alicia to the doctors on Tuesday. The doctor was very nice. His name was Dr. Charles McKenna and he was very sympathetic to our situation. He understood the circumstances and didn't look down on Alicia at all. I was allowed to accompany her into the room where she gave a urine sample and waited for the doctor to fulfill his duties.

He performed an ultrasound where we saw the baby, and we both smiled. "This is amazing," Alicia said staring in awe of her child on the screen. "Look at the little head." She was already a proud mother.

Back in the doctor's office he told us that she was due sometime in December. He gave us pamphlets on what to expect in the coming months and what to do in case something happened out of the ordinary. Now we were on our way to five months of waiting. Alicia's next appointment would be at 16 weeks.

The day was beautiful, the sun shone and the birds chirped. The air was a little chilly, it was a good thing we remembered to put on jackets before we left. We took a walk around the park and then headed to the store to buy some pregnancy books. We talked for a while and thought of nothing bad that had occurred in our lives. We barely ever talked about our father but today she asked if she should tell him about the baby.

We drove around town wasting time before we went back home, she sat in the passenger side seat and looked out the window and rubbing her belly. She seemed lost in thought so I inquired as to what she was thinking.

"A penny for your thoughts."

"I was just thinking about dad. Do you think he would want to know?"

"No, he left us; he doesn't deserve the right to know what goes on in our lives. As I see it he's not our dad, just the sperm donor."

"I feel obligated to though, what if he was really trying to get in touch with us all these years and mom told him some story to keep him away?"

"Well, if he really loved us, then he wouldn't have cared what she said, but loved us for who we were." I failed to mention her refusing to see him or my meeting with him. I also didn't see it necessary to share the conversation I had with our mother about his birthday return when she and I had arrived back home from Kira's house.

"I guess you're right," she said resuming her faraway look. She looked very down; she hadn't been her usual self at all.

We continued down the winding path until we reached an open field where we set up a blanket and opened our wicker picnic basket. We turned on the stereo and listened to some soothing music. We each had made our favorite sand-wiches, mine a tuna salad, and hers a roast beef with mustard. We drank our sodas, snacked on potato chips and Alicia ate some pickles. I guess the saying was true, pregnant women have strange cravings.

The two of us didn't say much during lunch, we just kept each other company for the remainder of the day and night. When we pulled into the driveway we noticed our mother had Jon Luc over to our house. We both looked at each other and rolled our eyes.

"Do you want to head out, maybe go to this club I know?" Alicia asked me.

"Aren't you tired? I don't want you to do something that will stress you out."

"Amber, come on, it's not like I'm going into labor tomorrow morning, plus it's not a dancing club it's more of a listen to music, talk to others kind of club. Please, I'm not in the mood to listen to Jon Luc talk about painting and his experiences traveling the globe."

"Ok, me either. Let's go. Here, you drive." We switched places and she backed the car out of the driveway and drove away. The club was forty-five minutes away and the parking was terrible. We ended up parking three blocks from the small building.

"I hope we don't see anyone I know," she whispered.

We walked up to the front door to the bouncer and I showed him my ID. Alicia showed him her fake. We were in. The 18+ club was filled with a mixture of people, some older, and some my age. There was a karaoke stage set up and a pool table in the back. The bar hugged the wall with several people who were seated on the red leather stools. "Oh great," Alicia said. "Look, there's Cynthia, I forgot she was working here. She's Brad's new girlfriend."

"Do you want to leave?"

"No, he won't be here. He hates it, says the environment is filled with too much idiocy for his well-developed mind. Plus, she's older than him she won't know who I am. I hope."

"Okay." We took a seat on the couches opposite the pool tables. Some college guys were having a competition, betting hundreds of dollars on their win. Cynthia came by and asked if we wanted something to drink, I ordered a rum and coke and Alicia ordered a diet coke.

"What's the matter, afraid to drink Alicia?" Cynthia asked. She had recognized her. "Yes I saw a picture of you in Brad's room if your wondering how I knew it was you. I can't believe you could show your face in here knowing I work here. After what you did to him I just don't get it. If I wasn't working I would cause a scene, but because I have too much work ethic I won't." She walked away to get us our drinks, "Oh and because you are just not worth it," she mentioned.

"What does she think you did to him?" I asked.

She sat there, a look of hurt in her eyes, "he's been telling everyone that I cheated on him with ten different men, and that one of them was his father. The whole school thinks that because I have no father that I needed to feel one inside me, that I needed the attention of an older man, someone who had experience, a replacement for all of my issues regarding dad. I tried to ignore it because I knew it wasn't true, and Missy, Ali, and Eric knew that I didn't so I didn't care."

"I cannot believe he would spread these rumors. I am really sorry Alicia; I wish I could have been there for you."

"You're here for me now."

The speakers came to life as the karaoke machine scrawled words across the screen. The person at the microphone sang along as her voice cracked and shook from drinking. Alicia and I laughed to ourselves, how embarrassing for that woman.

An hour later the owner of the bar came over, "last call for singers, karaoke will be over and the Talking Walking Dollies will be taking over."

"I'm going to do it."

Alicia stood up and walked over to the mike. Instead of singing along to the karaoke machine though, she sang a song that she had written herself. The song of her feelings, the emotions she had been holding inside for fifteen years. The words reflected what she looked like on the inside; they were beautiful, each and every one of them. The entire club was silent, including me. Every time she sang she took my breath away.

Everyone stared as this young girl belted out with this voice so incredible you'd think she was already a star. Through her song you could feel exactly what she has been feeling all her life, you could taste her tears, you could touch her soul, and it was amazing. By the finale of the song everyone was crying, including Alicia. The place was quiet, and Alicia walked off the stage and sat down next to me again.

The band that was scheduled to play took the stage and began their set, but no one listened. They kept coming up to us and telling Alicia how wonderful her song was and how she should go into the business. "But stay true to who you are, it would be a shame if you turned into those big business folks who only care about fame and money," was the mantra for almost every person's thoughts.

"Thank you," my sister responded. She was very humble and I could see how she attracted everyone who saw her. This was just another strap to the belt of admiration I held for her, another string on a guitar, and another clip in a movie. I stared at her; I still couldn't believe what I heard and saw. We stayed at the club until almost closing and then we headed home for bed. The lack of sleep nagged at my eyes.

Entry 67: <u>August 1998</u>

The weeks passed by, my mother still clueless as to Alicia's situation. She still hadn't gained enough weight to tell she was pregnant and she had been sick every morning. Our mother told her she was getting fat, but then shrugged it off.

In her fifth month, she found out she was having a boy and we had seen him on the ultrasound screen. The nurse printed out a copy. He was beautiful, and we couldn't wait for him to be born.

The summer months were hot and unbearable, especially for Alicia, she was getting bigger and bigger by the day.

I remember one day during the month of September Alicia telling me how our mother found out about her pregnancy.

It was a particularly hot day and she decided to sit in the bathtub in freezing cold water. She was now six months pregnant, and her belly looked like a basketball had been shoved down her throat. I was at work fixing a broken projector and listening to customers complain about the prices. The water felt good on her body, the coldness reached every muscle and limb and cooled her off. The baby was moving around, kicking and enjoying the relaxation of being in a bag of water all to himself.

While she bathed, Alicia heard the front door shut and wondered who it could be, her mother hadn't been home all morning and I wasn't due home until 6:00. Then she heard the sound of Jon Luc and knew her mother had come home early. And that voice, that annoying, pretentious, I'm better than everybody else voice bounced off the walls of their tiny home. Alicia put her head down onto the back of the tub and breathed deep.

"But my dear, why must you disagree with me? You know that I am right about this, you should admit it and then we can both go on with our lives."

"Jon Luc, please, stop. Why don't you go on living in the present, the time when nobody gives a shit about people telling them what they should and shouldn't like? Get over yourself, you are not the end all and be all of every situation."

"Oh Shelley, you have so much to learn."

"You aggravate me sometimes; I'm going to the bathroom." She turned around and walked toward the bathroom. Alicia, noticing she was coming her way and remembering she didn't lock the door yelled to mother that she was in there.

"I don't care," her mother said as she opened the door. Alicia had tried to get up and put a towel around her but it was almost impossible to do that in such a hurry. There was no position she could assume to hide her belly, and Shelley noticed.

Her eyes bulged at the sight, and she immediately gasped at the sight.

"ALICIA! You little slut! When did this happen? It seems as if you are pretty far along, why didn't you tell me?"

"Well gee mom, you didn't ask."

"Don't get smart with me, you are a little girl and I should have locked you away so this wouldn't happen. Who's the father? Was it that bastard? Was it Derek? Or was it someone else? God knows you've slept with half the town."

"Look who my role model is," she said curtly.

"Get out of the tub right now, you hear me?"

Alicia got out of the tub as fast as she possibly could, which wasn't fast at all. She put a towel around her figure and faced our angry mother with a hatred only she could feel at that moment.

"I am not a slut, I haven't slept with all those people you have heard, and I have definitely not slept with Derek. And I didn't tell you because honestly you don't matter to me. I could care less what you think of me."

"You bitch; I should have never had you. You were the reason David left me, you were the reason I started drinking and you are the reason my life is miserable."

Alicia's eyes watered; she had thought that her whole life and to hear her mother say it only made it true. She was angry, sad, and she was filled with a feeling she couldn't even describe. A feeling of abandonment, of loneliness. She felt broken.

My mother's eyes dug deep into my sister, seeing through her to the back wall, through her grandson, his innocence. They were both furious.

"I can't believe you have gotten yourself knocked up, and now you will have a bastard child. I hope it's a boy, girls are just difficult and not worthy of loving."

"Well for your information it is a boy, and you will have nothing to do with him, you are not his grandmother and he will never acknowledge you as a person. You will be plain old Shelley to him. I do not want to screw him up like you screwed Amber and I up."

"Oh don't you fucking give me this bullshit; the only one in life to blame is yourself." She screamed to the living room, "Hey Jon Luc, come look at my daughter, the whore!" she laughed. Jon Luc came in to the bathroom and looked with disgust at Alicia.

"Why Alicia," he stated in his dumb French accent. "You look dreadful. Look what you have done to your body. You are a mere sixteen years old and you are having a love child."

"Believe me, this is not a love child, I am most definitely not in love with his father."

"Oh I'm sorry dear, I didn't know that the baby was a bastard, please forgive?"

"Oh I'm sorry too Jon Luc, no. I cannot forgive those who judge others," she responded mockingly. How dare he come in here and treat her like someone who had a care in the world of what he believed in or thought of.

"Please come Shelley, let the girl live through her mistake, she'll learn and move on. Let's go have a drink."

Our mother turned and left with her boyfriend, but not before giving my sister one last dirty look.

I came home at my usual time to see Alicia on the bed, she wasn't crying but it looked like she had been. She told me the whole story. I couldn't believe how inconsiderate and unloving a person could be. I comforted her a little and then we drove around for a while. We decided to head to the club we had previously visited. We had been there a few times, and it seemed as if Cynthia was always working. She was what one called a 'workaholic.'

The band that played that night was a nice jazz band called 'The Jazzilicious Trio.' We didn't really listen to them, just sat on our usual couches and viewed our surroundings. We stayed there for a few hours until we decided that we needed to get our minds off of life, off of the night she had gone through. Although my mother didn't exactly show me how she loved me she had never told me that I was worthless, unwanted and a burden. My soul ripped apart; she had hurt my sister who was my other half. She was part of me, joined by the heart. I was her protector, her caretaker. I wanted what was best for her, and I knew that our mother wasn't the person we should be near, and definitely not the person we should allow to come anywhere near the baby.

We left the bar as Cynthia stared at us, especially at Alicia and her bulging stomach. Alicia was worried about her telling Brad about the baby but she didn't care, how could Brad think it was his? If in fact she did sleep with every guy in town, who's he to say it's his.

The night air was cool; the wind hit our faces with freshness, as if everything was right in the world. People walked the streets smiling and laughing, enjoying life. The restaurants were just closing; the bars were thriving, and the casino was lit up and flourishing with the people who just couldn't let the game go.

All over the world people lived their lives in peace and happiness, something Alicia and I had not had the privilege of doing since we were young. Shouldn't these citizens of the United States of America know about our pain? Why didn't anyone care? In this world filled with bodies posing as humans we were at the bottom of the food chain. We were the worms, we were the hopeless, the two girls who were thrown into the pile. What would happen to us?

The many neglected and abused children in the world, sat there waiting for someone to come along and take them away from the situation they have lived with. No one came, no one called, and most of all, no one cared. We were in a group all to ourselves and now another one was coming into the world, but Alicia and I would never let him become one of us, the elite group of unwanted children. He was wanted, he was loved, and we couldn't wait to show him the good sides of the world.

Alicia and I had hopes for the young one, we had dreams for him to become something, and show the world honesty, truth, and love. We, unlike our mother, wanted Alicia's child to do something in his life so that he could be remembered as a caring human being who helped society, made it better.

We went home and fell asleep.

Entry 68: <u>December 1998</u>

During the last months of the pregnancy our mother stayed away from the house, she was out with Jon Luc or any number of her other friends from morning until night. In September I threw Alicia a tiny baby shower and invited her friends Missy, Eric and Ali. I also decided to invite Emily, Beckah, Dylan and Lilly. The eight of us were the only ones there for her. Out of the years where she had many friends who flocked to her, the seven that stood by her side during times of pain and suffering were the friends that should be there in the first place. They were her real friends.

The shower was at a restaurant called The Image. Alicia loved the restaurant, the food was magnificent and she was thrilled that the owner had a table for them. They sat in the corner of the room that overlooked a tiny pond. We had a nice conversation and many laughs. We each had a chance to feel the baby kick and we played some games. Presents were opened and Alicia found herself with new baby clothes, bibs, bottles, diapers, and formula.

We each placed a piece of paper into a glass with a boy's name written on it. When Alicia drew the papers she found eight names that were unique to each person. Missy had put Elijah, Ali wrote Matthew, Eric had joked Jacob "wouldn't that be funny? Jacob Jacobs?" he laughed. Emily put Stevie while Lilly put Christian. Beckah and Dylan unknowingly put in the same name, Jack. And I wrote Brockton Oliver. For some reason that was her favorite name. So the baby was no longer called 'baby boy' we now referred to him as Brockton, or Brock for short.

Because of her pregnancy Alicia wasn't going to college. She didn't have the money to go and our mother couldn't afford to send either of us, she was too busy smoking and drinking her money away. She decided that after Brockton was born and after graduation she would go to work at the movie theater with me and work her way up to manager. We could make sure that we were never working together so that either one of us would be home for Brock.

I bought her a bassinet for the shower. We placed it in our room between our beds. We shopped for the many other objects and necessities for the baby and were finally all set. The time was coming fast, it was mid-November now and both of us were getting nervous. Our mother had repeatedly announced that she wasn't happy about this one bit. Alicia and I both thought, 'it's about time you're not happy about something.'

The final month went by quickly, yet seemed like it took forever to get there. The feeling was quite unusual and hard to explain. On December 13th Alicia woke up at 6:00 a.m. and complained of pains in her lower abdomen. We both knew she was having contractions. The doctor told us at her last appointment that we should wait until they were 2-3 minutes apart before going to the hospital. When they reached 4 minutes apart we headed out. The drive seemed longer than we had practiced. Alicia screamed in pain and I was breathing in and out. My hands were wrapped tightly around the steering wheel, and blocked the blood from reaching the fingertips. Needless to say my entire hands were beet read by the time we arrived at the hospital 15 minutes later.

Alicia was admitted immediately and was given an epidural as per her request. The contractions were strong and fast. Alicia was in a lot of pain and finally the epidural took effect. It seemed as if a million bricks were taken off of her body all at once. She seemed peaceful and she slept for ten minutes. The doctor came in after seven hours of labor and told her she was ready to push. Thirty minutes later Brockton Oliver Jacobs was born, and he was the most beautiful baby we had ever seen. He weighed 6 lbs. 8 ounces and he was 18 ½ inches long. He looked like Alicia. He had a head of reddish brown hair and green eyes. His fingers and toes were all there, so tiny and so gorgeous. He tried as hard as he could to open his eyes and look at his family but it was too much trouble so they closed again.

The nurse wrapped him tightly with the blanket provided and put a cute blue hat on his tiny head. He looked warm and snuggly. Alicia stared at him in awe; she couldn't get enough of her son. She kissed him on the head so much it was as if she thought that if she didn't he would disappear. I stared at my sister and nephew with such admiration. "You're such a brave person Alicia," I whispered into her ear. "You are my hero."

"I'm not the strong one Amber. Thank you for being my sister."

"Wouldn't have it any other way, you are truly the best person, sister, human being anyone could wish for. And now you can share your talents with someone else."

"Would you like to hold him?"

She placed him into my arms and I felt an incredible amount of love for such a small person. At that moment I forgot all about my pain and thought only of my beautiful nephew. I couldn't believe that a minute ago he hadn't been there, and nine months ago he was nothing. I was so happy, a true moment of joy in my life. I was thankful for everything, thankful for Alicia, and her health, thankful for Brock and thankful that for the most part he didn't look like his father. He did have Brad's mouth, but everything else was Alicia, not that she would have loved him any less if he looked like Brad.

"He's beautiful isn't he?" Alicia asked.

"Yes he is. Hey Brockton, I'm your Auntie Amber and I love you so much." I kissed him on the head and realized that Alicia had known what she was doing when she kissed him so much. "He has this thing about him, you just can't seem to let him go, he's special Alicia."

"I know he is, and he will always be special, won't you sweetheart?" She rubbed his little arm, which had sneaked out of the blanket, and held onto his hand. He was definitely a gift from God.

Alicia's green eyes sparkled with pride and joy, she loved him completely and she wouldn't allow him to grow up like she had. She would keep her promise to him and he would live a fairy tale life.

The nurse took him to the nursery where she let him spend time with the other babies. With a bracelet on his foot that matched the bracelet on Alicia's wrist he was off to make new friends. The nurse had told us that she couldn't believe how good Brockton was, he barely cried and constantly looked around, checking out his surroundings. He was a sweet infant. She didn't have to tell us that more than once.

I spent half of my time at the glass window staring at him and the other half making sure my sister was comfortable and not in any pain. Nothing could bring me down anymore, all I had to do was look at my nephew and I knew everything in the world was right.

God worked in mysterious ways, a tragedy turned into a beautiful event that brought about a human so perfect in every way. It amazed me to think about the formation of a child. From tiny cells comes a living breathing being that will some day be able to walk and talk, to make decisions. I was at the window again perplexed and my mind had wandered to the mysteries of life. I couldn't wait to take him home with us and help Alicia take care of him. He wasn't just hers he was mine as well. I was happy.

Entry 69: <u>December 1998</u>

They released Alicia and Brockton two days later and we were on our way home. What would our mother do? She knew about the baby but had refused to acknowledge the fact that it happened. We could both picture her screaming and yelling about the crying and late nights.

We bundled him up in a blue one-piece pajama and wrapped him in the blanket. His hat was placed on his head and we were ready to go. I held a sheet of instructions, 'call 1-800-fix-baby if there are any problems,' and a pile of pictures in my hands while Alicia held her son. She placed him carefully into the car seat in the back and buckled him tight. She sat in the front seat and I drove.

When we arrived home our mother wasn't there, surprise. surprise. We were thankful and we walked inside. Brockton had fallen asleep on the way home and so we put him in his crib. I went to the store to grab some diapers and more formula. When I returned home I made some bottles and placed them in the refrigerator. I checked in on Alicia and Brock, both of them were sound asleep. I went in and shut the door quietly, I wanted to take a nap so I fell into a dreamless sleep the moment my head hit the pillow.

An hour later I awoke to crying. I got up off the bed and picked up Brockton. Alicia woke up, I told her to stay asleep. I would feed him and change him. I knew that she hadn't slept since the night before he was born so I wanted to help her out. After I fed and changed him, I held him and talked to him. We had a nice conversation, he told me he liked the house and he loved his mom and his aunt. I told him not to be afraid when he met his grandmother. He actually forced a little cry when I mentioned her, which I thought to be very odd.

He fell asleep in my arms and I placed him across my chest. We slept on the couch, an both us felt each other's heartbeats. The beauty of innocence shone around him. Alicia came into the room and found us both sleeping sound; she grinned and took a snapshot, a memory of his life. The bright light caused my eyes to shutter and I awoke. For a moment I didn't know where I was or who it was that slept on me, but as soon as the sleep tore away from my eyes it all came back to me full force.

Alicia grabbed Brock from me and sat in the rocking chair across the room. He was still asleep. We talked for a while until he woke up and required more food. His tiny cry was the best sound in the world.

Around one in the morning while Brock was up for another feeding Shelley stumbled in the door, Jon Luc in tow. She was drunk as usual and they were loud and obnoxious. I heard Alicia trying to whisper to them to keep the volume down, he was just falling asleep and she didn't want him to wake up. Our mother looked right at Alicia and the baby and gave them the look of death. Both of them stood there in silence as if they never knew that Alicia had ever been pregnant, and the sight of a baby was preposterous.

"Oh, so the bastard finally arrived?" she asked. She walked over to her daughter and grandson and poked her face up close to his and then turned and walked back to Jon Luc. "Looks just like Alicia, don't he? Poor kid."

"It is a shame dear, a child so young having an infant to care for. What is the world coming to?"

"Alicia, make sure he doesn't wake us up or else he's on the streets."

"He's a baby, he's going to cry, and if you throw him out I go too."

"Oooh, is that supposed to be a threat? Come on Jon Luc; let's go turn the sheets down."

I walked out of the bedroom and straight into my mother. She pushed me down and I hit my shoulder on the doorframe. "That's what you get when you don't look where you're going, try to be more careful next time," she smirked.

The family room was dimly lit and very quiet. Alicia cried in the corner as Brock sucked down the milk in his sleep. I sat next to her and wrapped my arms around her as I had done on more than one occasion. "She hates him."

"She hates everybody who threatens to disrupt her life; it's not about him it's about her. She hasn't spent enough time with him to truly make an assessment on his personality."

"But she said that he looks like me, and then said 'poor kid' as if I'm ugly."

"Think about that for one second and you will find your answer. She is jealous because you are beautiful and your son is gorgeous. She can't stand that you could ever be happy with your life so she has to find some way to bring you down, to make you feel inferior."

"Amber, she hasn't looked at me since before I even knew how to feel. She talks to me but when she looks at me she doesn't really look at me, you know? Her eyes become distant and unfocused. I feel like I'm not even there, that I don't even matter to her. She looked at him the same way tonight."

"She can't stand to look at you because you look like her, and you remind her of herself sober and what it was like to be happy and healthy. I know it's not easy but at least she doesn't smack you around anymore. Now you have Brock to think about. Just forget what she says to you, let it go because nothing she says matters Alicia, nothing."

"Thank you," she said. "You're right, who cares what she says? Huh Brock? You don't care do you?"

"Oh by the way, I forgot to tell you, when I was talking to him earlier this afternoon he cried when I mentioned his 'grandmother.'"

"Really? Wow, he already knows she's evil. Give me five!" she said to him as she grabbed his hand and slapped him five.

It rained for the next few days so we were stuck inside, which was nice and relaxing. Brockton loved the sound of the raindrops hitting the roof and flowing down the gutters. He opened his eyes as wide as he could to find where the noise was coming from, that kept him busy for a while until he gave up.

After a month passed we couldn't believe how much he had grown, he was now 9 pounds and 21 inches. The doctor said, with each appointment, that he was an excellent baby. He never cried when he had to get his shots and he didn't fuss when he was placed on the cold scale. His hair was growing and his eyes hadn't changed color yet. He was looking more and more like Alicia with every passing day.

That night we had decided to go to the club for a night out on the town. We dropped Brockton off at Missy's house; she was delighted for the opportunity to watch over the baby. She told us to enjoy ourselves and we promised to listen. Then we picked up Madison who had been bugging me to take her with us.

The club was crowded tonight, our seats weren't available. We decided to get a drink at the bar. I ordered my usual rum and coke; I don't like drinking or the taste of alcohol. The rum was hidden behind the taste of the coke. Alicia ordered a margarita and we waited until our seats were empty.

Suddenly the owner of the bar came over to us. We looked at each other; did he find out that Alicia was under age? We had nothing to worry about; he introduced himself and got right to the point. "Hello, my name is Jordan Nicholas," he shook our hands. "Are you Alicia Jacobs?"

"Yes," she said curiously.

"Well I was informed by Cynthia that you were the young girl who sang here a while ago, is that correct?"

"That is correct."

"Great, I am so glad I finally got the chance to meet you. Would you mind singing for us tonight? If you don't feel up to it then that's okay, but I would greatly appreciate it. You were fantastic!"

"Sure, I would love to. How long do you want me to sing for?"

"How about three songs? And if you want to do more, go for it. How's that?"

"Wow, thank you. Do you mind Amber?"

"Not at all, go for it, you deserve it."

She got up on stage with all the confidence in the world. Her smile spread ear to ear as she took the mike. "Good evening everyone, my name is Alicia Jacobs and I will be singing a few of my songs for you. I would like to dedicate this to my son Brockton and my sister Amber," she pointed to me. Everyone turned and looked at me, they clapped.

She sang with all her might, the first song a ballad written for Brock, which brought tears to the eyes of all the parents in the room. The second song was a faster song, where everyone got up and danced. It was during this song that I noticed him sitting at the bar. It was Brad; finally it was my chance to tell him what I thought of him.

I walked over to the bar and tapped him on the shoulder. He turned around and looked at me. His hair was slicked back and he smiled at me with lust in his eyes. He looked me over and gave me some dumb one-liner. I suppose he noticed the anger in my face because he snarled at me and asked, "What's your problem Amber? You know I could help you get over your anger, loosen you up a little."

"You fucking asshole!" I screamed.

His face registered utter shock and he lifted up his hands in defense. "Whoa there, calm down. What did I do to you?"

"It's not what you did to me it's what you did to my sister. How dare you think you are so awesome that you can take advantage of a girl who didn't want to do it? Do you actually believe you have the power to do whatever you want?" By this point my voice had become louder and louder, as if someone was pressing the volume button. Alicia was off the stage and headed my way. Brad was angry at being humiliated and Cynthia listened intently at what I was saying. "You fucking moron, how could you do that to my sister?"

"Amber, stop," Alicia said to me. She tried to grab me but I was out of control. I hit him and he blocked my punches. He looked at Alicia and gave her his snake-like smile.

"What are you looking at? Don't even look at her, you pig. How could you rape her? Do you realize what you did to her? And now she has a son, a beautiful boy whom you will NEVER see."

The whole place went silent, especially me. Alicia looked at me with hurt in her eyes. I had promised her I wouldn't tell anyone and in one instant I had told everybody. Cynthia eyed Brad and me carefully, deciding who to believe. If Brad gave any indication that what I said was false, I didn't see it.

"I didn't rape her, she wanted it. She was begging for it, and then when it was finished she was all upset and angry at me."

"That's bullshit Brad and you know it," my sister said. She was furious that he wouldn't admit that he raped her.

"No I don't know it, and you have no right to accuse me of doing such a thing. I am innocent, no blood on my hands." He raised his hands up and dangled his fingers. He came toward her and whispered in her ear, "Plus, who is going to believe you? I am a baseball player going to college on a full scholarship and you are just some bitchy whore who wanted to get back at men for what her father did to her slut mother. Good luck sweetheart."

Alicia's clenched her hands by her side; my eyes burned with hatred.

"I can't believe you would do this to someone," Cynthia finally spoke.

"I didn't. You can't believe everything you hear Cyn, it's just stupid. She's lying, just because she wanted to get back at me."

"For what?"

"For falling in love with you of course. I had stopped paying attention to her because you came into my life and she was jealous, she wanted me all to herself."

"Oh go screw yourself Brad, we're over. You met me a month after she broke up with you. If you ever come near me again, call me, or talk to any of my friends about me I will hurt you more than you can possibly understand," she had said in a soft voice, almost intimidating.

We stood back and watched the scene between them. Brad looked astonished that another girl was breaking up with him, considered it to be my entire fault. If you don't want to blame yourself blame someone else. I was there to take it.

"You bitch, you'll pay for this you hear me? You will regret you talked to me, that you mentioned anything to me." He was in my face, pointing his finger into my chest bone. "Don't have your back turned for a moment because you will pay, and pay dearly." As he left the building he knocked the crowd down and almost broke the hinges off of the door.

"I'm sorry for being such a bitch to you Alicia, and I am so sorry he did this to you," said Cynthia after Brad left.

"Thank you. What made you believe me?"

"Because he almost did it to me the other day but he stopped when I punched him."

"Oh my God, why were you two still together?"

"Well, I thought that he would never do that again, and I certainly didn't think he had done it before. What's your son's name if you don't mind me asking?"

"Brockton. He's adorable. You'll have to come by and see him some day, he loves people. And, thank the Lord, he looks like me and not that son of a bitch."

"Yeah, I would love that," Cynthia said. It seemed as if the two of them would become friends. And she would have another babysitter.

"Okay, well we're going to head out, have to pick him up from the babysitters. I'll see you soon. Have a good night."

"You too Alicia, bye. And, watch out for him."

"Thanks I will." She said and we left the club.

Entry 70: <u>May 1999</u>

Months passed and we still hadn't heard anything from or about Brad. We were more than happy. Cynthia was a regular visitor to our house and she babysat when either of us needed to go out and have fun. Brockton was getting so big, he now knew how to roll over and he made cute baby noises.

On my 19th birthday when Brockton was five months old, we all went to the zoo and looked at the animals. He loved the elephants and he laughed at all of the monkeys swinging in the trees. That day was a great day. We ate lunch in the picnic area near one of the dozens of gift shops and Brock had his bottle along with some baby food. His red hair glowed in the sunlight and his green eyes sparkled with joy.

Our next stop was a show about alligators and it was starting in five minutes. We gathered our stuff and headed over to Gatorland. The trainers fed the alligators fish and we watched as each snapped their jaws and dug their teeth into the slimy water creatures.

The sun was hot and both Alicia and I were getting burned. Brock was getting fussy; it was almost time for his nap, so we decided to head back. Alicia had a surprise for me; she was taking me somewhere later that night and Cynthia was watching the baby. I was a little nervous, I didn't like surprises. But since I trusted Alicia I went along.

We brought Brock over to Cynthia's house around 6:00 so he could spend some time with her before his bedtime. Alicia took me to dinner at Alec's Place, a restaurant downtown. It was crowded, but we had reservations. The food was delicious, I had ordered a pepperoni pizza with a side order of fries, it was the best pizza I had ever had. Alicia had a meatball grinder, which was also very tasty.

After dinner we went down to one of her favorite dance clubs, Every Night Fever. I had never been there but excited to try out a new place. The music was loud and fast, and it was excellent for dancing. We ordered a drink first and then went straight to the dance floor. Everyone was bumping and grinding and having a great time. Alicia and I were having so much fun dancing, forgetting about our lives, pretending that she didn't have a child, that I didn't care what others thought of me.

Three different men came and tried to dance with us, we didn't let them. We didn't want men to screw up our lives any more than they had. Around midnight a boy about my age came up to us. He had blonde hair and blue eyes and he was rather good looking. He seemed familiar, like I had met him before, but I just wasn't sure where.

"Hey, can you talk for a minute?" he screamed over the blare of the speakers.

"Sure," I answered. Alicia nodded that it was all right. She kept on dancing.

Outside the air was what I needed. The heat from the club had caused me to sweat, and now I cooled off. My ears rang but at least I'd have a break from going deaf before I went back in.

"So, what did you want to talk about?"

"I just thought you were so beautiful, and the way you were dancing caught my eye," he said. Oh how romantic.

"Thank you," I responded shyly. "Do I know you from somewhere?"

"I believe you do, if you are the person I think you are. My name is Chris."

"Oh my God, Chris? I can't believe it's you!" I jumped up giving him a huge hug. I hadn't seen him since he had moved away when we were in fifth grade. We wrote letters throughout the past decade, but for some reason had never shared pictures. He had grown up, of course. He must have weighed 170 pounds of pure muscle. "You look good."

"You do too Amber. So, what's been going on? Is your mom still psycho?"

"Well yes, that won't ever change unfortunately." I wished he hadn't ever brought up my mother but I couldn't change my past. Alicia has a baby, his name is Brockton."

"What? Isn't she young?"

"Yeah, but it wasn't her fault. Don't even get me started. He's beautiful though, I'm glad he's here. That's all that's going on, how about you?"

"Well, I moved back here on my own to finish up school. I'm a political science major; I plan to run for governor after I finish up law school. Janie is doing well, she just graduated. I can't believe how big she is! Was that Alicia who was dancing with you?"

"Yup, that was her."

"Wow, she looks so different, so old. I still can't believe that she's a mom! It blows my mind."

"You're telling me. She's grown up a lot in the last year; I admire all she's gone through. She's a survivor. Alicia's my hero, and my best friend."

"I always remember you complaining to me of how she used to boss you around, you hated it."

"I know, but now that we're both older, and wiser I might add, we've become very close."

"That's really good, you need that. Hey I'll let you get back to your party, we should get together soon. I would really like to catch up on stuff, in person that is, and I would love to meet your nephew."

"That would be great," I said; I couldn't believe he had come back into my life. "Here's my number, call me anytime. Bye Chris, it was excellent seeing you."

"Bye Amber, and Happy Birthday," he kissed me on the cheek and we hugged again before I went back inside to find Alicia.

She sat in the back drinking another drink. I sat with her and told her all about what just happened. She couldn't believe that it was Chris and immediately told me how happy she was for me. We talked a while longer and then returned to our places on the dance floor where we danced until closing at 2:00 a.m.

Our car was parked a few blocks away, being a Saturday night the streets were filled with cars and the parking lots were full. We liked to walk, it was a beautiful night. It seemed like yesterday I was eleven years old lying in bed hugging my nine-year-old sister while we both cried over a ruined birthday. I reminisced over the years my sister and I spent together. In retrospect our horrible life wasn't so horrible because we had each other. What we thought was a tragedy was a life lesson, one that was meant to help us along in our journey of life. I had come to grips with my life over the last year. I couldn't change the past, couldn't change the fact that my mother was an alcoholic, couldn't change the abandonment of my father, couldn't change the death of my grandmother, couldn't change the sudden loss of my writing class with Ava, and I had to leave it all behind me. It was finally time to look to the future, Brockton's life, maybe a marriage of my own, and though I have never thought about having children of my own maybe that would be an idea.

I realized I didn't have any power of what others thought of me. I had to be myself and think about what would make me happy and not others. Future, here I come. The first day of the rest of my life had been staring me straight in the face for years and I had ignored it, but now was the time to embrace it and let it come.

We walked down the street on the cement sidewalk. I thought about my future and Alicia thought about going to school. A few blocks from the car we heard someone behind us. Both of us turned around to see who it was, but we couldn't see anything. We thought it odd but we kept walking.

A few yards up we reached the parking lot; it was empty except for our car and a few others. Alicia thought that we should hurry up and get in, she had a funny feeling. I wish I had listened to her. I told her we had nothing to worry about, it was a safe neighborhood and we were okay. I regret that more than anything. My life changed in an instant.

Out of the corner stepped Brad and two of his friends. They looked satisfied, like they were going to do something that they had planned for a long time. We were both afraid.

"What are you doing here Brad? Leave us alone, we just want to go back home."

"Oh I'm sorry; I can't let you do that. It's your birthday Amber; I could never let you leave without giving you a present. That would just be rude, right guys?" The two boys next to him nodded in agreement. "We're going to have our own little party."

"Brad, come on she's not the person who you are mad at, it's me," said Alicia. "Just leave her alone."

"Oh Alicia, I'm not mad at you, you didn't do anything except break up with me. I'm over that, but now your fucking sister here, forced Cynthia to dump me, throw me in the doghouse and I warned her she's going to pay, and now's the time."

We tried screaming but nobody was around. I felt so stupid. I felt like a naïve little girl who had thought that nothing could happen to her, only to someone else. I should have known better, I shouldn't have forgotten my past so quickly.

"What are you going to do? Show her you're powerful by raping her too? That shows maturity, intelligence. Now why is it you didn't get into Yale?"

"Shut up Alicia, don't get into this."

He walked toward me and took out a gun from his jacket pocket. I gasped.

"What the fuck are you doing?" asked his two friends. They obviously had no idea what the plan was. "Brad, don't do it. She's not worth it."

He turned around and pointed the gun at his friends, told them to be quiet. Fear tensed through my body; I felt my knees buckle. My legs felt like they were going to give out at any moment. My whole life flashed before me and tears streamed from my eyes. Alicia was stood there, stunned. She couldn't believe this; she thought he was stupid, that he would actually be willing to kill someone over a little fight that resulted from his mistake.

She knew he was going to kill me, she knew he was out of his mind. At this point in time he wasn't himself. He was a crazy person and once he did it he would regret it and ask for forgiveness. God would never forgive him, she would never forgive him and she wanted revenge even before something terrible happened.

She prayed with all her heart that he would stop and think it through, that he would realize what he was doing and walk away. "WALK AWAY YOU SON OF A BITCH," she screamed.

He didn't listen to her. He pointed the gun at me again, as the barrel stared me in the eyes. He was ten feet away. I couldn't believe what was happening. "I love you Alicia," I said accepting my fate.

Brad cocked the gun back.

Brad aimed.

Alicia screamed, "NOOOOOOOOOOOOOOOOOOOOOO!"

Brad smiled.

I cried.

Alicia ran in front of me.

Brad fired.

The bullet hit Alicia in the chest at full force, it was not what Brad or I expected. The force of the shot rocketed Alicia into me causing us both to fall backward. Brad dropped the gun and the boys ran away as fast as they could.

I picked up my sister and held her in my lap. She bled profusely from her chest. She was coughing blood and wheezing in pain.

"Why did you do that?" I was angry at her for taking it for me, I was heartbroken for my sister, and I was in a state of shock at what had just happened. I got my cell phone and dialed 911.

"Amber," she spoke in slow soft words. She was having trouble.

"Don't talk, it's too much trouble."

"Do something for me,"

"Anything," I cried.

"Get away from mom, bring Brockton and leave this place."

"We'll both get out of here; just hang on the ambulance is on its way."

"I don't think I'll make it," she coughed. Her whole body shook. I held her closer, and tried to stop the bleeding. She took a break from speaking for a second.

"Please I don't want you living with her and hurting, you deserve to be happy," she coughed again. "Please Amber, be happy. That's all I want for you, all I've ever wanted for you. Don't be sad for me, live a life where you don't have to put your needs aside for mom. Leave and never look back." Her eyes were rolling back, she was slowly losing herself. I could feel her weakness, I could feel her fading.

"Don't go Alicia, I love you. I need you."

"You don't need me, look inside yourself and I'll be there. I am inside you; I will be your happiness. I love you Amber, I've loved you my whole life." She coughed up a lot of blood this time; I turned her so she wouldn't swallow it. "Always remember Amber; always remember how much you mean to me, I love you so much," she said again. Her body went limp. She had taken her last breath, spoke her last words.

I rocked back and forth, my thoughts only on my sister, who was gone from this world. I screamed a silent scream, I had lost my voice. My eyes were red and bloodshot, and burning from my tears. I was soaked with my sister's blood and my arms throbbed from the pain of holding my hero in my arms while her soul lifted and went to a happy place to live with our grandmother.

I held her close to me, and knew this would be the last time I would ever hold her, touch her, see her. The ambulance came and told me I would have to let them have her. They gently pried Alicia off of me, placed her on the gurney and just as they had done with my mother put her in the back of the ambulance. I went with them. The entire ride I stared at her, my only real family besides Brock. Poor Brock, to grow up without a mother. I promised myself I would always be there for him like a mother but he would always know his real mom. I would never allow him to forget her.

Alicia's hand had flopped off the gurney so I grabbed it and held it until we arrived at the hospital. While I held her hand, I prayed that she would be happy wherever she was, that she would be our angel, she would watch over Brockton and I. I also promised her in that moment that I would take care of her son with all my heart and soul. I promised her I would leave my mother to live by herself and take Brock somewhere far away. We would get a new start, a new life, and I promised her I'd be happy.

"For you Alicia, I will be happy. I love you so much and I will never forget you. You are my sweet angel."

Entry 71: <u>May 1999</u>

During the 911 call I told the operator who shot my sister. The police searched for Brad and his two friends. I didn't know what would happen to them, I just hoped against hope that it would be what they deserved. He had taken my sister away from me and I would fight for her rights.

That night at the hospital was the longest night of my life. They tried to revive her but they were unable to. It was the same as when our mother was in the hospital; the old couple awaiting the news of their son only to be told their efforts had worked to no avail. I was the old couple, sitting in the back of the waiting room waiting for some miracle.

The doctor came to me as he came to them, and with a grim look on his face and a tear in his eye he told me she was gone. They couldn't save her just like they couldn't save the old couple's son. I knew deep in my heart that they wouldn't be able to save her but it still caused a deep sadness in my soul. He asked if I wanted to sit by her side until the people came to take away her body to the funeral home.

I sat down next to her bed and looked at her. They had folded back the blanket so I could see her face. She looked as if she was in peace, no more sadness, no more hurt. Our mother could never look at her as if she wasn't there anymore. "You are always here Alicia," I whispered. "No matter what she thought I always knew you were there and you will never disappear."

Around six in the morning I drove to Cynthia's house. "Where have you been? I've been calling you. I was worried." She and Brock had been up for an hour. "That's unusual, isn't it?" she had asked. Then she noticed the sullen look on my face.

"What's wrong?"

"He killed Alicia," I said.

Cynthia knew exactly who I was talking about. She broke down, brought her hands to her mouth and cried. She hugged me and didn't care that I didn't return the hug. I was emotionally drained, I had nothing left inside of me at the moment but I knew it would return full force soon enough. I went inside and picked up Brock from his playpen and held him tight.

He was a smart baby and knew my pain even at five months. He didn't try to push away, he placed his head on my shoulder and he stayed there until I let go a little. He looked at me with his beautiful eyes, his mama's eyes. I couldn't help but smile, she was still here with me. "Your mama loves you Brock. She told me that, she loves you more than life itself." He smiled as if he knew already.

The funeral was very emotional for me. I had seen my sister the last time the night before and I would never see her again except in my dreams and in the pictures I had of her throughout the years. I planned the entire funeral, down to the very last chair. I had called my father, as hard as it was, I did it. He sobbed on the phone and told me he'd be there.

Our mother sat in the chair next to me and looked straight ahead, a blank expression on her face. I couldn't tell if she was sad about the loss of her daughter or happy because she no longer had to deal with her. Jon Luc sat next to her, his fingers intertwined with hers. I stared in anger; he was the last person I wanted here. Alicia had hated him and here he was pretending to cry for her.

Cynthia stood in the back holding her hands in a prayer-like shape. Missy stood next to her, tears in her eyes and Brock in her arms. Eric and Ali stood next to them, unbelieving of why they were there. Kira, Mark and Bailey sat next to me as they supported me and grieved for Alicia. The twins stayed at home with Uncle Jerry. They were family and it was only right for them to be sitting next to me. Lilly, Beckah, Dylan, Madison, Deana, Matt, Andrew and Austin sat a few rows back; they were all there for me. Even Ava, Jenn, Cassie and the rest of the writing group came to show they cared. The flowers were around the casket, some sunflowers, red roses, and her favorite, white lilies. I had ordered a single white rose dyed a shade of amber and placed it in her casket with her. That way I could be with her for eternity.

The priest said a beautiful prayer for Alicia and the ceremony ended. They lowered my beautiful, caring, loving, seventeen year old sister into the ground next to our grandmother. I threw in some dirt and watched as everyone disappeared to their cars. We were having a special dinner at Cynthia's house to celebrate Alicia's life. I stayed by myself by the grave, said my last goodbyes and headed to the house.

When I arrived everyone was there talking to each other and reminiscing about their times with Alicia. Chris was there. He walked over to me.

"Hey Amber, I am so sorry about what happened."

"Thank you. I am glad you came." We embraced and he held me while I cried a bit more. "Did you get to see Brockton yet?" I asked.

"No, I didn't. Where is he?"

We walked over to Cynthia and she told us that Missy had him. "Here he is, isn't he beautiful?"

"Yes he is. Hey Brock, I'm Chris. Wow, he looks exactly like Alicia."

"I know, that's why he's so gorgeous."

The party lasted the rest of the afternoon and I mingled with everyone, including my mother and Jon Luc. I decided to make a speech; I yelled above the crowd and asked if they'd listen.

"I would like to thank all of you for coming. We all know that Alicia was a very special person and she showed her wonderful personality through everything she did. She was beautiful inside and out, and although some of you couldn't see this in her," I looked at my mother, "it was there." My father was sitting on the couch with his new wife and their two children, Connor and Ella. They all listened intently to my speech.

"I plan on taking Brockton and moving to a different part of the state, or maybe even somewhere else. I promised my sister I would be happy and living with you, mother, isn't making me happy."

The room was quiet and my mother seemed angry. She came up to me after the speech was over.

"What makes you think I'd let you take Brockton? He's my grandson he should be raised by me."

I was flabbergasted. "You don't even like him, why would you want to have him? You were never a good mother they would never place him with you. And if I have to fight to make sure of that I will. I would rather lose him to someone else than to lose him to you."

"I kept you two alive for this long, her death wasn't my fault. She would want me to raise her son; she loved me and respected me. Alicia thought I was a good mother."

"Oh yeah? Then why did she write this note a few months ago?"

"What note?"

I reached into my pocket and took out the note she had written on her seventeenth birthday. It was dated.

"To Whom It May Concern,

If anything should happen to me, I wish to have my sister, Amber Katherine Jacobs as my son's legal guardian. Under no circumstances should my mother be awarded custody, it would not be in the best interest of Brock.

This is my wish, Alicia Kristine Jacobs, Brockton's mother."

The look on my mother's face could have killed someone. She couldn't believe what she had just heard. "Where did you get that?"

"She gave it to me when she wrote it. When she found out she was pregnant she had promised the baby she wouldn't let him grow up and be miserable like we did. So if you would do me one favor, in my whole life this is all I ask of you, let it go. Tell the judge you don't want custody. Please, do this for me, your only surviving daughter, and do this for Alicia. We deserve this from you."

My father walked over to the two of us. Both of us stared at him, I had avoided him the entire day and my mother didn't pursue him either. "Shelley, do this, let him live with Amber. Give her custody. We owe her this. Both of us have to stop being selfish. Alicia is dead, our youngest daughter is no longer with us and we should respect her wish to have Amber raise Brock."

She surprised me; she agreed with my father and promised she wouldn't pursue custody. I was so happy that I would be able to fulfill my promise to my sister.

The crowd diminished after a few hours and only the people closest to me and Alicia remained. Cynthia offered to take care of Brock that night and I acquiesced. I needed to be alone to mourn my sister.

Bailey came up to me with tears in his eyes. "I'm sorry about Alicia. I'm really going to miss her."

I leaned down and took him in my arms holding him tightly. "I'm going to miss her too."

He cried into my shoulder as Kira and Mark looked on. "Why did she have to die? She was my sister."

"She was my sister too and I ask myself that every day. But you know what, she'll always be here even if you can't see her. She is in your heart," I patted his chest where his heart is located. "She is also part of me and a part of Brockton so every time you see us you will see Alicia too."

We stood face to face. The little boy from seven years ago was gone and now stood a handsome and intelligent ten year old. He nodded to me and we hugged again. When he was safely by Mark's side, Kira came to comfort me. The emotion I felt after the conversation with Bailey was strong and powerful and coursed through my body and soul. I knew this was the beginning of a very painful process of grieving.

"I can't believe how incredibly strong you are Amber."

"I'm not strong, I'm falling apart with every breath I take. I can't fathom the idea of living without her. How am I going to do this? How am I going to raise her son by myself and live up to his mother?" I was still crouched down close to the floor and Kira had leaned down so we could be face to face. She had begun to pull my hair behind my ears and wipe the tears from my face. "She was my best friend Kira. She was everything to me and to Brock and now he is going to grow up not knowing her. He will never feel her loving arms around him or her sweet kisses upon his cheek."

"He won't have that but he will have you there to remind him every day of her. He will know her through you and I know that you won't let him forget his mom. You are going to do a wonderful job with him. You helped me with Bailey and the twins and they are better for that." She was now closer to me and holding my hands in hers. I could feel her trembling and could hear the tremor in her voice when she spoke. It wasn't just me who had lost a sister it was also Kira who had lost a daughter. "I can't believe she's gone. My little Alicia, so sweet and caring. I don't know what I'm going to do knowing that I can never see her again, but I know I still have you. We have each other Amber, we have each other." And with that last word she leaned into me crying. We sat there on the floor in each other's arms rocking back and forth trying to put the loss we were feeling to sleep.

Twenty minutes later Mark held Bailey by one hand while helping Kira out of the house with his other arm. "I love you Amber. Come visit soon, promise?"

"I promise. I love you too Kira."

After they left Ava gave me a hug and shared her sympathy. We talked for a while about what I planned on doing now. I told her that I would look at a few apartments in the next few days and for another job.

The night went by fast and pretty soon it was just me, Madison, Deana, Matt, Andrew, Austin, Lilly, Beckah and Dylan. They decided they wanted to keep me company while my mother and Jon Luc went out.

We reminisced about the good times we had with Alicia; the night we ran away from Kira's and spent the night at Beckah's as fugitives, the nights at the karaoke bar while Alicia sang her heart out, and the baby shower we were all a part of. We laughed and we cried but mostly we just had a good time spending time with each other. We had all realized too tragically that life was too short to not keep in touch or get together.

As the night came to a close we fell asleep on the floor, our heads all close and our hands clasped. Friends forever.

EPILOGUE

Entry 72: <u>July 1999</u>

The day we went to court proved I was right all along. The judge read the note and agreed to Alicia's wishes. He had asked both my parents if they wanted custody and they both declined. I was nervous that my mother would change her mind out of spite, but she didn't.

They found Brad and his two friends in a bar four days after the murder. They have been convicted of Alicia's murder and are currently serving a life sentence. He confessed in the interrogation room. The guilt was eating him alive.

The judge awarded me full custody and Brock and I were on our way to live our new lives. For once in her life my mother put her daughters' and grandson's needs first, and I was grateful for that.

The following morning I packed my car with my belongings and Brock's baby paraphernalia. I left a note thanking my mother for her kindness, although I didn't need to; she owed me this and a lot more. I put Brock in his car seat and looked around my house for the last time.

I remembered all of the times Alicia and I had spent in this house; birthday parties, study groups, fights, and late night talks. We shared secrets and consoled each other in times of hardship. Alicia was in this house; she was all around, but I had to leave. I took a picture of us when we were young and brought it with me. I also had pictures that I had taken just a few months ago.

I felt as if she was on vacation having the time of her life and she would be back in a week or two. I missed her, my heart was aching that she wasn't in my life anymore. Every time I thought of her I would look at Brock, who had grown tremendously. He was crawling around everywhere and lifting himself up using the furniture already. And when he smiled I saw my sister; she was telling me through him that she was happy.

I drove away, leaving my past behind and drove towards my future. Before I left I stopped to say goodbye to my sister. The graveyard was quiet, no one was visiting that day. I drove up to her site and stopped the car. We walked to her gravesite, where I placed a bouquet of red roses and told her that I loved her and I was going to be happy. Brock and I sat down beside her and we had a picnic, as we had done while she was pregnant.

An hour later we said our goodbyes and tearfully we left her body behind, but we had her soul with us.

I rented an apartment for the two of us about an hour away, just twenty minutes from Kira and Mark. I secured a job at a daycare center as well and Brock stayed with me while I worked.

The apartment provided a place to sleep and eat and play, which was good enough for the two of us. Brock had his own bedroom; it was painted in a light blue shade with sheer white curtains framing the single window. When we arrived at our new home we started unloading.

"Hey there," a voice said from behind. I immediately jumped, ever since the incident many little things startled me, especially people coming up from behind.

I noticed it was Chris and I calmed down. "Hi, what are you doing here?"

"I knew you were moving in today and I thought you might need help with your stuff, there is no way you can do it by yourself with the baby."

"That's really nice of you, thanks."

"My pleasure."

Chris brought up the crib and the large items while I grabbed the smaller stuff. It was difficult to carry a nine month old as well as luggage and odds and ends. I didn't know what I would have done if Chris hadn't shown up.

Everything was in the apartment and the car was finally empty. I parked the car in a safe spot and then we all ate dinner. Brock was exhausted from his busy day and went down at 8:00 on the dot. We finished unpacking and talked for a while. We had a great time together and he spent the night, on the couch of course.

I had placed a picture of Alicia and I on the nightstand next to my bed and I said goodnight to her before my eyes closed. I was finally on my own, without my mother. I smiled in my sleep. The first day of the rest of my life, I thought for the second time.

🍁   🍁   🍁

Entry 73: <u>October 2002</u>

Dear Readers:

It has been three years since Alicia's death and my life has turned around completely. I have enjoyed my freedom, and am now at peace with my life. Brockton will be four years old in two months; I can't believe how big he has grown. He is the smartest toddler I have ever known, and I'm not just saying that because he's my nephew.

He took his first step at eleven months and he said his first word when he was a year and a half. We were at my sister's grave giving her flowers and he said "mama." He didn't say it to me, he said it to Alicia. I was so proud. He knows I'm his Aunt and he calls me Auntie, I wouldn't have it any other way. He is a happy child, living a great life.

We visit Alicia's grave three times a year to bring flowers; on her birthday, my birthday and Brock's birthday.

I haven't spoken to or seen my mother since I left nor have I had any inclination to. My father and his new family have come by a few times; ever since he lost a daughter his priorities changed. I am trying to repair our relationship, although it has been difficult.

Chris and I were married last year and have been blessed with a brand new baby girl, Katia Alicia.

Every Friday night the four of us go to family night at Kira's house and during dinner we say grace to show our appreciation for each other and to give thanks for Alicia. She is always a part of our thoughts and prayers.

I speak to Ava regularly; Emily is five now and her youngest daughter Lanie will be two next month. She is pregnant with her third child and is due at the end of August. She and her husband are expecting a boy. They plan to name him Charlie. Madison, Deana, Matt, Andrew and Austin visit us a lot and love Brock and Katia almost as much as I do. We also see Beckah, Dylan and Lilly at least twice a month. Life so far was going well and we had found our routine.

My life was never easy; I chose not to let it stop me. Writing has helped me deal with my past and has brought me to the point I am at now. By telling my story I have brought about a change, I have released my demons and am now able to truly move on with my life. I still have moments of anger and depression but they aren't as bad as they once were and now I have Chris, Brock, and Katia to help me through it all.

I hope you all have come away with this tale with a sense of family. It is very important to be there for your children, show them you love them, and never allow them to feel neglected or unwanted, it is a truly horrible feeling. Patience is a virtue that you must cherish or else you will drive yourself mad.

For the teenagers, if you see someone in your school who is quiet, or has a parent(s) who has a disease, such as alcoholism, don't judge that person on that. Realize that every single person has his or her own personality and they deserve your respect. Find something that will make them happy, make them feel like they belong and use it. They might just need a simple 'hello.' If you help others you will be happier with yourself.

Respect everybody; do not take them for granted because you don't know when they might be suddenly taken away from you without a single word. Keep those you love in your heart forever. Never leave the house angry; your parents care for you, they are only ruining your lives because they love you.

If someone says no, listen, they mean it. It is not fair to anyone if force is pushed upon him or her. It is their right to hold their own wants, needs and opinions and no one except God can take those away from them.

Most importantly, find something you love doing and do it no matter what anyone says. Don't fall into something you hate because it's easy, go full force to find out what it is you want to do and do it. Don't go into a profession because your family members or friends tell you that is what they want you to do; your life isn't theirs to decide.

Live life as if every day was the day you have been waiting for, as if today was the day miracles were going to happen. Don't let one second go by where you don't think about what's good in your life. If you do the sadness will take over; I know that from experience.

And lastly, remember I love you all.

Love,
Amber Katherine Jacobs
XOXO

978-0-595-39557-6
0-595-39557-0

Printed in the United States
54894LVS00003B/58